THE MASTE.

ARTHUR RUSSELL THORNDIKE was born in Rochester, Kent in 1885. Although his sister, Sybil Thorndike (1882-1976), was the better known actor, Russell Thorndike also acted both on the stage and in a number of films, but his first love was writing books. Thorndike finished his first novel, *Doctor Syn: A Tale of the Romney Marsh* (1915), around the same time he enlisted for service in the First World War. After being severely wounded at Gallipoli, Thorndike was discharged and returned to acting. Perhaps surprised at the perennial popularity of the first Doctor Syn novel, Thorndike revisited the character several times in the 1930s and 1940s, in addition to publishing a number of other novels, of which *The Slype* (1927), also available from Valancourt Books, is probably the best.

In the final twenty years of his life, Thorndike wrote no further novels, but continued to act, appearing frequently as Smee in productions of *Peter Pan*, and made a few film appearances, including minor roles in Laurence Olivier's *Hamlet* (1948) and *Richard III* (1955). Thorndike died in 1972.

MARK VALENTINE is the author of several collections of short fiction and has published biographies of Arthur Machen and Sarban. He is the editor of *Wormwood*, a journal of the literature of the fantastic, supernatural, and decadent, and has previously written the introductions to editions of Walter de la Mare, Robert Louis Stevenson, L. P. Hartley, and others, and has introduced John Davidson's novel *Earl Lavender* (1895), Claude Houghton's *This Was Ivor Trent* (1935), and Oliver Onions's *The Hand of Kornelius Voyt* (1939) for Valancourt Books.

Cover: The cover reproduces the scarce jacket art of the first edition published by Rich and Cowan in 1947.

BY RUSSELL THORNDIKE

Doctor Syn (1915)
The Slype (1927)★
The Vandekkers (1929)
Herod's Peal (1931)
The Water Witch (1932)
Jet and Ivory (1934)
Doctor Syn Returns (1935)
The Further Adventures of Dr. Syn (1936)
Dr. Syn on the High Seas (1936)
The Amazing Quest of Dr. Syn (1938)
The Courageous Exploits of Dr. Syn (1939)
Show House—Sold (1941)
The House of Jeffreys (1943)
The Shadow of Dr. Syn (1944)
The Master of the Macabre (1947)★
The First Englishman (1949)

★ Available from Valancourt Books

THE MASTER OF
THE MACABRE

by

RUSSELL THORNDIKE

With a new introduction by

MARK VALENTINE

VALANCOURT BOOKS

The Master of the Macabre by Russell Thorndike
First published London: Rich and Cowan, 1947
First Valancourt Books edition 2013

The Publisher is grateful to Mark Terry of Facsimile Dust Jackets, LLC
for providing the reproduction of the original jacket art used for this
edition.

Published by Valancourt Books, Richmond, Virginia
Publisher & Editor: James D. Jenkins
20th Century Series Editor: Simon Stern, University of Toronto
http://www.valancourtbooks.com

Library of Congress Cataloging-in-Publication Data

Thorndike, Russell, 1885-1972
 The master of the macabre / by Russell Thorndike ; with a new
introduction by Mark Valentine. – First Valancourt Books edition.
  pages cm
 ISBN 978-1-939140-47-0 (*alk. paper*)
 1. Haunted houses–Fiction. I. Title.
 PR6039.H78M38 2013
 823'.914–dc23
          2013011048

All Valancourt Books publications are printed on acid free paper
that meets all ANSI standards for archival quality paper.

Set in Dante MT 11/13.5

INTRODUCTION

Russell Thorndike and his sister Sybil, who both became eminent and much-loved actors, spent some of their childhood holidays at their mother's cottage by the sea wall at Dymchurch, a village in the middle of the Romney Marsh, and they continued to go there in later life. It was an area they loved and often evoked, an expanse of one hundred square miles, much of it flat wetlands, reclaimed from the sea. Russell Thorndike used the Marsh as a setting for his most colourful and memorable character, the dastardly smuggler Dr. Syn. The cottage was also the destination, never then reached, of the writer-narrator of *The Master of the Macabre* who has to seek shelter instead at the remote house of the title character, the enigmatic recluse Charles Hogarth, a scholar of the occult.

His sister envisaged Dr. Syn as "poking his head out of a dyke in our dear beloved Marsh" and proclaimed his appeal for "the souls like us who love a thrill," who "will be jollier for the meeting" with the swashbuckling villain. The Master is a sort of successor to Dr. Syn in her brother's literary career: but instead of smuggling, his business in darkness is the supernatural. Indeed, Dr. Syn and his crew make use of the strangeness of the "devil-ridden marsh" (as Thorndike describes it) by spreading rumours of phantom horsemen, to warn people off from witnessing their own nocturnal rides after contraband. But these are just ingenious spectral subterfuges: the Master deals in the real thing.

The Thorndikes were children of the church. Their father was a minor canon at Rochester cathedral, the Kent city which had been a favourite haunt of Charles Dickens (he set the unfinished *Mystery of Edwin Drood*, 1870, there). Arthur Russell Thorndike was born on 6 February 1885 in the cathedral precincts, and he recalled that for them as children these were not solemn and sacred, but a wonderful playground, "our scenes for plays and romances." He and his sister were deeply attracted by the theatre from an early age, writing and performing in their own plays as children. This sense of the church as a sort of historical "playground" is still reflected over fifty years later in *The Master of the Macabre*, his 1947 book, where a former Archbishop's palace has been turned into the quaint home of the title character, a chapel is a bedroom, and an old tomb has been made into a bath. The religious house has become a theatre for the story: for Thorndike, all the past, sacred or secular, is a pageant of incidents and imagery.

This instinct had started early. The precocious boy's earliest literary productions were religious plays, showing how his imagination mingled the matter of the church with a delight in the theatre. This could only have been nurtured further when he became a chorister at St. George's, the Chapel Royal, Windsor, accustomed not only to holy services but also to regal and state occasions, full of elaborate costume and ritual: he sang during the magnificent obsequies of Queen Victoria's funeral in 1901. Thorndike later wrote a history of the Chapel and the choir, *Children of the Garter* (1937; the title reflects that St. George's is also the chapel of the Knights of the Garter).

In their early twenties, both he and his sister, who had been training for the theatre, joined a Shakespearean company touring North America, and they were away for several years. Later tours took them also to India and South Africa, and they performed in London over the next ten years. During the American tour, on the road to a rather volatile Southern town, Russell spun a fantasy to his sister about Dr. Syn: she later recalled she was "rigid with fear and thrill, open-mouthed" as he unfolded "horror upon horror." On their return, Russell Thorndike began to write the book. This too revealed his dual fascination with the theatre and the church. For Dr. Syn is a most dramatic, cavalier villain by night; but he leads a double life: for by day he is the pious and kindly parson of the parish. He epitomises, with a grand flourish, the two great impulses of Thorndike's life, the religious background of his upbringing, and the two siblings' devotion to the stage. Something similar might be said of the Master of the Macabre too: a secular scholar, flamboyant in costume and address, but also a seeker after the things of the spirit.

The First World War intervened in their lives, and it brought sorrow: their brother Frank was killed in action, and Thorndike, who had joined up in the First Westminster Dragoons at the outbreak of the war in 1914, was badly wounded at Gallipoli and invalided home in 1916. He had used some of the time at the front to complete the book he and Sybil had planned so long before: and in 1915, *Dr. Syn: A Tale of the Romney Marsh* was published by the young and adventurous firm of Robert Holden (they also took early work by Claude Houghton and Australian fantasist Vernon Knowles).

Thorndike married Rosemary Dowson, a daughter of an actress, in 1918, resumed his acting career and was soon in demand as a leading man, though he was also involved in theatre management and directing. Amongst many major roles, he took both lead and character parts in Shakespeare productions, appeared in the English premiere of Ibsen's *Peer Gynt*, and was also in demand for modern plays. In film, he often portrayed characters much older than himself, including Dickens's miser Scrooge, and he could also be relied upon to provide what actors then called "a bit of the 'old,'" in a different sense, meaning the grand, melodramatic style of Victorian theatre.

He also became an industrious writer, perhaps sometimes simply because he needed the money: not all his theatrical projects were a financial success. As well as his adventures and mysteries, amongst his miscellaneous books were a series of adaptations of Dickens for children, a biography of Sybil, by then even better known and adored than he was, and two guides to Shakespeare's country. But he remained best known as the creator of Dr. Syn.

It can be as hard for a writer to make a truly memorable villain as it is to come up with a believable hero, but a few authors have certainly succeeded. E. W. Hornung's Raffles, Guy Boothby's Dr. Nikola, Sax Rohmer's Dr. Fu Manchu and George Macdonald Fraser's Flashman have all won favour with readers. And Thorndike's Dr. Syn is certainly among their number. In seven swashbuckling adventures and several films, this ruthless rogue rides with his eerie horsemen across the night marshes, ever eluding the watch of the Excise men.

It wasn't only the splendid title character that attracted readers. It was also the setting, finely evoked by Thorndike, among the remote wastes of Romney Marsh, a place which already had an uncanny reputation. Nor was the double life of Dr. Syn entirely an unrealistic romance, for in coastal parishes it was not unusual for the local parson to at least turn a blind eye to, if not actually condone, smuggling activity. There's a story of one church service cancelled because there was no room for the congregation: the nave was full of bales of tobacco and the pulpit stacked with barrels of brandy.

However, Thorndike had made the mistake of apparently killing off his villain in the first book, presumably not realising how popular he would be. He found various ingenious ways around this in the six subsequent titles, but it was twenty years before Dr. Syn rode again, in *Dr. Syn Returns* (1935; the other books in the series followed quickly after). In the intervening period, however, Thorndike wrote a handful of other strange and thrilling yarns, starting with the fine murder mystery, Dickensian in atmosphere and set around the cathedral in Thorndike's home town of Rochester, *The Slype* (1927, also available from Valancourt). He went on to write further dark romances after the Dr. Syn series finished. In all, there were nine novels that were not about the diabolical parson, concluding with his historical adventure of the 11th century Saxon rebel Hereward the Wake, *The First Englishman* (1949). Most of them are crime novels, though all with peculiar and sinister aspects.

The long shadow of his immortal villain has tended to obscure these other books, which can be as full of picturesque characters and strange adventures as the Romney Marsh titles. *The Master of the Macabre* is Thorndike's first fully supernatural story, and as atmospheric a tale as you could want for an autumn evening or a winter's night, full of foul weather, processions of phantoms, sinister assailants, *diablerie* and intrigue. Who is the Master? He is, says the narrator, "the most curious, the most uncanny man I ever have met or ever shall meet." Like Dr. Syn, he leads a sort of double life. He is a scholar, a visionary, a dreamer: but he is also an active investigator of the strange, a collector of legends, and their associated curios, across the world. And these he recounts to his chance acquaintance, the narrator, over a roaring fire in his lonely house.

Thorndike's publisher for this book, Rich & Cowan, noted that "Russell Thorndike has himself been named 'The Master of the Macabre,'" and said "this volume of strange happenings enhances his reputation in this line of literature." A contemporary notice, in one of the first journals of the field, did not wholly agree. *Fantasy Review* (February-March 1948) conceded "the individual stories are

well told" but thought there was too much of "graveyard worms
and putrefying corpses" which "merely induced a slight feeling of
disgust." The tales of Poe, Machen, Lovecraft and Blackwood were
thought to be better, as they only "hint darkly of such things"—
suggesting perhaps a not very close familiarity with their work.

The great authority on supernatural fiction, E.F. Bleiler, thought
the structure of the book was a problem, calling it a "hodge
podge," but the reader should not find it difficult: it unfolds quite
easily in the narrative. There are three clear strands, gradually
revealed to the narrator, Tayler Kent, biographer and adventurer,
who ends up a guest of the Master after a car accident in deep
snow while delivering a mysterious package to him on behalf of a
friend. The first concerns hauntings associated with the Master's
ancient house and its hidden mystery, linked to a renegade monk.
The second plot line is a duel between the Master and rivals who
want a relic he has got. And the third is a set of self-contained
episodes in the Master's career as a sleuth of the supernatural,
told to the convalescing writer by firelight. The scheme is rather
like that of Arthur Machen in *The Three Impostors* (1895) or Robert
Louis Stevenson in the *New Arabian Nights* (1882): a major plot
and conspiracy, augmented by piquant minor side-adventures. If
Thorndike is hodge-podging at all, he's doing it in good company.
The idea of a character who was an investigator of the uncanny
had begun almost as soon as detectives of crime became popular
in fiction, in the late Victorian period. This coincided with a surge
of interest in the spirit world, and psychic research, with many
formal investigations of haunted houses, séances and poltergeists,
by learned bodies to which eminent scientists and scholars sub-
scribed. One of the first to take advantage of this climate was the
mother and son team of Kate and Hesketh Prichard who, under
the pen-name E. & H. Heron, created Flaxman Low, an early
occult detective. Fantasy novelist M.P. Shiel took the genre to its
most outré form with his exiled Prince Zaleski, secluded in his
Monmouthshire abbey, full of exotic relics. Others soon followed,
and noted Edwardian examples were Algernon Blackwood's rather
solemn psychic physician, Dr. Silence, and the resourceful and
energetic Carnacki, the Ghost Finder created by William Hope
Hodgson. By contrast, Arthur Machen's Mr. Dyson is a flâneur and

idler who rather languidly lets mysteries come to him, inspired by an ingenious theory of coincidence.

Many more such characters followed, and Russell Thorndike's *The Master of the Macabre* is a late flowering in the field, which draws upon the qualities of several of his illustrious predecessors. He has the scholarly, scrupulous rigour of Dr. Silence, and some of the sybaritic, connoisseur-ish nature of Mr. Dyson: his medieval Archbishop's palace with all its strange and ancient talismans and monuments is like Prince Zaleski's abbey tower, full of curios in a "half-weird sheen and gloom." But he also has the courage and hardihood of Carnacki, and one or two clues perhaps suggest Thorndike might have had Hodgson's hero in mind when he created his own occult detective. One is that the narrator has, like Carnacki, a Chelsea apartment: perhaps not all that striking, as the artistic, bohemian quarter would be an obvious choice for such characters. But the other is more of a hint: the narrator's friend, the adventurous, enigmatic explorer who sends him to see the Master in the first place, is Captain Carnaby. True, that surname is also a London street name, later famous in the Swinging Sixties, but it's so close in look and sound to Carnacki that some tribute might well have been meant. Certainly, *The Master of the Macabre* is a worthy successor to the classic stories of supernatural sleuths: vivid, richly imagined, and lively.

Though he wrote no more books in his last twenty years, from 1950 onwards, Thorndike continued to work in the theatre and cinema, with a regular seasonal role, aptly enough, as Smee in *Peter Pan*, and a few last film appearances in cameo roles in the Fifties. Russell Thorndike died at his Norfolk home on 7 November, 1972, aged 87, after a colourful and somewhat hectic career. Sheridan Morley wrote affectionately of him that he "remained devoted to his wife, sister, and overacting, in approximately that order, across more than half a century of greasepaint touring," and he will always have a place in theatrical history. But it is likely that he will be remembered just as much as a fine, full-blooded teller of tales, as much a master of the "old" in his storytelling qualities as he was as an actor.

MARK VALENTINE

May 4, 2013

THE MASTER OF THE MACABRE

CONTENTS

CHAPTER ONE

GHOSTS DRIVE ME FROM TOWN

IF it had happened once, I should have paid no attention to it. But when it went on—every night—stretching into the fourth week—I began to worry.

In all my fifty years I had never experienced such a thing before.

"Tayler Kent," I said to myself severely, "this is Anno Domini—nothing more nor less."

Of course, I had been working hard—that might have accounted for it. The particularly complicated biography which I was just completing, had undoubtedly taken its toll, and my nerves were a bit jumpy. Could it be nervous dyspepsia, the curse of so many writers? I pooh-poohed the idea. Mental strain had never affected my digestion, so it could not be a blot of mustard, a crumb of cheese or a fragment of an underdone potato, as Old Scrooge so eloquently describes it. And for four weeks running—that was the strange thing. Always the same—no matter whether I went to bed early or late—it was always the same.

I used every sort of subterfuge to elude them. I tried to trick them by keeping my light burning all night—sleeping in my great leather arm-chair—using the spare bed instead of my own comfortable room with its great windows overlooking the Chelsea Embankment—but no matter what I did they would not be fooled.

I turned night into day, but I could not escape. Every time I closed my eyes and dozed off, there they were. Always the same. The woman pleading—the man in turns commanding and servile. Was it a dream or an actual visitation by some tortured spirits? They seemed to be trying to convince me of something—desperately in need of release from some horror.

This dream—if it can be described as such—never lasted long—and on waking I found that the strange feeling of hypnotism remained. Their figures were shadowy—and I was never able to make out whether they belonged to this age or not. But their faces were vivid, and their eyes seemed to be compelling me to obey them. I began to fear I might be mesmerized into an act of violence. Then I began to see those suffering, haunted faces when I was *not* asleep, and I knew there was only one thing to be done. I might have consulted my doctor, but I knew that the hard-headed old Scot would have laughed at me and prescribed a good strong tonic. I might have told the story to those sceptics at the Club and been ragged out of my fears. I might even have sought aid from the Society of Psychical Research. But I did none of these things. I decided—coward that I was—to run away. I would not spend another night in the place. I would go to my cottage on the Romney Marsh, and let them follow me there if they could; that is, if I ever succeeded in getting there myself, as the weather was not promising—eleven o'clock and it was already snowing hard. The eight o'clock news had pronounced several roads impassable, and the papers, never missing a chance of pessimism, were heralding depressions everywhere and recorded the fact that it was the worst November for forty years.

All this in no way damped my determination to escape, and as time went on I began to feel quite elated at the thought of really having tricked my possessive ghosts at last. They were driving me from Town in a biting blizzard, but at least in my lonely comfortable cottage in New Romney I should get a good night's rest and be able to finish my work in peace and quiet.

So an hour later, like a truant schoolboy, I sneaked into my club in St. James's for an early lunch.

I successfully avoided the Club bores—found a quiet table and had an excellent if hurried meal, for I knew there was no time to waste, and in this steady snow it was very doubtful if I could get out of London at all.

On leaving the Club I collected my letters and gave instructions to the hall porter.

"You've not been in for some time, sir," he remarked. "If you hadn't come in to-day I was going to give you a ring. There's been a package here waiting for you for the past ten days or more. I hope it's not important because Captain Carnaby, who left it, told me to lock it up till you come." So saying, he unlocked his cubbyhole and handed me a well-sealed parcel, with an accompanying letter, which I opened straight away.

My Dear Kent,

Ages since we met. Must get together soon. I'll contact you, as my movements uncertain per usual. Do me a great favour. When next you go down to the coast by car, please take the enclosed package and leave it at address named. Won't take you out of your way, as you pass Wrotham. You'd find the bloke it goes to very interesting, if you see him. As I daren't send it by post, you'll know contents are not without value. Anyway, I've risked my old carcass to get it. Bless you & Good Tenting.

Carnaby.

PS. I am learning at last to be cautious. So please burn this note after reading.

I turned to the blazing fire and obeyed instructions, after lighting a cigarette with it as excuse. Then I asked the porter how the Captain was looking.

"Just the same, sir. Hadn't seen him for six years, when in he walks, with his 'Morning, Bill, how are you? Any mail?' Just as though he'd been in every day. Both them Carnabys was nice members. Proper gentlemen always—and clever. But one never knew what either of them was going to be up to next."

I agreed, and stuffing the package into my overcoat pocket, went out to collect my car from the garage, wondering what joke Carnaby was practising upon some gentleman at Wrotham, for I had read the address. No name—but just:

To/The Master of the Macabre
At/The Old Palace of Wrotham.

CHAPTER TWO

I MEET THE MASTER

Snow—that had been piling up for days . . . then Rain and Sleet and a bitter cold Gale . . . a Blizzard that swept the Sunny South and ranged up across the Midlands to the North, turning the roads of every British county into icebound tracks of peril.

The manager of the Old Chelsea Garage certified me as insane for taking out the car. "New Romney?" he scoffed. "You'll never make it, sir. If you send me a telegram to-morrow morning telling me you've got there—I'll wire you a fiver."

"And if I don't—I'll send you the same amount," I replied boastfully.

I lost my bet, as you shall hear—though the obstinate devil that drove me to the attempt did me the best turn in the world—for had I not been so foolhardy, I should never have met the Master.

Yes—Snow—Rain—Sleet and a shrieking Gale.

But the star turn of that tempestuous troupe did not make its appearance till my car, after hours of ploughing and bulldozing, skidded a waltzy way to the top of Wrotham Hill—and then—*Enter Blanketing FOG*—a fog that obliterated the whiteness of the snow and showed the dark night what the phrase '*Pitch Darkness*' really meant.

Knowing the road well, I decided not to attempt the steep and very dangerous descent, but the car took things into its own hands (or rather wheels), for it began tobogganing broadside-on—down and down. Neither brake nor steering wheel had any control, and the chains, which the garage man had insisted on lending me, refused to function. I tried to keep to the left of the road which had been cut into the steep hill-side, for to skid to the right meant a sheer drop into the valley below.

Beyond the windscreen I could see nothing. The fog was black velvet. I confess I was afraid. Yes—very frightened. Then there came a succession of bumps, followed by a terrific jerk which threw me sideways across the next seat and against the door.

There followed a sound of soft thunder—as though some playful giant had emptied a gasometer filled with castor sugar. A heavy thud—and out went my lights. A gigantic snow-slide had fallen from the hill and enveloped the car. I was completely buried. At the same time an excruciating pain began to shoot in my ankle. I tried to wrench my foot clear from the brake and gear handles, but it was firmly wedged. I managed to get at my lighter from the car pocket, and by its glimmer freed my foot from its steel grip. The car was lying on its left side, so that the right doors and windows were above my head. The driving-window and windscreen showed heavy packed solid snow, but the back window was but thinly covered at one corner, and I realized that this door would be my only chance of escape. I had fortunately provided myself with a flask of whisky against the cold, and after a deep pull at it, I felt better able to combat the red-hot needles shooting in my ankle, which was either broken or badly sprained, for it was already swollen. To ease it I kicked off my right shoe, though realizing I should never get it on again. I put out my lighter to save the precious light, but found the darkness too overpowering, so lit it again for a cigarette, by the glow of which I started operations to extricate myself.

I got over the seat and using the near door as a floor, I stood upon my left leg, and pressed my shoulder against the door above my head. It gave about half an inch, only to bring down a fresh avalanche, but I at length lowered the glass and set to scooping the snow clearer with my hand.

I suppose it must have taken me half an hour to get out of the car, close the window and door again, and to abandon all hope of getting at my luggage, except for my beloved typewriter which had travelled under the seat. For the rest—I left them locked up in the 'boot.'

How cold it was as I rested for a few minutes in the drift which was piling up in the fast-falling snow, but I tilted the contents of the flask down my throat, said "Good night" to my car which I could feel had already vanished beneath its chilly pall, and set off, half crawling, half hopping and falling, down the dangerous road.

At first I had no means of guessing how far down the hill I might be, since the fog was too thick for any sight of the village lights, so my only hope was to keep to the road if possible until I could feel its steepness running out on to the level. More by the grace of God than my own feeling, I eventually reached this objective with many a tumble and more bad language, but without rolling down the precipice on my right. No sooner was I sure that I had made flat ground than I began groping for the finger post at the crossroads, which directed one off the main road towards Wrotham Village, but this I failed to find, so turning sharp right I plunged on blindly, sinking waist-deep in snow pockets and floundering into submerged hedges and fencing, which proved I had missed the road and was crossing the fields.

At last I made out that I had involved myself in a farmyard, for I fell into a pig-sty and was indignantly snuffled at by a ferocious sow who objected to trespassers near her squealing litter. My next lap of crawling and stumbling was taken up short by my knocking my nose against the door of a shed from which came the plaintive lowing of a sick cow, and through the chinks I could see the welcome light of a hanging lantern, which I promptly made up my mind to borrow, in order to find the farmhouse the easier.

This I soon did, and a fine old place it seemed, built of grey stone. Passing a mullioned window, I reached a heavily iron-studded oak door with a huge knocker. Either I was so weak from pain and my late exertions, or this implement was weighty and stiff, but I remember the effort it took to lift it. It slipped from my wet gloves with a resounding thwack, which struck me as being too abrupt for politeness, and it was while wondering if I could manage to lift it again that I noticed by the lantern's light, an iron bell-pull at the far side of the door. I hopped across to it and with my last ounce of strength, as I afterwards discovered, gave it a tug, and heard a deep bell echoing through the recesses of the building, which brought to life animal noises from the farmyard. Then I found that I could not release my hold. My fingers were frozen and would not unbend. I heard steps echoing across what proved to be a flagstoned hall, but before the door could be opened, the lantern fell with a crash on the paving, and I sank down against the wall with the bell-pull still in my clenched fist.

It was certainly a surprise to Mr. Hoadley when he swung open the great door, for there I lay in a grotesque attitude, my clothes white with snow, one shoe missing, and my face blue with cold, torn, scratched and bleeding, a broken lantern one side of me and a neat typewriter case on the other.

Not a word could he get out of me, because I had fainted. Checking up later with Mr. Hoadley, I found that it took about three minutes for me to unthaw, physically and mentally. When I came to myself I found myself sitting in a high-backed Jacobean oak arm-chair in front of a fire of logs, in a bare but handsome flagstoned hall.

An elderly man hovered over me, and as the last thing I remembered was the tread of the farmer crossing the hall in answer to my knock and ringing, I gathered that he was the man himself. But anything less like a farmer I could not imagine. True, he wore heavy iron-shod boots, which echoed on the stone floor, but his black suit gave the impression of an old-fashioned butler. I will go further for a more accurate description. Put him in a gown with bobbles on it and no sleeves, faced with black velvet upon black alpaca, and you would have the perfect Dean's Verger for any cathedral. His face was pale and thin, surmounted by a shock of flowing white hair, which gave him great dignity, but softened into good humour by a pair of somewhat weak eyes whose crow's-feet danced with merriment. His nose was long and seemed to be twitching after distant scents, while his slender hands would have given credit to an artist. All this I took in by degrees, for at first I was absorbed in gazing at a large besocked and besoaked right foot which came between me and my vision of the comforting fire. It was looking at me from the top of a much-cushioned stool. As I stared at it, a sharp pain made it clear to me that this curiosity belonged to me, as its red-hot needles, mentioned before, brought back recollection of what had happened to me.

"Drink this, sir," said the gentle voice of the Dean's Verger.

It was then that I noticed his delicate hands, as they fingered an exquisite tear-drop glass of life-giving brandy. "I managed to get a little of it through your clenched teeth—but you was not able to help yourself—not that I'm complainin', sir—it's you what ought to do that—what with your broke ankle and tored face. That's right, sir, now another little sip, and if you could manage to make it a gulp you'd feel the benefit. I don't know what you think, sir, but it seems to me that storms didn't ought to be so aggressive—at least, not with private individuals like yourself, sir. 'Tisn't as though you was a Lord Mayor's Banquet or a political meetin' in the Albert Hall. You was all alone with only one shoe, a very good make of portable typewriter, and a lantern you brought from the cowshed. Now, sir—try again—and if I may give you a toast? Down with stormy aggression against individuals."

I then told him about my escape from the car, and began to apologize for the trouble I was giving him and to thank him for his kindness, but he soothingly dismissed this, telling me not to worry my head over nothing.

"Persevere with the brandy, sir. It will set you up again, before we deals with your poor foot."

He was interrupted by the most violent shrieking of the storm. He chuckled. "You're quite safe here, sir. These walls have stood up to storm since the thirteenth century. They built thick and strong in them days. Still, I doubt if they ever heard worse wind than this." He listened for a moment, shaking his old head, then turning to me nodded slowly and deliberately as he added: "It's my belief you only just got here in time, sir. There's a limit to what the strongest can stand, and you must have reached it when you reached up for our bell-pull. Lyin' down in a storm like this is puttin' money in the undertakers' pockets, and who wants to make them rich? Don't do it again, sir. It's a bad habit."

I told him it was the last thing I wanted to do. "I was up in the Arctic two years ago—pretty tough going, too—but as I crossed those fields between the main road and your farm, I came to the conclusion that the Land of the Midnight Sun was Margate Sands on a hot summer's day compared to this. Worst snowstorm I ever met. If I hadn't stolen your lantern from the cowshed, which at least showed me your door, I think your local undertaker would have made a deal out of me."

"And now, sir," went on the old man, "if you feel strong enough I'd like to take a good look at that foot. By a cursory feel over it with the sock on, which I took the liberty of doin' while you was 'out,' I should give it as a 'clean break,' and should be set at once, if you are willing for me to attempt it. I tried to get the doctor who lives some way from here, but the storm has put the phone out of order. I feel quite confident in setting it as well as he could. You see, sir, I started life as a doctor—a ship's doctor. That, of course, was before I met the 'Master' and turned servant."

"I see," I nodded. "I didn't think you looked the typical farm owner."

"Farm owner? Me?" repeated the old man. He smiled and went on to explain: "And this place isn't really a farm, neither. Just a fine old house which the Master bought, and there happened to be a farm-yard that went along of it. I know very little about farming, though the Master has a smatterin' if I may so say. He has a natural smatterin' of everything. I've seen his smatterin's at work—all over the world, and without boastin' on his behalf, I assure you that his smatterin's in many walks of life as often as not have beat the professionals at their own games." All this time he had been tenderly removing the sock, and passing his slender fingers over my injured, swollen foot. I felt that he was chatting quietly to take my mind from the pain, which he knew I was suffering.

"So you were a ship's doctor?" I inquired.

"And I look no more like one than a farmer, eh, sir?" he chuckled. "I sensibly give it up—two or three voyages, that's all—but I felt there was no career in it for me. I had not got that bedside manner so essential."

"I disagree with you there," I said. "You are handling my misfortune to the manner born."

"Very polite of you to say so," he replied, "but I know my limits, and my manners such as they are would never have opened a door in Harley Street. You'll laugh when you hear what the Master says I has the manners of. Not in these boots, mind you, which I put on to light the oil-stove in the cowshed, but in me house pumps—says I looks and carries on for all the world like a cathedral head verger."

"How very strange," I said, smiling.

"No, sir, I can see what he means and I don't dislike it. You don't think so, sir?"

"I do, and since you like it, I'll confess that I thought exactly the same thing. When I could not somehow place you as a farmer, I thought what a wonderful figure for a dean's verger. That's why I said 'how very strange.'"

The old man shook his head. "Not so strange as you'd think, sir, as you'll probably find out when you've slept in this old place for a few nights, as it looks as though you will. There's something remarkable about this house, sir, apart from its historic interest. To use an old-fashioned word in keepin' with it—this house is very susceptible."

"Susceptible?" I repeated.

He nodded gravely, adding, "To susceptible minds. It makes you—dream. Strange dreams."

"Haunted?" I asked with a smile.

"So they say—and so we've found," he stated gravely. "This house has—influences."

"Nice ones?"

It struck me this time that he nodded doubtfully before adding, "And other ones."

"Sounds interesting," I said. "Please tell me more. By the way, what is your name, Mr. ——?"

"Just—Hoadley, sir. But if you don't mind, I'd rather leave it to the Master to tell you about the house. He's very interested in it, sir, as you will appreciate when you know who he is and what he does—but if you'll excuse me, that, too, I would rather you hear from his own lips. I know he is anxious to tell you himself. You see, sir, he was—well, we was—half expecting you to-night, and that's why I didn't change back into me house pumps after returnin' from the shed. The storm warned me you'd have difficulty, and I kept prepared to run out, as I did, sir."

A practical explanation occurred to me before I had had time to register surprise.

"Is this house called by any chance 'The Old Palace'?" I asked.

"That's right, sir," replied Hoadley.

"And did a Captain Carnaby let your master know that he had commissioned me to leave a package here on my way to the coast?"

"No, sir," answered Hoadley. "At least, the Master didn't mention it to me. But I remember a Captain Carnaby—in India—some years ago—a friend of the Master's. We've heard nothing of him for some time."

"Strange," I muttered, "and since putting it in my pocket I hadn't given the thing another thought. It suddenly came back to me. That's strange, too."

I felt in the breast pocket of my driving coat which I was still wearing, and handed over the sealed packet.

"May I ask why the Captain gives your Master such a curious title?"

"No doubt the Master will tell you that too, sir," said Hoadley. "And now, sir, I must warn you that this may really hurt. Think you can stand it?"

"Go ahead," I nodded, as I leant back in the chair, gripped the arms tightly and straightened out my leg.

Hoadley make a quick, sure job of it, and, as time showed, a good one, but I must have been all in—and the added sharp pain knocked me out again.

When I came to myself, Hoadley was still hovering over me, but I was feeling more comfortable—for instead of gripping the oak arms of the Jacobean chair, I was lying in a luxurious deck-chair, which I soon discovered was on rubber-tired wheels. Beside me, in the glass socket, was a fine old rummer filled with excellent brandy, which Hoadley immediately commanded me to sip. I was still drawn up in front of a flaming log fire, but it was a different fire-place, elaborately carved in stone and reaching to the heavily oak-raftered ceiling, whereas the first fire-place I had seen was plain to severity, and only relieved by a circular shield of arms let into the stones of the chimney-piece. This was altogether a different affair—an ornate array of niched effigies—saints and bishops—emblazoned in the rich, mellowed tones of ancient heraldry, and illuminated by the soft, steady flames of two fat wax candles burning in a pair of massive brass sanctuary standards which stood on each side of the hearth.

My attention was drawn from the blaze of heraldic shields which filled in the gaps between the effigies, by a deep, somewhat nasal voice, asking, "Ah—do you feel better now? I am sorry you have had such a rough passage, but you have had a short, sound sleep which we thought best not to disturb. Hoadley took the opportunity, however, to clean up your face, so unfortunately torn and scratched, and I assure you that you now look quite respectable. I am very glad to meet you, Mr. Tayler Kent. My name is Charles Hogarth and you are now in the library of the

Old Palace of Wrotham, where you are very welcome."

The speaker was sitting a little back from the fire in a high, padded wing arm-chair with his feet on a footstool. To save me turning my head to look at him, Hoadley turned my wheel-chair gently so that I could address my host more conveniently.

He was a remarkable-looking man; elderly, tall and thin, though conveying immediately the great strength and energy which I afterwards found him to possess. His clean-shaven long face was aristocratic, with a fine forehead and a sweep of silver hair. His features, though finely chiselled, had a gauntness that added to his power. My first impression was that his vivid personality had stamped itself upon his servant—the one-time ship's doctor—for Hoadley was somehow a gentle edition of his master, but whereas I found Hoadley's mind to be placid and contented—the Master was alive as though driven by fierce fires in his soul.

All this I took in as I apologized to him for the trouble I was causing.

"Nonsense," he replied, "I owe you a debt of gratitude for coming here. I have read all your books with great interest, and I only wish I could have come to your rescue personally—but as you see—I'm crocked too. Never had a day's illness before—and now—all of a sudden I get pinioned in the grip of what Hoadley here calls neuritis. But I know better—it's to do with this house. So I don't mind so much."

"One can put up with a certain amount of dampness in such an enchanting place," I said.

"Dampness?" he echoed. "This is the dryest house I've ever lived in. Hoadley had to clean the brass every week in our Oxford house—but here it keeps bright for a month or more without a rub. No—it's not exactly the house—it's the influences in it."

Hoadley looked at me as though he would say, 'What did I tell you?'

"No—we must both thank Hoadley," went on my host. "He somehow got me out of that wheeled contraption you're now in, for certainly your need of it is greater than mine."

"I don't remember being moved at all," I said amazed. "How on earth did he manage to lift me by himself?"

Hogarth laughed as he looked from me to his servant. "Ah—don't be deceived Mr. Kent. Hoadley looks as if he were in the next world singing anthems, but he's got the strength of the Devil."

Hoadley smiled seraphically and left the room, saying it was time I took some refreshment. In his absence Mr. Hogarth told me the names and history of the carved figures over the fire and explained that the present house was the only habitable wing left of what was once a vast palace belonging to the Archbishops of Canterbury.

"It was demolished in the thirteen hundreds by an Abbot Islip of Westminster fame who, wanting a strong sanctuary on the river, took such wood and stone as he needed and had it carried ten miles away to Maidstone. When you are well enough to hobble over the grounds, you will see some interesting ruins, which will give you an idea of what the place was like in the days of its glory."

As he rambled on about local history, Hoadley brought in an invalid's tray with soup, fish and chicken, and at the Master's orders a bottle of champagne. When I asked him to convey my toast of thanks to the cook for taking such pains at so late an hour, he blushingly replied that he had done his best.

"Oh, yes," went on the Master, "Hoadley is a good enough chef for any royal palace, let alone an old left-behind ecclesiastical one like this. You see," he explained, as Hoadley disappeared with the empty decanter of port, "although we have servants in the daytime—that is a gardener and his wife and daughter, and help from their small boy—none of them will sleep here."

"Why not?" I asked, though guessing at the answer.

"For the same reason as made me buy the place," returned Hogarth. "Rumours of—ghosts—and queer goings-on. There is no one who will visit me at nights except the doctor and the rector—and I don't think they feel too happy about the place after dark."

"And you?"

"Oh, I love poking my nose into things I don't quite understand," he said, rather in the manner of a naughty little boy, who having started a mischievous adventure, means to follow it up.

"And have you encountered anything—alarming?" I asked.

"Speaking plainly?" he queried, then with an emphatic nod, "Yes."

"May I ask of what nature?"

"I would rather not answer that—yet," he replied seriously. "You see, I want you to give me your impressions—and in order to receive them, you must keep an open mind. If I tell you what I think—it cannot fail to prejudice you. No—don't bother about anything, but just keep an open mind. That, I think, is the best way for you to get things to happen to you. Do you mind if things do happen—to happen to you?"

"Not knowing *what* things—I can't say," I laughed.

"But you are not afraid?"

Suddenly confronted with the question—I was not quite sure. I think I was a little—no, a good deal. But I put a good face on it, replying in his tone, "I would rather not answer that—yet. I shall endeavour to keep an open mind, and if things do happen to happen to me—well, then, I'll give you my impressions."

He smiled—I thought a little grimly—and so did I, for here already I was doing what Hoadley had apparently been forced to do for goodness knows how long—copying the man's personality.

Hoadley had drifted back with another decanter of port, and the Master asked him, "Did you light a fire for Mr. Kent in the Tapestry Room?"

"No, sir. I have prepared the Abbot's Chapel. I took the liberty of thinkin' it the more convenient, sir."

I detected a queer look pass between them, but the Master covered it up with a casual enough, "How so?"

"Absence of stairs, sir. I can wheel Mr. Kent along the corridor—straight to his bed."

"That is certainly a good idea," nodded the Master. "My friend Hoadley is so full of bright notions. And what I said about the dryness of this house, Mr. Kent, certainly goes for the Abbot's Chapel; so don't let the name conjure up any fears of—damp. There's nothing to be afraid of—there. You will certainly have the handsomest room in the place, and the most convenient, too. Hoadley will show you all the gadgets. I hope its influence will inspire you to a new book. Now that your war-work is finished, we require a new book from Tayler Kent as quick as you can give it to us. Oh—and perhaps I had better explain why I elected to turn a chapel into a bedroom. It was forced upon me by the bed itself—a unique one—museum piece—a four-poster worthy of the name. When I came here I found it in pieces in the apple-room, and it was much too good for that sort of treatment. I was not able to put it upstairs as the ceilings were too low, but the Chapel has a lofty groined roof and carries lofty bedposts and carved tester well. You will be the first one to sleep there since the days of the abbots, and their sleep was different to yours."

"You mean their last sleep," I said quizzically, not quite relishing the idea, "lying in state when the Chapel was itself."

"Exactly," he replied. "But many hundreds of years ago. Don't worry on that score."

"I'm not worrying, Mr. Hogarth," I laughed. "I've slept in stranger places in my time, I expect, and I am sure more uncomfortable ones, and I don't mind telling you that I am very sleepy now, due to your excellent dinner and good vintage."

"Then I will not detain you any longer," said my host, "Oh—except to thank you for safely bringing this package to me," and from the table at his side he picked up Carnaby's sealed communication, which I had noticed he had not yet opened. "If you knew how eagerly I have waited for this, you would realize my appreciation of your kindness. I suppose that old oyster didn't mention what this contains?"

"Only that it was important to you," I replied. "And certainly I have known Carnaby long enough to be as close an oyster in asking him questions that don't concern me."

"But I rather fancy that the contents of this will concern you, and I confess my fingers have been itching to break the seals ever since Hoadley handed it to me."

"Then please do so," I urged. "Though why you should think it may concern me I have no notion."

"Just a vague guess of mine, that's all," he smiled. "But I am resisting the temptation to-night. You know as well as I do that Carnaby does not waste his own time or other people's, and breaking silence of some years in which I have not heard from him means that he has accomplished something important to my work which I asked him to do for me when I last met him in Egypt.

At the moment, however, I am worrying out another long problem to its conclusion, and I really must not confuse the issue. So Carnaby's solution, whatever it is, must wait with my patience till I have an open mind to deal with it, though I confess I shall be glad to get rid of a matter that has not only puzzled me but irritated me too for a vast number of years. Perhaps I shall be able to deal with it to-morrow, meanwhile it must remain a mystery in my strong-room."

"I admire your strength of mind," I said. "I was telling Mr. Hoadley that from the time I put the packet into my pocket I forgot all about it, and it was only when he told me that you had been expecting me, that I imagined Carnaby must have told you that I was bringing it. As this is not so, may I ask how and why you did expect me?"

"That will take me a long time to explain to you," he replied. "May we also leave that to the morrow? I am not going to keep you from your rest any longer, so allow Hoadley to pour you out a night-cap."

But I shook my head. "Not another drink, I assure you, sir. I have taken quite enough, and with great appreciation."

"Nothing else?" he asked.

I hesitated and he was quick to notice. "Ah—now what? Please don't be diffident. We and the house are at your command."

"Only another question," I said with a smile. "But there again I am content to wait for your answer in your own time. But I must own to being devilish curious about the nature of your work. Carnaby told me nothing, except that I should find you interesting if I was lucky enough to find you at home. I asked him what your name was, and all he said to that was, 'I'll write the name and address on the package.' Naturally, I looked at the address when I picked it up at the Club, but all the name I read was, The Master of the Macabre."

The Master laughed—a rather forced laugh, I thought, as he tried to explain. "We know Carnaby's whimsical ways and he always avoids using names unless he issues a warrant—that's the policeman in him. Master of the Macabre, eh? Referring to my work. When you get to know me better, Mr. Kent, you'll understand what my very peculiar life's work has been. I started in on it when I was at school, and maybe before that, and it has been the passion of my life. All other things I have let slip by. Such things as marriage, for instance, became impossible, for mine was not the sort of job to share with a woman. I should have driven a wife insane. Get to know me better, Mr. Kent, if you find the patience and the inclination, and you shall be the judge of whether or no I have been wasting my time. And now I think Hoadley is ready to take you to the Chapel. Good night."

"Are you ready, sir?" asked Hoadley behind my back.

"Yes—you can lie me in state like an abbot, Mr. Hoadley," I laughed, and with a further good night and thanks to my queer host, I was pushed slowly out into the hall and along a corridor by the Dean's Verger, while the voice of the Master of the Macabre called from the Library, "Sleep well."

The Verger behind me was intoning, "The ecclesiastical door—Gothic, I think, sir—at the very far end of the corridor—that is the Chapel, sir."

CHAPTER THREE

THE ABBOT'S CHAPEL

EVEN from the distance of the long corridor I could see it was a fine old door, and when Hoadley left my chair to open it I saw how thick and strong it was. The lights were on—concealed electric flooding that showed up every detail of the beautiful stonework—and a log fire blazed and danced. A thick, plain red pile carpet covered the floor. I had noticed the same shade of pile in the Library showing beneath handsome silk Persian rugs. There were some fine rugs in the Chapel, too, which created a feeling of luxurious comfort. Now although I was anxious and apprehensive about entering this unique bed-chamber in which I was to sleep, I was subconsciously thinking how little I knew about the Library I had just left. True—the fire-place was fresh in my memory, with all its attendant effigies in detail—but apart from that I could only clearly say that I had noticed my host himself, with a white cambric stock round his throat tucked into a quilted collar of a black velvet dressing-gown. I remembered his great chair, and the corner of a sturdy oak table by which he sat. But his face and figure were enthroned amidst vague shadowy shapes of books and glass cases. Hoadley, having opened the door wide, returned to the back of my wheeled chair and guided me into the room in which I was to encounter many strange experiences.

Its chief feature was the bed—huge—handsomely carved—with old gold velvet damask hangings from the heavy oak canopy. These were open so that on my first entrance, no part of the Chapel was hidden. The back of this great bed was against the wall—otherwise there was space all round it. Hoadley steered me alongside and then closed the door, while I looked round. As my host had said, the fire-place was a replica of the one in the hall.

"An interesting shield of arms, sir," said the Dean's Verger, following my gaze. "It is what is called a 'rebus,' and a very famous example. As you are probably aware, sir, a rebus is a heraldic joke—a sort of pun. This is a double rebus—two jokes in one. You can tell the original owner of the shield by the picture. What do you make of it, sir?"

I described to him what I saw—a sun in the shape of an eye looking at a tree from which was falling a man, to whose mouth was attached one of those balloons in which nowadays comic newspaper artists write their captions. I was too far away from the fire, however, to read this ejaculation.

"The sun, sir, is God's eye, like the masonic sign," explained my guide, "and the tree is but a slip of a one. I SLIP. On the other hand, and so as there won't be no mistake, the poor gentleman falling out of the tree is callin' out, "I slip." That's the name, sir, same as in the hall, and same as in the Islip Chapel at Westminster Abbey. Abbot Islip, sir—Abbot of Westminster—Archbishop of Canterbury—and the last man to renovate this Chapel—well—no—not the last, because the Master has restored it in our time from bein' used as a hen-house. But, you know, the old Abbot wasted his time and labour, because the records say that no sooner had he restored this chantry than he changed his mind and pulled down the rest of the monastery to cart it over to Maidstone."

"And that, I presume, is his tomb," I suggested, indicating a carved stone canopied shrine let into the wall beyond the bed.

"Yes, sir, it is a tomb—but——"

"How cheerful," I interrupted. "I suppose, then, I share a double room with Mr. Islip."

"Oh—no, sir," Hoadley contradicted quickly. "His remains are not there, sir. I'll show you in a moment. No, sir—no remains is there, sir. That tomb was built for a tomb, but never has been a tomb. Abbot Islip lies in Westminster—in his own chantry— whereas this was built for another party—a predecessor of his—but you see, sir, all along of his being a gay dog and a dark horse combined, as it were, he was forbidden Christian burial. The Master has a very entertainin' copy of his record, which was distinctly black. Abbot Porfirio's the name, sir. Sounds Italian to me. Well— this Porfirio apparently dabbled in devil's magic—and at the same time carried on with the pretty novices under his charge. Them days seems to have been the ones for carryin'-ons. And there was no *News of the World* neither to show 'em up."

"Ah, well," I sighed, "I confess I didn't relish doubling up with a corpse."

"No fear of that, sir," pointing to the tomb. "Never put to its proper use, wasn't that tomb. When we first come here it hadn't even got a cover to it. We found it used for mixin' pig-wash and a trough. But now, sir, the Master has put it to a more comfortable purpose. You lifts up the lid——" and suiting the action to the word he hinged back to the wall a heavy mahogany top—"and there's as fine a bath as I ever have seen. All modern appliances too and a nice polished marble interior what the Master had let in and calls Ali Bastard like them Forty Thieves. And when you've seen the doctor, sir, we'll fix you up a sling for your foot so that you can try the bath out."

The old man then helped me to undress into a pair of pyjamas that were already warming by the fire, after which he opened a door of a long, tall, oak cupboard ecclesiastically suited to a vestry and unhooked a Paisley shawl dressing-gown which he lay at the foot of the bed. He then indicated a pair of crutches that stood in a corner of the wall by the bed and advised me "not to get about too much till we know just how the ankle does."

"You seem to have had everything ready for my reception," I laughed. "What made you think of crutches? You didn't know about my ankle, I take it?"

"Well, sir," hesitated the Dean's Verger, "the Master, if I may say so—was advised. The house kind of influenced him."

"Do you mean he was told of my accident in a dream?" Indeed, in the atmosphere of that strange house I felt anything was possible.

"The Master will no doubt tell you all about it, sir," and Hoadley changed the subject by showing me how to turn the lights off from the bed and urging me to have no compunction in pressing the electric bell if I was in pain, as it was connected with his own room and he would be pleased to wait upon me. "For if I may say so, sir, there is nothing so tedious as an ache that keeps one awake."

"I'll grin and bear it rather than disturb you," I replied. "You have been more than kind already."

"You will not be disturbing me, sir. I sleep very light—especially when the Master is working all night which, in spite of his surprising attack of neuritis, he is about to do now. On such occasions, sir, he takes coffee—quantities of it—and as he does me the honour to say that I make it more to his taste than he does himself, I get up every two hours and a half and replenish it. Even if you do not ring, sir, I shall take the liberty of tiptoeing along the corridor at coffee times, just to ascertain whether you are asleep or awake. It will be no trouble, sir, I assure you. There is a fine crypt beneath this room, sir, in which the Master very often works at night, but owing to his malady, he will not be there, but in the Library. In fact, sir, his work to-night will be very silent—merely contemplation and puzzling over a problem which he is hoping to solve."

"Strange to have a crypt under one's bedroom," I said.

"I mention it, sir, because the Master uses it as his workshop—experiments and the like—and I felt relieved that he wouldn't be usin' it to-night, as there's sometimes echoin' up here when he uses a hammer or such-like down there. No—*that* will at least be all quiet to-night, sir; and the wind is dyin' down—gettin' more gentle—because the snow's failin' straight again though heavier than ever."

"My poor car will have quite disappeared by morning," I replied ruefully. "Won't do it much good."

"Don't worry about that, sir," went on the old man. "Keep it nice and tucked up. Snow's warm, you know, when heavy, and the sleet gives over. I'll get the garage man at the Bull Hotel next door to tackle it. He's a first-rate man with cars—and his old father—still alive, sir—was the best man with horses—the very last man, he was, to drive the Dover Mail. Quite a picture they makes together, sir. Father and son. Ancient and modern they stands for—like the hymn book. And such a contrast, in looks as well as habits. Son's thin—father's stout. Son's small—father's huge. Son's pale—father's red. Son oozes of petrol—father of stables."

"Drove the mail?" I asked astounded. "Do you mean a coach?"

"That's it, sir—and they say it was always dead on time when Daddy Swift handled the ribbons. He's ninety odd and still looks well on a box seat."

"Wrotham seems a more than interesting place," I ventured.

"It is that, sir," he nodded.

"And I've only considered it as a place to drive through on the way to the coast."

"And you'll now know it as a place to stay in, sir, and I'll be surprised if you don't find it more than interestin'. You may find it one of the queerest spots, sir—queer and—disturbin'."

"Disturbing, eh?" I echoed. "Well—I doubt if anything could disturb me to-night. And thank you again, Hoadley, for all your help. Your Master will be wondering what has happened to you."

Hoadley shook his head. "Not while he's contemplatin' and concentratin', sir. He'll be sittin' quite still, drawin' briskly at his pipe and just thinkin'. What's more, he won't move till he's got the better of his thoughts or wants more coffee. But I must take his wheeled chair and get him into it, because in between coffees he may have need to navigate hisself to the bookcases to refer to notes. And now—as Mr. Pepys says, 'So to bed,' and good night, sir, good night."

He and the wheeled chair went out silently into the long corridor, and he then closed the door gently behind him, leaving me
alone in the Islip Chapel, but not for a very good night as you shall
hear.

CHAPTER FOUR

FIRE—WORMS—AND THE DEVIL

EXACTLY when I went to sleep, I have no idea. I know that for some
time after switching off the lights I lay and admired in the bright
flickerings of the log fire, the superb architecture of the Chapel,
and fell to wondering how it looked when filled with chanting
friars.

I pictured the Abbot glancing thoughtfully at the bath, or tomb
as it was then, and cogitating as to when he would be called to lie
there—or did he have any inkling that he would be buried with
honour in his own chantry in Westminster? I saw him smiling at
his heraldic joke above the fire-place, and then glancing furtively
around to see if any of the brothers had noticed his attention
straying from his book of office.

Well—if in those days they had a serving monk to make such
a skilful log fire as Hoadley could, the community would have at
least been warm and cosy in their chantings. My thoughts also
wandered to my host—the Master of the Macabre—wondering
what his mysterious profession might be. I explored all possible
and impossible theories. What, for instance, were the notes which
Hoadley said he would wheel himself to fetch between the coffees? What did he hammer at in the crypt when free of neuritis?
What sort of information had I brought him from Carnaby? Of
what nature were those richly bound volumes that had peeped
through their glass cases at him from the shadows of the luxurious
Library? I tried every calling to fit his background from criminolo-
gist to the public hangman, and felt that none of them was right.
He had owned during my dinner that he was descended from the
great Hogarth. This was a possible line—that he was a painter

of macabre pictures? I felt, however, that if this were the case, I should have heard of him and seen his work. He had the face and hands of an artist. Was he a sculptor that he used a hammer in the crypt? Yet Hoadley had used the expression 'experiments and the like.' I pictured him sitting stiffly in that Library chair—thinking. What about? I tried to stage in my mind his first meeting with the curious Hoadley, and found it easy to imagine his strong personality compelling that Dean's Verger of a ship's doctor to leave all and follow him to be his disciple. And I presume that it was in this puzzling that I slid into sleep.

My next reaction was being soothed awake by a soft caressing sound within the room. Something or someone was moving in the Chapel.

It was a ghost, of course. The house was traditionally haunted, and here it was. I had only to keep quiet and wait for it to materialize.

Yes—there it was again—a rustling of silk. Strangely enough my certainty that it was a ghost did not alarm me. Had I considered for a moment that it might be a male ghost, I should no doubt have been very apprehensive, but I had been brought up to imagine that masculine spirits built up their dramatic entrances by a clanking of chains, while the same tradition had taught me that the female of the species resorted to a rustle of silk skirts, no matter what period her habit as she lived might have been. And yet—what was a female doing in a monastery? I answered that to myself out of Hoadley's mouth, 'those was the days for carryin's-on.' As the sound continued I grew more and more curious, and more cautious, too, not daring to move for fear of scaring her from an appearance. Then I wondered if this could be her exit rather than her entrance. She might have been disporting herself materially while I slept. This gave me an acute feeling of disappointment which proved to me I was not afraid. How long then had I slept? Some little time, evidently, since on looking at the fire I could see that the big log that had been burning at the top had broken and fallen into the glowing coals.

Still the silk rustling continued—now very faint—now very clear.

Then a new thought came to me. Silk robes. A monastery. Perhaps the ghostly robes of a cardinal were more probable. I began cudgelling my brain for dates. The only English cardinal I could think of who had spiritual reasons for haunting a Kentish monastery was Wolsey. I ruled him out when I remembered that this palace had been dismantled before his time.

Ruminating on these things for a considerable time, during which neither beautiful novice nor cardinal appeared, I fell asleep again, for how long I cannot guess, to be awakened by a fierce crackling noise which proved to be a fresh strong log upon the fire, causing shadows to dance amidst the arches of the groined roof. The log had been put there by Hoadley, for he stood before it checking the figures on a tape measure. Not in any mood for a renewal of conversation, I kept quite still, feigning sleep, but through half-closed lids I saw him tiptoe quietly to the bath and measure its breadth from the back of the carved niche to the front of the tomb, which gave me the uncomfortable feeling that I was watching my undertaker preparing for my burial. He then went back to the fire with his thumb pressed against the correct measurement, which he read and evidently committed to his memory.

It was then that I heard again and most distinctly the same sound of rustling silk that had puzzled me before. I saw him look round as though to assure himself that it had not disturbed me, and I closed my eyes tight. It took me a long time to open them again, for I seemed to have lost the power to do so. Of course, what had happened, I had fallen once more into sleep, for the new log was half-burned through, and to my astonishment Hoadley still stood there with his back turned towards me. He no longer held the tape, at least I couldn't see it, for both his hands rested against the stonework above the fire, and his body leaned forward with his head down as though in distress. I was about to speak and ask him what was wrong, for I imagined I heard him sigh, when as though with a great effort he straightened his back and stood to his full height.

It was then that I knew it was not Hoadley at all. Neither was it my host. Whoever my visitor might be, he was dressed in a long gown reaching to his feet which were bare. No—it was not Hoadley, for this figure was much too tall—neither was it Mr. Hogarth, whom I remembered was very slim, whereas this person had a colossal breadth of shoulder. If I had had no sort of fear when expecting to see a female visitant from another world, I could not be so boastful now, for I found myself in a sweating terror of the man turning round, lest it should be the face I knew so well. I knew he was going to, although at first I could only see the back of his skull which frightened me because of its unnatural size. Such a breadth of shoulder hinting at a chest like a gorilla, demanded a huge head to set off such a giant frame, but the terrifying part of it all was that the head was much too small, exactly as though a pygmy's head was joined to the body of a colossus.

The back of the skull was bound with a sort of rolled cloth which exposed a circular bald patch, surrounded by thick and curly black hair. It was the figure of a monk—for the patch was not natural, but an obvious tonsure, and the robe was that of a black monk. Then the house was haunted and this was a ghost, and to my shame be it said, I was in terror, and this terror increased when the head began to turn, slowly. In my own excuse let me say that I was weak. I had gone through a good deal even during my drive down, and although in the end it would appear on the surface that I had landed on my feet and gained a haven of outwardly good comfort, even luxury, the whole evening's adventure had been, perhaps, too macabre for an exhausted soul.

But when that face looked straight at me, and I turned on the lights full, to find it still looking at me, I cannot begin to tell you how I was shaken to the core. But first it is important to this story and in mine own defence that I should try to describe the face, since much is to come of it later in this history, a history—not of myself—but of Charles Hogarth, whom this book is mainly about, and who will always be, I think, the most curious, the most uncanny man I ever have met or ever shall meet.

Let me be brief. The cheekbones were very wide, the eyes very large, the mouth far too small and turned up at the corners, the nostrils almost facing one and showing great holes at the end of a long straight nose, and certainly resembling the nostrils of some beast. Added to this the large eyes were of pale watery blue colour, and as I said before the whole face and head much too small for the features and the huge frame to which they were supposed to belong.

Much to my horror, the figure with his pale eyes fixed upon me, began to glide towards the bed. Had he touched me I should have cried out, but fortunately he stopped beside the bed and beckoned with a commanding gesture. Still keeping his eyes upon me he then retreated towards the window which was built in the eastern wall over the carved stone altar. Turning his back on me to my great relief, he knelt down uttering the strangest prayer which came to me like a series of groans that seemed to arise from the man's tortured soul. At the end of this lamentable litany, he slipped his monk's robe from his shoulder and grasping a scourge from his girdle, he began to belabour his bare back with all his strength. As the lead-loaded thongs cut into his muscles he screamed like a wounded beast, and I saw the blood trickling down from the scarlet weals of torn flesh. It was the most horrid sight I had ever seen. After some time he finished this self-punishment by pulling his rough gown over his wounds, and still grasping the bloody scourge, got to his feet quickly, and once more fixing me with his ghastly stare, pointed imperiously towards a door in the wall at the side of the altar. Striding towards it, he flung it open, regardless of the heavy snowflakes that swept in upon him.

I knew what he wanted. He expected me to follow him out into the storm. With the best will in the world, which I certainly had not got, I could not have obeyed him without crutches, which I remember hoping that he would not see. To distract his attention, I threw off the bed-clothes, and feebly pointed to my swathed and broken ankle. He seemed to understand my difficulty, for much to my horror he came close to me and peered down upon Hoadley's handiwork, putting the scourge in his left hand so that his right one would be free. I had lost all power of speech, and as I saw his huge fingers, hovering over the bandages to find where they were fastened, I found that I could not even scream. It was then that a more alarming thing saved me, for although I could not scream, someone or some*thing* else could. A piercing scream rang out in the night. It seemed to me to come from outside the great window, but of this I could not be quite sure. It certainly came from outside the Chapel, and from the direction of what I learnt next day was the Old Orchard. This surprising noise cutting the silence had a ghastly effect upon the cadaverous monk, who rushed towards the door through which Hoadley had wheeled me earlier. But before he could reach it there sounded three deliberate blows upon it from outside which brought his mad rush of panic up with a jerk. He stood stock-still—rigidly staring, as the knocks echoed once more through the Chapel. Although to me he was still a figure of the utmost terror, I could see that he in his turn was terrified by something outside the door more powerful even than himself. This—I realized—was the dread of Rome and the awful consequence of being solemnly cursed by the Catholic Church represented by a full conclave of monastic colleagues. I gathered this because a deep voice from the corridor was intoning the name *"Porfirio."* Then, after three more blows upon it, the door opened slowly to the accompaniment of a Gregorian chanting of a most fearsome and impressive Rite.

Looking down the corridor I saw an endless double column of monks all bearing candles. As they chanted, they slowly filed into the Chapel. The Litany, or whatever the rite was, being in Latin, gave me no hint of what it meant, for I was not a Catholic and not quick enough to translate the various phrases except one that seemed to be a general response repeated over and over again, and which even in my terror I was able thus to construe:

"Fire—Worms—and the Devil."

As they intoned they came slowly in—filling the Chapel. The strange thing was that the bed on which I lay did not exist for them. They walked through it in orderly files, till I—ignored with the bed—was crowded out by their numbers, who were now standing, now kneeling, all about me. This, however, in no way prevented me from watching the condemned monk, for his colleagues were transparent, while strangely enough, he was not.

Had I not taken such a loathing for him, due to the sweating terror he inspired me with, I should have found it in my heart to pity him, for, at the first chanting of that curiously awful phrase,

"Fire—Worms—and the Devil,"

he had rushed towards the open door at the side of the altar and through which the snow was still falling. But he had no sooner reached it than he sprang back with a cry of horror, as a further party of his colleagues, covered in snow, and holding crucifixes before them, stepped into the Chapel to cut off his retreat. Like a trapped animal he cowered down against the altar, and then suddenly all the monks blew out their candles simultaneously and all was dark, save for the tiny red glow of smouldering wicks, which filled the building with a stench of smoking wax.

Fire—Worms—and the Devil.

That was all I remember—for once more I had slipped into unconsciousness.

*   *   *   *   *

An excruciating pain in my ankle woke me. It burned. Hot needles. The fire was now lower than I had seen it, but there was enough glow to realize that the Chapel was empty, and how relieved I was. The crowd of monks had gone—though I told myself that I preferred the full conclave rather than to be left alone with the huge body and tiny head of Porfirio. Had it all been a dream or an actual manifestation? I longed for morning—hoping to get an early chance of discussing it with my host.

Hoadley had evidently been in the room again during my last sleep, because the curtains round my bed were all closed except those facing the fire. These I closed too by pulling a cord, hoping that if I could sleep again it might make me forget the acute pain in my ankle.

I had no idea of the time. There was no clock in the Chapel, and my wrist watch had been broken when I had capsized with the car. The only way I could gauge the time was to wait for the hour to strike on the church clock. This I determined to do, vowing to keep awake until I heard it. I failed dismally. I slept, and calculating afterwards, found that I missed the striking of both three and four. Through this period of sleep, however, I was conscious of my throbbing ankle. Then I *did* hear it. It struck five, and before the last stroke had ceased to vibrate, I was conscious of footsteps coming along the corridor, and of the door being quietly opened.

I heard another log being placed upon the fire which crackled up, for I could see the brightness through the crack where the curtains had not quite joined.

My ankle still gnawed. Perhaps I groaned aloud under the nagging ache—for I heard Hoadley cross from the fire and gently feel for my bandages. Had this remarkable butler got a healing touch? I was ready to vouch for it in Harley Street itself, for as he manipulated my foot, which had burned like high fever, grew suddenly cool as though he had sponged it with cold water, and the pain had gone.

Without even thanking my old guardian angel I relaxed into the relief of a sound and undisturbed sleep. No more dreams, for I was claimed at last by the freedom of real rest.

CHAPTER FIVE

THE MASTER'S TITLE

WHEN at last I opened my eyes and pulled the cord of the bed curtains I found the Chapel bathed in sunlight. Hoadley was there, having just opened the heavy curtains which disclosed the great east window. I had seen it already in my ghastly nightmare, but now with the morning light behind it, I could enjoy the rich colours of the fine old stained glass.

Without turning round, Hoadley seemed aware of my appreciation and said, "Yes, sir, I always say to the Master that any cathedral could be proud of it." He wasn't looking at it himself, for he was arranging the necessary toilet requisites—brushes, comb, safety razor case, etc., laid out on the stone table beneath it—the same altar of my dreams, though now covered with a white cloth.

Beside the bed stood a trolley with morning tea, *The Times* and *Daily Sketch*, cigarettes and matches.

I realized then how I longed for a smoke. To me there is no

cigarette in the day like the first, and I lit one while he poured out my tea.

"Yes," I agreed in answer to his remark about the window.

"And it looks better with the sun behind it than it did from in here last night."

Hoadley's brow puckered. "But you never saw it last night, sir. The curtains were drawn."

"No, of course they were," I said lamely. "What's the time?"

"Five-and-twenty to, sir."

"To what?"

"Eleven, sir."

"What?" I cried aghast. "Eleven? Why didn't you wake me before? I'm a disgrace."

"The Master ordered that you were not to be disturbed till ten-thirty, sir. He was so sorry that you had such a bad night."

"I had some horrid nightmares, certainly—my own fault—I ate and drank too much. But how did your Master know I had had a bad night? He was too crippled himself to come along here to see. Or was I noisy? I'm told I never snore, but I may have talked in my sleep or cried out, for I remember I tried to scream in my dream. By the way, how is your Master?"

"Completely cured, sir—very remarkable—he'll tell you all about it. He was very distressed though that you suffered pain in your foot, sir, but is glad it is better now."

"Yes—thanks to you, my friend," I said. "The last thing I remember was you readjusting my bandage, and I'm ashamed I was too weary to thank you then."

"Me, sir?" Hoadley looked puzzled. "I never touched your foot in the night, sir."

"Well, early this morning then," I corrected. "It was after you'd made up the fire again—yes, it was after you had closed my bed curtains."

Hoadley still wore the puzzled expression. "*Me*, sir?"

"Yes—it was after five o'clock—I was in agonies then—foot burning like hell till you cooled it."

Hoadley shook his old head. "Not me, sir. You was dreamin'. I thought you would. All susceptible people do in this place."

"But you *did*. Don't you remember—the fire—these curtains?"

"I put on a log at five o'clock, sir—but I never came near your bed—neither to pull the curtains nor to see to your ankle. I thought you had pulled the curtains yourself. Didn't you, sir?"

"Only this side after the others had been done. I say, Hoadley——" I had broken off suddenly at something I had seen or rather could not see in the room. "Where's that door gone? The one to the right of the altar. It *was* there. The snow came in—and he tried to make me go out into it."

A look of wise understanding came over his face. "Oh—yes, sir—door? Of course. *He* wanted you to go out? And you couldn't because of your ankle. A lucky thing, after all, that ankle. He wanted the Master to go out too—only *he* couldn't neither because of his neuritis. Another lucky misfortune, too, perhaps. A door, sir? You must ask the Master about that. I've never known no door there. Only the one there into the corridor. I think I gets the other business though. P'raps he had the power to cure you for his own ends—your foot—so you could trot after him—and then the Master's immobility—cured that too so that he could. If he ain't as cunnin' as a fox like I always thought him. Would never do no one no good turn unless he could get twiddled for a good turn too. No—I never liked him—nor never trusted him, neither."

"Who are you talking about?" I asked, wondering whether they had seen anything in the night, and whether there really was a ghost.

Hoadley bit his lip. "I'm talkin' a bit too much, I'm afraid, sir, and the Master don't like me to. But it's ever so queer. The Master was cured before you then. Yes—for he was down in the crypt about three, makin' you a foot-sling for the bath. I come in here and measured it up and then he went to the crypt to hammer it up. Here it is, sir, and very neat, I thinks."

"What?" I cried, scarcely looking at the contrivance made with great care for my comfort. "Then you weren't a nightmare with the tape measure. I thought you were an undertaker. And did you say 'hammer'? Then that must have been the awful knocking at the door before the monks filed in. I shall never forget the smell of their candle fat. Had there been a candle burning in here I could understand it, but not with electric light."

"Well, I brought a candle in here, sir. I'd been mendin' a fuse in the corridor, and came in to make up your fire. I blew it out, so as not to wake you, sir, with too much light, and now you mention it, I didn't snuff it till after I'd dealt with the log."

"They say there's always a cause for any effect if you can only find it," I said wondering.

"And that's funny, too, sir, because them were the identical words the Master said to me at about three o'clock, when he moved in his chair, after solvin' a problem. That was queer too, because he never thought he'd get it by the second coffee-time, being disturbed as he was. Perhaps the Disturber helped him—to suit his own turn, of course. Still, he enjoyed the disturbance—thinkin' it was that what cured him. I go further, sir. I say it was Porfirio's hand that touched him same as he touched your foot."

"What?" I cried out again. "Do you mean to say——"

"Didn't mean to say nothin' sir," he interrupted quickly. "The Master will tell you about the hand."

"The hand?—oh, all right—but please tell me this. How did your Master know that I had suffered in the night—and then got better? Did he come in here at all?"

"Oh—no, sir—no one came in here but me."

I laughed. "That's what you think, eh? But I think that you really think more—a good deal more—only you have made up your mind not to do any more talking on the subject. Is that it, Hoadley?"

He smiled. "If I have a fault, sir, it is perhaps that I do talk too much upon occasions. I suppose, though, I can ask questions, sir? That's different to talkin', I take it, and the Master never told me to avoid that."

"Well—all right then—ask?"

For a few moments Hoadley looked steadily at me before saying, "So you saw the Abbot Porfirio."

"Yes," I replied grimly. "Who told you?"

"He did," said the old man grimly.

"I suppose I shouldn't ask when and where?"—for I had seen how nervous he was of being led to talk behind his Master's back.

"Well, sir," he hesitated, "it seems only fair that I should answer you, when you've done the same for me. I have seen him many times, but he was never so persistent as last night. He followed me about. Wouldn't let me sleep between coffee-times. He made me understand quite plain that he wanted the Master or his guest or both, to follow him out into the night. I told him plain that thanks to his cruelty neither of the gentlemen under my charge could walk—that the misfortunes he had brought upon them had made them too ill to brave the night, especially in such a storm. He didn't deny his responsibility, so I know he is the cause. You see, sir, after long association with my Master I have gathered something of the Laws of Witchcraft as practised in the Middle Ages, and it seems that God for His own purposes is not above making bargains with the Foul Fiend. You gets an example of it in the Book of Job. God gave Satan the power to use the Winds of the Wilderness to blow against that patient old man for the destruction of his house. And in mediæval times it was given to witches to ride the storms. Even to-day tempests are wicked perks of the Devil. You don't tell me that belchin' volcanoes, typhoons and the like ain't the properties of Hell itself? And old Porfirio ain't no fool neither. Hand and glove with the Devil he was, and to my belief still is, and he don't get the Master nor you, sir, hoppin' about the grounds at night in his service. And might I ask you not to mention this to the Master? He's rather fond of laughin' at me—callin' me pixylated, and it's a word I don't like, sir, me bein' in all things very practical if I may so say."

"Pixylated," I echoed, laughing. "That's nothing to what I'll be if I stay here many nights. I don't mind confessing that I feel pretty shaken by what I dreamt last night."

"Dreamt or saw. I wonder which. And now, sir, if I may suggest," he changed the subject hurriedly, "you'll keep quiet till you has your breakfast, which I can have served for you straight away, and then there is the matter of shavin', which no doubt you would like done, and when you've seen the doctor we can ask him whether he recommends a hot bath or no. I managed to get through to him just now, as when I was out I saw they was repairing the blown-down posts."

"You've been out already then? Is the snow still deep?"

"Very, sir. But it's clear and bright and sunny. Pipin' for the blood to dance, too, as Charles Dickens says. A very good writer, too, sir, if I may express an opinion. You see, sir, knowin' you was anxious about your car, I went over to the 'Bull' and got Young Swift—though he ain't so young—to hop up the hill and locate your car. I was lucky enough to be first in the queue for his breakdown appliances, and him bein' a quick worker got her clear in less than an hour with shovels, and she's lyin' now snug in his garage. In the night I had taken the liberty of providin' myself with your keys, and we opened the boot and got your cases out, which I unpacked, puttin' your clothes in the airin' cupboard, so that if the doctor allows you to get about a little in the house on crutches, you'll at least feel warm and dry."

"My dear Mr. Hoadley," I laughed, "I shall begin to believe in your Master's accusation of pixylation as far as you are concerned, for you seem to be a positive wizard, which is something akin to witches, magicians and the like. And do I see my own hair-brushes, et cetera, on the high altar there? I do—and you certainly are a wizard then. Thank you. And God bless Magic."

The door opened and a cheery voice cried out, "And how is my guest feeling now? A better morning to you than last night. And hearing you mention the word magic as I came in, do tell me, is 'thirteen' an unlucky number for you? For me it's a good one, and I like it—Fridays too, and isn't it Friday the thirteenth of November?"

My host looked quite a different man. He was now dressed in riding breeches, stock and tweed coat. His face looked a good deal younger now that his features were not crippled with pain. I had not seen him move very much upon the night before, but now I discovered that he walked about with an easy stride that might have been borrowed from a Bedouin chief. It conveyed dynamic purpose. He went over to the window in the west wall. I saw that it had casements to open, and though lead-rimmed, there was no stained glass. He stood there looking out at the snow while he talked, expressing his regret that I had passed a troubled night.

"You may wonder how I know," he said, smiling, "but you'll find that this house has the strangest properties—powerful, insidi-

ous ones. I am sure that your mind will be strangely influenced by
it. While Hoadley fetches your breakfast perhaps you would tell
me exactly what you dreamt. But first let me assure you that I had
no subtle designs on your rest by consenting that you should spend
the night in this room. The most active—if I may use the word—
yes, certainly the most active room in the whole house so far, has
been the one in which I sleep. It is called the Spanish Chamber
because its walls are decorated with very fine old Castillian leather
embossed with queer designs of the fifteenth century. Had it not
been for your ankle you would normally have been put in the Tapestry Room, which in my experience here has the most peaceful
atmosphere, for its haunt according to legend is that of a beautiful novice, more sinned against than sinning. However, you have
had enough of ghosts. We'll see what the doctor says about your
foot, and then contrive to get you up there to-night. I have slept in
the Tapestry Room and assure you, have neither seen nor dreamt
about the young lady. You'll be peaceful enough you'll find, and I
am sure Hoadley and I will be able to hoist you up there. Meanwhile I should suggest that you use the wheel-chair and spend the
day in my Library. Hoadley will bring your lunch in there, and you
will have it to yourself, as I am intending to combine business with
pleasure, indulging in my passion for riding in the snow. I wish
you were able to accompany me, but if you like horses we can
postpone some rides together till you are healed. I'm going over to
Maidstone across country and shall call in at West Malling Abbey
on the way back. You see something occurred to me last night too,
which has set me wondering, and I wish to dip into some records
in the Old College there—Islip's river stronghold which I mentioned to you over dinner. But come along—please tell me your
experience of the night, before that fanciful old gentleman hovers
back with your breakfast."

He lit a cigarette while I quickly told him of my dreams. He made
no comment, for I was scarcely finished when the butler returned
conveying my breakfast and telling his Master that his horse would
be round in a few minutes. And what a breakfast—and how beautifully served. Grapefruit, Scotch porridge with cream and brown
sugar, then, such a kedgeree as I have seldom tasted—only to be

followed by real buttered eggs, rolled bacon and a kidney, sup-
ported with French rolls (made, I discovered, by Hoadley and not
the local help), hot toast done to a turn, home-made marmalade
that really did taste of orange peel, and all washed down with
plenty of excellent coffee, kept hot like the dishes on one of those
glorious Victorian copper conveniences so well nicknamed Slug-
gard's Friend, whose gentle smell of methylated spirits served to
remind me of luxurious and leisurely breakfasts of the past. My
host did not keep his horse waiting, it was not the weather for
that—but during Hoadley's hoverings in and out he managed to
enlighten me with something of the reason for the title he bore
upon the packet superscribed by Carnaby.

"I promised to tell you about my life's work, didn't I?" he said,
"but you must get to know me better before judging whether I
am worthy of such a grandiose title as Master of the Macabre.
No one has a better right to criticize me than Carnaby, for he was
my fag at school, and a queer little beggar he was too. He was
the perfect policeman even in those days, and a personal friend of
every fictional detective from Holmes to Sexton Blake. I always tell
him that his brilliant career started the day poor old Middleston
was expelled. This was the climax to a number of money thefts
that had been going on in our House. Well, certain marked coins
planted by one of the masters were found in his locker, and since
he would not deny his fault he was for it. But, thanks to little Carnaby believing in him, he was only at home in disgrace for five days.
Carnaby got to work and proved conclusively that the master who
had planted the coins had been the thief all along, but because
Middleston's sister was engaged to him, the boy had kept his
mouth shut. If it hadn't been for our sleuth, Middleston would not
have been Governor of whatever-he-is at the moment. My own
tastes, though on a different line, ran parallel with Carnaby's. But
whereas he was a solver of mysteries, I merely sought them—a
collector of things and matters macabre. In my youth, far from
being afraid of ghosts and goblins, I hunted for them. At the age of
seven I nearly passed out with pneumonia, contracted through a
habit of climbing from my bedroom window into the churchyard
which lay next to my father's vicarage. With an overcoat over my

THE MASTER'S TITLE 41

night-gown I would lay hidden in the long dank grass amongst the tombs, hoping to see the bodies come out at midnight. As I grew older I sought out people and books that could tell me queer things, and as I believed adventures came only to the adventurer, I went about the world adventuring, collecting the material of odd happenings—mine own and other people's. You will find that a large portion of my book space in the Library is filled with vellum-bound books of mine own manuscripts. Some are in handwriting, some in typescript, and some—my choicest experiences in my line, printed in the old Caxton style from a press I made myself, which I run in the crypt below here. I print two copies—then dismantle the type for the next one. I should like you to bring an editorial mind to bear on some of them, for I find it rather difficult to pick and choose, since most of them being personal experiences have an equal interest for me. And there are such a lot of them, and I think none devoid of something a little unique."

"But how many have you had published?" I asked.

"None," he snapped back. "Good God, no. I couldn't bear to see my carefully selected incidents bastardized in commercial print on paper more suitable for lavatories than lecterns. Besides, it would go badly against my fastidious grain to be put to the mercy of commercial readers and editors, who would rob the stories of their truth just to suit the taste of their particular public. No, Mr. Kent, my selection is for the few—such men as yourself—since I judge you by your own work."

"I can appreciate your irritation against commercial publications," I replied diffidently, "but I find commercialism in our trade is able to supply something which I find far from irritating—money."

"Well, in that respect I am luckier than most," he said with a charming smile. "I have plenty—and I am glad to say I have made it myself—quite on the side—while pursuing my own self-imposed calling. I have been most things in my pursuit of the macabre, as Carnaby would say. There are damned few jobs I haven't had a cut at in my world-wide search, and in some I have been more successful than I deserved, though I gauge my success not from the fortunes I have made in various schemes, but whether or no that line of business supplied me with a worthy story for my collection.

But I see Jack Ketch being led out of the stables, so I must be brief. Doesn't do to keep him waiting in the cold."

"The name sounds macabre enough," I laughed.

"My favourite horse," he explained. "A grand animal but with a sadistical sense of humour. Hoadley suspects that his cherished ambition is to break my neck—hence my name for him. And by the way, Mr. Kent, before I go I must apologize for having talked so much about myself, but it seemed only fair to you that I should satisfy your mind about my background. You knew nothing of me nor of my work, whereas you being a public man, I had the advantage of you. But please bear with me a few minutes longer, because in telling you of my stories I find I have omitted what to me is the most fascinating side to it. For every story I have collected I have acquired a mascot, for want of a better word. That is to say, I have bought, borrowed or stolen, begged and accepted, something in connection with each yarn that can claim to have played its part in the happening. It's a queer collection. All manner of things around which the macabre hovered. Some of these 'props,' as they would call them in the theatre—yes, I was once an actor—are exceedingly valuable in the commercial markets, while a lot of the specimens appear to be mere junk. But their face value soars through association, so that some of the more ordinary objects are more precious to me than others adorned in gold and precious stones. For instance, you will probably agree that a thorn from Christ's Crown or a nail from His Cross would be a far more precious possession than the Koh-i-noor or Hope Diamond. If I may say so without sounding blasphemous—the story value of that thorn or nail would be far more valuable to a collector like myself. In the Library you will notice a glass case of curios. Each evening you are here you shall pick out one that rouses your curiosity, and I will tell you the reason I have given it a place. And one more thing, Mr. Kent. What happened to us both last night seems to indicate that I am about to ring up the curtain on a new happening bequeathed us from the past. In which case I am very happy that you are here to share the excitement with me. And now don't hesitate to call for all you want and I shall be with you again this evening for dinner. Take care of that ankle and don't let the doctor interfere too much with Hoadley's care of it, for I sometimes agree with Stevenson's Billy Bones that 'doctors is all swabs'—though you can take my word for it that Hoadley isn't. And now for the snow and Jack Ketch."

And he was striding along the corridor calling loudly for the Dean's Verger.

*   *   *   *   *

I think that day was one of the most peaceful I have ever spent. Shortly after I had finished my belated breakfast, the local doctor arrived to examine my ankle. I was expecting something quite frightful by the attitude my host had taken of him, but I found I liked him. I think because he was so generous in his praise of Hoadley's setting.

"Couldn't have made such a good job of it myself," he said.

However, he substituted plaster of Paris for the temporary splints Hoadley had put on, and in apology, praised the homemade sling for the bath and told me jocularly that I could lie in the tomb when I liked so that the water was hot enough for hell, adding, "And they say that when one doctor calls in another for consultation, the best thing for the patient is to get into his grave and save time." Certainly I couldn't imagine a tomb being more pleasant. After my luxurious bath, and a comfortable shave, Hoadley helped me to dress, and I finally re-entered the Library in the wheel-chair with time to drink an excellent dry sherry before lunch.

Attracted as I was towards my absent host, I was glad of my solitude that day, and there was no question of being bored in that delightful room, for, with the exception of the manuscript book-cases, I was able to open what glass doors I chose, with a master key left by the Master himself, and as Hoadley had given me a lesson in how best to propel and navigate myself in the chair, I had great fun doing a grand tour of the book-shelves, making a list of such volumes that attracted me most.

The Library by daylight more than came up to expectations. The fire-place upon closer inspection was even a more perfect relic of the past than I had thought it the night before, and I found a beautifully bound book in red leather printed from the crypt press lying on the table, and giving in the Master's own conversational style a full account of the effigies and heraldic designs. A lovely thin volume, pleasing to hold and read. Indeed, that was, I found, the chief feature of the Master's bookcraft. Each work was as delicately beautiful to the hand as to the eye.

Through one of the three large windows I looked up to Wrotham Hill carpeted in rich deep snow with the sun glistening upon it, and felt relieved that through Hoadley's foresight and organization, my car was no longer buried up there. I saw, too, the fine old stables flanking one side of the old tilting yard, and the majestic ruins of what had been the banqueting hall in the days when the archbishops had entertained royalty on their way to Canterbury. One wall stripped of the ivy that covered other pieces of crumbling masonry, showed the arched entrance approached from the sheltered fruit garden. The trees in the orchard, where I was to meet a great adventure, looked like fairyland, and I longed for my ankle to heal quickly so that I could explore so many fascinating nooks and corners. There were two smaller windows, let in to give light to two embrasures, built on, as I learnt, by the Master, to give the lofty chamber more wall space for books. In both of these, running the whole length between the bookshelves, were glass-covered specimen cases, one of which was filled with pottery, coins, weapons and trinkets dug up by the workmen when the Master had restored the place. But a very large case at one end of the main room interested me more, for in it were obviously some of the mascots the owner had mentioned. To this I found it easier to navigate my chair, since there was plenty of floor space around it, and through the glass sides and top I saw for the first time some of his macabre relics.

Yes—a curious mixture indeed. Just like looking through the window of a more than interesting curiosity shop. An eastern dagger—two human skulls—one of which had an Elizabethan clay pipe thrust incongruously through its teeth. A large key with its wards in the shape of a shield, the arms of some house cut into the bright steel, and the quarterings divided by the spaces of the key itself. It lay upon an old scarlet cushion of rich velvet. Near this lay a highly jewelled snuff-box, reclining on a volume of Cæsar's Gallic Wars—a French translation. Looking dull and cheap in comparison was a brass button dented and corroded. It was fixed to a card upon which was written the one word—*Zanzibar*. Then an old piece of gold cord twisted into a loop with a tarnished tassel hanging from it. This reclined upon a coarse-haired grey wig. Next to this was a white moth with a pin through its head and one wing broken and missing. There were lots of other things and all differing, but the one that intrigued me most, perhaps because it took up most room and looked out of place, was a heavy-looking sharp-edged spade with a huge horse-shoe fitted to the handle.

Even before I examined it more carefully, I vowed that I would make the Master tell me its story before any of its case companions.

It seemed to me that the horse-shoe had been put on to strengthen the wood of the right-hand grasp—and quite a useful idea too. Above the upturned iron horns, across the horizontal part of the handle, a date was printed in poker-work—I confess it made me jump as I read it—for burnt deep into the wood I read 13 *Nov.* 1846. The Thirteenth of November—Hogarth had spoken of the date when he had first come into the Chapel. It was the date of this very day, but a hundred years ago.

I refrained from questioning Hoadley about it. I felt he would only say that the Master would tell me in his own good time, and I was already getting tired of that sentence. So I tried to forget about it. But there was another thing which set me wondering about it—a thing which I hadn't noticed at first. Lying in the circle of the horse-shoe handle space was a yellow curl of hair, plaited with pink silk. Whose could it have been, and what connection was there, if any, between its owner and this ugly shovel? I also thought it very strange that my first day in this house where the spade reposed should be upon the identical date.

However, there was quite enough to occupy my mind in the Library, and I contrived to ignore my curiosity, turning the chair with its back to the case, and delving into a volume of local legend and folk-lore, so that I was surprised how time had slipped by when Hoadley brought me in tea, with the news that his master would be back within the hour.

As a matter of fact it was at least two hours before he came in, seemingly very pleased with his day's work and his ride.

"I began to fear that Jack Ketch had given you a last drop," I laughed.

"On the contrary, my dear fellow," he replied. "I have never known him so well behaved, perhaps because we went a-calling on the charming Lady Abbess at Malling Convent. She too was in such a good mood that I not only stayed to tea, but persuaded her to lend me certain archives they possess upon the neighbourhood, dealing with our disturber of the peace, Abbot Porfirio. I am going to translate and print them in English, and on the promise of a copy for the Abbey Library she has broken the rule of letting them go out of the building. Perhaps we shall discover why the old rascal is so desirous for us to go walking out at night." And putting a packet of papers and two books bound in old calf upon the table, he suggested getting ready for dinner, and it was then that I found Hoadley had moved me up into the Tapestry Room. I confessed later at dinner that although I should like to spend another night in the Chapel, I was not sorry to postpone the treat. At last dinner was over and we were once more in the Library with our port and cigars.

CHAPTER SIX

CONCERNING A MAD SEXTON, A DRUNK HANGMAN AND A PRETTY GIRL

At last—and at my repeated request, for his mind was full of Porfirio—my host got up to unlock the specimen case. "Yes—certainly the old spade can lay claim to precedence over the other stories this night, as it celebrates the centenary of the deed it took part in a hundred years ago. Another appropriate reason for telling you the facts to-night is that I rode past where it happened to-day on my road to Maidstone. Do you know the little village of Aylesford? It's a gem—perched on the steep river bank, the old church crowning it above the chimneys of the High Street. A place full of legend and folk-lore, rich in history. It was where the beautiful Saxon bridge now stands that the Angles forded the Medway to battle in the days of Hengist and Horsa. Hence the name—Angles ford."

As he talked, he lifted the spade from the case and leaned it against his chair. Then he tenderly picked up the lock of yellow hair.

"I don't know whether you think that inanimate objects placed near one can made the recital of an occurrence in which they were concerned more vivid—but I do, and that is why I am going to lay this lock of a girl's hair on the table here beside you." As he suited the action to the word, and went back to his chair, he added, "A hundred years ago that little curl was growing on the head of the fairest village beauty of Aylesford. Rich—spoiled and courted, she should have married and had children and grandchildren—and that curl should have gracefully changed from yellow to silvery white. Unfortunately the thirteenth of November proved to be an ill-starred date for her. But let me tell you what happened."

He picked up the spade and pointed to its handle. "By the way, about this time in the evening a hundred years ago, when that curl was alive, this horse-shoe, obviously made for a great shire beast, was not on here. It was put on later. But let me get on with the tale.

"Everyone in the village of Aylesford knew that there was bad blood between a certain Farmer Quested and the Sexton—of that day. How the quarrel had originated nobody knew, but it had grown ever since the Farmer had been elected vicar's warden and as such read the lessons every Sunday. It became violent when Kitty Quested returned from service abroad and set all the lads' hearts hammering at her beauty.

"The Sexton's daughter was a poor sickly imbecile, and when she died the village pronounced it a good thing and laughed when they saw the old man transfer his affection upon the churchyard horse, that pulled the great stone roller, nibbled the grass and was called Scraggybones. That, his beer and his hatred for Quested were the only things the Sexton loved. Now upon this very night of the year when the village was drinking at the 'Chequers,' the Elizabethan inn which lies beneath the church on the opposite side of the street, some wag asked the Sexton, whose beetroots he had been stealing.

" 'Beetroots?' repeated the Sexton. 'Don't like 'em.'

" 'Then why steal 'em?' asked the wag.

"'Haven't,' snapped the Sexton.

"The wag pointed to the Sexton's spade. This very spade, my dear Kent. Just here on the corner of the blade there was a red smear.

"'If you've been amongst my beetroots, old 'un,' put in Farmer Quested from his corner by the fire-place, 'I'll have the law o' you.'

"The Sexton chuckled. 'If ever Cephas Quested takes the law o' me, it'll be over something more serious than beetroots, I promise you.'

"Just then the Vicar came in and called for a glass of old ale. He was popular because he was not above drinking in his own parish inn. His arrival checked the angry retort which his warden was about to make to his sexton. But it did not check the Sexton's chuckles, which developed into a sinister giggling as the old man cleaned the blade of his spade with his thumb, flicking the bits of dirt across the Farmer's knees into the fire. The Vicar having nodded to all the cronies, addressed himself to his warden.

"'You'll be glad to hear, Quested, that we have started carrying out the improvements you suggested *re* the churchyard at our last council meeting. Our worthy Sexton has been digging up the bones from behind the old wall above the Bier-Walk. Such a pile.' He turned to the Doctor. 'As a man of science I should like you to look them over. Your judgment must sort out the Christian from the heathen. I think they're all heathen, buried there before the church came, and if so they need not harbour up consecrated ground when we're so short of space.'

"'Very foolish to have built a churchyard on the side of a hill,' laughed the Doctor. 'Naturally the bones work their way through the cracks in the old wall. Many's the mischievous limb I've prevented from tumbling out upon the Bier-Walk.'

"'Yes, it's quite uncanny the way they work themselves out,' agreed the Vicar. 'I suppose it's something to do with the wet soaking through to the lower level. It carries them along.'

"'It's not the wet,' contradicted the Sexton, still flicking bits of dirt into the fire. 'If you wants to know what it is, I'll tell you. It's the worms.'

"They all laughed at this, which annoyed the old man.

"'I tell you *they* finishes what the Sexton begins. When I buries you there,' and he struck the floor with his spade [and so did the narrator] 'I don't flatter myself you'll stop there. *They'll* come and scatter you, and never leave you till they've got you where they wants you. They're always on the march manœuvring the dead.'

"'Horrible thought,' laughed the Vicar.

"The Sexton ignored this and continued, 'If there's any truth in parsons' yarns about the dead rising again with their bodies, I'll guarantee some confusion in this churchyard, where Smith's finger-bones have been feeling their way into Jones's eye sockets. The Quested marble slab won't keep Cephas still for all his weight. His mother ain't under it now. They'd shifted her sideways last time I give her a look-up. Creepy-crawly their way. Always *making room for the next.* Ha! Ha!'

"'Stop your blasphemy,' shouted the Farmer.

"'Now then. Now then,' warned the Vicar.

"'More ale,' laughed the Sexton.

"'No, you've had enough. Go home,' ordered the Vicar.

"'All right, sir,'' answered the Sexton. 'But if Farmer Quested wants to see for himself, he'll find me up in the churchyard. I'm going to put away my spade.'

"The Sexton slapped the blade of it with the flat of his hand, then looked at his enemy and said, 'Beetroots, eh? I like that.'

"He turned the spade upside down and began to walk it about the bar parlour. [My host got up and suited the actions to the words in a most convincing manner.] He looked like a child playing with a doll. 'I never had a pretty daughter, I didn't. Mine was as ugly as sin, as I heard Farmer Quested say the day of her funeral. But my spade ain't ugly. You're a beauty, ain't you?' He kissed the blade, and catching it up in his arms, hugged it. (Like this, my dear Kent.)

"'Go home at once,' commanded the Vicar. 'You're drunk.'

"'That's good too,' sniggered the Sexton. 'But the best thing I've heard to-night was *beetroots,*' and clutching his spade in high glee he trotted towards the door, where he collided with Johnny Jolt, the Hangman.

"'Wait till I gets *you*, you clever stringer,' chuckled the Sexton.

"'Birds of a feather,' laughed the Doctor.

" 'You needn't talk, you old poisoner,' chaffed the Vicar.

"Everybody laughed and the wag capped the joke with, 'Where's the body? For the vultures are gathered together.'

"Johnny Jolt, fresh from a job at the county gaol, enlivened the company with gruesome details. Cephas Quested was not listening. No. Cephas Quested was sniffing. Sniffing audibly.

"Mister Jolt broke his talk to scowl at his interrupter.

"Quested sniffed again.

" 'I recommend hot Hollands for a cold,' snapped the Hangman.

"Quested took no notice, but sniffed again, then said, 'Can any of you smell anything? What did that Sexton flick in the fire?'

"A faint crackle came from the hearth. Cephas Quested leaned forward and stared.

"Just then young Piper came in, looking very sorry for himself. The wag had a new victim, for the whole village knew that he had been captivated by the Quested girl.

" 'Cheer up,' cried the wag. 'There's more than one rosy apple in any orchard. Besides, I ain't sure but that Miss Kitty don't favour you above us all.'

" 'Then why did she appoint a meeting which she never meant to keep?' answered the dejected lover.

" 'Where were you to meet my daughter?' demanded the Farmer.

"Young Piper was too miserable to care whether the father was annoyed. 'By the churchyard wall above the Bier-Walk. I was late. I warned her that I might be. She promised to wait.'

" 'God grant she didn't,' muttered the Farmer, still staring into the fire-place.

" 'But she did, and she is,' laughed the wag, looking through the casement. 'You gave up too soon, my lad. She's up there now. Look.'

"Young Piper ran to the window.

"On the other side of the street, high above the chimneys of the shops, stood the church with its burial ground braced with an ancient wall, from the top of which was suspended a lantern which gave light to the Bier-Walk beneath. The silhouette of a girl stood out against the sky-line. She was sitting on the wall with one arm leaning upon the lamp-bracket.

"'I could only just have missed her,' cried young Piper, bounding towards the door.

"'Stop,' thundered Cephas Quested.

"Everyone thought that the Farmer was about to play the heavy father against young Piper.

"'Do you love my girl?' he asked.

"It was not a reasonable question to put in a public bar, but the young man answered bold as brass, 'I do.'

"'Then what is the colour of her hair?' asked the Farmer.

"Everyone thought this an odd question.

"'The harvest moon tries to copy it, sir,' replied the lover poetically.

"'The harvest moon, eh? And what is the colour of this?'

"The Farmer plunged his hand across the fire and drew out a piece of dirt from the hearth-back. He did not seem to notice that he burnt his hand. With his finger and thumb he dangled a piece of dirt from a hair which stuck to it.

"'Don't do that,' laughed Johnny Jolt. 'Is a man always to be reminded of his work?'

"'If this is what I think it be,' whispered the Farmer, 'your work ain't finished to-night, Johnny Jolt.'

"The Farmer's manner was very odd.

"'Have they all been drinking?' asked the Vicar of the Landlord.

"The door swung back. Everyone turned at the bang. Young Piper had run out. The wag looked through the window, but started back with his hands over his eyes. The window glass had been shattered in his face. A large bone fell on the floor. The Doctor picked it up. 'A human thigh-bone. Very ancient,' he said.

"'The Sexton's throwing bones into the High Street,' cried someone from the door.

"Then there arose a murmuring like the rumble of an accumulating storm. It rose and rose. The screams of women pierced the growling of the men. Doors banged. Lanterns waved. Lights in every window and casements thrown wide. The wag calls for someone to pull the glass from his eyes, but everyone is looking through the smashed window up at the churchyard.

"The limp form of a girl is being swung to and fro. She was suspended by her skirt, which the little Sexton was gripping with both hands as he stood upon the wall.

"From the Bier-Walk beneath, young Piper was leaping, trying to get the girl from the Sexton's grasp. He looked like a dog jumping for a bone. The news spread like wildfire. The quarrel of the Sexton and the Farmer had come to a head. To what had been the very pretty head of Kitty Quested, but was now horrible, nearly severed as it had been by the Sexton's spade.

"There was a great pot-hook hanging in the chimney.

"The Farmer dropped the piece of hair and dirt upon the floor. Somebody repeated young Piper's words: 'Copies the harvest moon.'

"Quested seized the pot-hook and wrenched it from the chain, bringing down a quantity of soot and a bat which flew about the room.

"Up under the churchyard wall the young man snarled and leapt. He leapt high and touched the body several times, and then the skirt ripped, and what should have been the light form of a girl leaning shyly against her lover, dropped heavily upon a maniac and knocked him to the gravel.

"The Sexton had no time to gloat upon this horror, for the whole village swarmed like a pack of wolves into the Bier-Walk. They were met with a fusillade of heathen bones.

"In the deserted parlour of the 'Chequers,' Johnny Jolt took his tankard of ale to the fire-place, kicked up the logs into a blaze, seated himself in Quested's corner and stretched his long limbs towards the warmth. It was not his business to arrest a murderer. He was the Hangman and had to wait for the Law to take its course. Besides, it was pleasant to get the chimney-corner to himself after a trying day, and everyone had rushed out of the inn in such excitement, neglecting to finish their tankards. The Barman brought them one by one for the Hangman to drink. At the risk of offending the whole parish, it was his maxim to keep on good terms with the Hangman.

"That gentleman of ghastly trade closed his eyes.

"'What are they doing now?' he yawned. Beer was good. The

fire-place was warm. He decided not to return to his lonely cottage till the inn closed for the night.

" 'What's all that infernal banging noise?' he asked.

" 'Fireworks,' answered the Barman from the window. 'The boys have cleared out the stock left over from Guy Fawkes' Day.'

" 'I wonder there's any left,' drawled the Hangman. 'Today's the thirteenth, ain't it?'

" 'That's right, Mister Jolt.'

" 'And what are they letting off fireworks for?'

" 'Shooting them up at the old Sexton. The kids hate him because he never lets them play around the churchyard, or throw stones at Old Scraggybones. I say, you should look. Everything's ablaze round him and he don't seem to care. He's flinging bones. They're flinging fireworks. Roman candles, squibs, crackers, flares and what-not. He don't half look horrible.'

" 'Why don't they go up and get him?' yawned the Hangman. 'I wouldn't let no Sexton throw bones at me.'

" 'There's no stopping him while that pile lasts,' answered the Barman. 'And when that's done he's got his spade. Perhaps he'll start the coffins going soon.'

" 'Don't be silly,' laughed the Hangman. 'He couldn't get 'em out in time.'

" 'Unless he's got 'em ready,' suggested the Barman. 'Sort of humour that would appeal to him.'

" 'They should attack him from the other side.'

" 'Climbing up from the gravel pits ain't so easy,' argued the Barman. 'Besides, it lands you right by the mortuary, which ain't cheerful. Hallo. That's what some of them's done. There's shapes on the dodge in and out behind the gravestones at his back. They've got up by the mortuary. Ah! Now they've got him.'

"A terrible shriek made the Hangman open his eyes.

" 'What now?' he asked.

" 'He's just seen 'em in time. Hurled a pick at one. Got him, too. Now he's over the railings of the Boggesses vault. Swinging his spade. Slicing their fingers with it. They're pulling the railings down with a rope.'

" 'Oh, they've got a rope, have they?'

"'Yes, and they've got him too.'

"A great shout arose. The Barman turned quickly to the Hangman. 'They're going to hang him from the lamp-bracket.'

"This aroused the Hangman's professional curiosity.

"He got up and swayed unsteadily in the fire-light.

"'I must see them do that. Hanging ain't so easy. Let's have a quick noggin of rum, just to keep out the cold, and then go along.'

"The Barman served the Hangman quickly with two or three noggins. Then they went unsteadily along the High Street and up the churchyard steps.

"The steps proved to Johnny Jolt that he was drunk. When they reached the Bier-Walk, the Barman thought they would never get through the crowd. He reckoned without his companion. Mister Jolt was well known, but his trade made folk avoid him, especially on a day like this, when it was known that he had launched a human soul into eternity. Thus a way was made for him, some shrinking from fear or loathing, others from a desire to see a real hangman carry out the job in hand.

"'Here's Johnny Jolt,' they cried to the amateur executioners, who had already fixed a knot to the lantern-bracket and a noose round the Sexton's neck.

"'We'll do it ourselves,' answered Quested. 'This is lynch-law, and no interference.'

"'Aye, our turn now, Mister Hangman,' called out young Piper, who was staggering about aimlessly, with the body of the unfortunate girl clutched in his arms. He refused madly to put her down, and fearing for his reason, they left him alone.

"'Go ahead, then,' laughed the Hangman. 'Only you won't make no sort of a job of it, I can see, and you'll have the constables after you before you can say "knife."'

"'No, we shan't,' answered Quested. 'The police sergeant rode off with the parson for help. They found it convenient to be out of the way. There'll be no rescue here, I promise you. We'll have finished with the devil by the time they gets back.'

"'Not at the rate you be going,' scoffed the Hangman. His professional eye was criticizing not only the noose and the length of rope, but the rope itself.

"They threw the Sexton into the air over the wall. The people on the Bier-Walk pushed back to get clear, but the Sexton fell on top of them, causing a panic in which women were trampled. The Sexton scrambled to his feet, and without removing the noose from his neck, climbed up the rope and caught hold of the iron bracket in the wall. But they soon dislodged him with a pole, and then they tried pulling him up. He got his fingers inside the noose, and by swinging out from the wall, managed to kick several people in the face with his iron-tipped boots. At last Johnny Jolt's patience was exhausted.

"'It's a sin not to work a man off on the first jerk,' he cried.

"'You do it. What's wrong?' they answered.

"'It's all wrong,' shouted the Hangman. 'To begin with—the rope—where did you get it? Out of the Ark?'

"'It's his,' they cried pointing to the hanging Sexton. 'Used it for lowering coffins.'

"'Well, it's too thick for a neck like his. Get a bell-rope from the tower. He keeps the key in his pocket.'

"The Sexton was lowered. 'Bind his hands behind him with his neck-cloth, which you should have took off in the first place.'

"The expert was obeyed.

"'Now two ringers up the tower with me to choose a rope.'

"Going round and round up the turret steps to the belfry convinced Johnny Jolt how very drunk he was.

"He chose a rope by lantern light, and sent the ringers up the ladder to the bell-chamber to cut it down. It slipped through the ceiling hole and lashed the Hangman in his face as it fell, which put him in a rage.

"Out in the churchyard again the fresh noose was adjusted. They offered no prayer, but Churchwarden Quested pronounced a curse that was shuddering to hear. Young Piper held the corpse of his beloved high up in his arms. It looked as if he were being civil to the last and giving the dead girl every chance of seeing justice done for her.

"Nobody troubled about the after results. The whole village was in it. Johnny Jolt cared for nothing. He was drunk. Everything was ready.

"The nerve of the village was strung to breaking-point, when a great white horse came trotting across the churchyard, in and out of the tombstones and caracolling over the graves. Right into the crowd it kicked its way, which scattered screaming till someone shouted: 'It's only Old Scraggybones, the churchyard horse. The only thing he cares about. String it up beside him.'

"Over the branch of a great elm, which stretched across the Bier-Walk, the Sexton's discarded coffin rope was thrown, and before his eyes the Sexton's whimpering pet was pulled up. It was his last Woh-ho. The poor beast, like his master, managed to lay out more than one of the villagers as he was swung off his feet. Yes—he died game to the last. 'Courage, Scraggybones,' cried the Sexton. 'I shall be with you in a moment, and then we will ride the Bier-Walk together.'

"Johnny Jolt waited for the Sexton to see this piece of savagery completed, and then he made ready the knot. But his victim's words sobered him. He did not like them.

"Mockingly asked if he had anything to say, the Sexton turned to Quested and said, 'It is November the thirteenth. I shall not forget that date in the place where I am going. I shall ride the horse of Death, and trample you upon the Bier-Walk. Remember.'

"The Hangman tightened the noose and adjusted the knot to his final satisfaction. As he did so, the Sexton spoke to him in a voice that sounded dead. 'It would have been better for you, Mister Jolt, had you stayed within doors. It is an unlucky night for you to be abroad, and before the calendar has run round many times, you will know that my last words are true. I shall be riding—and you will be thinking—"November the thirteenth. The thirteenth of November. I wish I had kept within doors."'

"The body was jerked over. The Sexton was dead.

"When the Vicar returned with the rescue party, the whole village was abed, but they found the Sexton beside his horse over the Bier-Walk.

"The whole village being implicated, nobody was punished, and all kept mum throughout the inquiry; and after a half-hearted attempt on the part of the authorities to make someone speak, the matter was dropped.

"A few years went by.

"People died and people were born, and the dread night was effaced by more recent happenings.

"Young Piper never mentioned it, as he had married someone else and did not care to mention Kitty Quested.

"*And then one night Cephas Quested did not return home.*

"It was in November, and there was snow upon the Bier-Walk. They found him there on the morning of the fourteenth. He had been trampled by a horse; for the marks of a great shoe showed livid on his temple. Yes. *He had been trampled to death on the Bier-Walk*, which was significant.

"From that day Johnny Jolt became a wreck. He drank more heavily, and his eyes were haunted with a fear. He sought company, but there was none where he was welcome. He was always asking people what day of the week the thirteenth of November fell on, and whenever that unlucky day came he moved from his lonely cottage and bought board and lodging at the Chequers Inn for the night.

"The inn changed hands, and the new landlord did not approve of Johnny Jolt. He thought that the presence of a drunken hangman kept good custom away, and he did not intend to give the creature house-room upon the thirteenth of November. The day came, and with it the Hangman.

"He was drunk by noon, but had the sense to sit quiet and soak in the corner. It drew on towards midnight and the cronies left. The ex-Hangman—for he had lost his job—steered himself to the bar.

"'I always sleep here upon this night,' he enunciated slowly. 'I have done so for many years. It is the night when I cannot sleep in the cottage by myself. I dare say you know the reason.'

"'Ah, yes, sir,' answered mine host. 'That is quite right. You honour the house every thirteenth of November, I remember. Now please, sir, I wish to close the doors. Drink up if you please.'

"'I will have one more before going to my room.'

"The Landlord gave him another. 'I will prepare your room for to-morrow night, sir.'

"'No, for to-night,' corrected the ex-Hangman.

"'I thought it was for the thirteenth you ordered it.'

"'Well?'

"'It is the twelfth now, sir.'

"'No—the thirteenth.'

"Looking at a calendar the Landlord shook his head. But the drunkard wanted to see for himself. The Landlord brought the calendar and leant across the bar.

"'Here you are. November. That's right. Here's the thirteenth. Tuesday, as large as life. To-day's Monday, and as you see, the twelfth.'

"'So it is,' admitted the drunkard. 'Even the Constable told me wrong.'

"'To-morrow, then, sir?' queried the Landlord, putting away the calendar. 'I'll get the pot-boy to light a lantern for you and pilot you up the church steps. It's your quickest way.'

"When they had gone, the Landlord chuckled to his wife: 'I'll tell him to-morrow that we were looking at the calendar for next year. I got it to-day on purpose.'

"Johnny Jolt chuckled to the pot-boy as they climbed the steps. 'Nearly let myself in for two nights at the inn. Couldn't have run to that, with prices as they are now.'

"The pot-boy asked him why he wished to spend a night at the inn when his own cottage was so near.

"'For company, lad. Did you never hear the tale of the mad and murderous Sexton?'

"'Never, sir,' lied the pot-boy, who wanted to hear it first-hand.

"'Then sit down here in the porch, and I'll tell you while my legs get sober.'

"The pot-boy thought it stupid of Mister Jolt to drink any more brandy if he really wanted to get sober, but he kept his mouth shut while the ex-Hangman talked and drank from the bottle in his hand. The story was finished about the same time as the brandy. Then Mister Jolt turned to the pot-boy and said, 'Now you see why I spend the thirteenth at the inn. If there is such a thing as ghosts that there Sexton will be one, and I ain't taking chances with him.'

"'But you are. It's the thirteenth now.'

"'What do you mean?' screamed the Hangman. 'What's to-night?'

"'Well, yesterday was Sunday, and we had psalms for the Twelfth Evening. The parson don't make mistakes, I hope.'

"'If that's true, I'll break that Landlord's neck. But are you sure?'

"Before the pot-boy could answer, there came the sound of a galloping horse, and at the same time the church clock began to chime for midnight. Mister Jolt's teeth chattered.

"'Listen. What's that?'

"'A horse galloping,' whimpered the boy.

"'Coming close, ain't it?'

"'Yus!'

"'Stopping, ain't it?'

"'Yus!'

"'What's that noise?'

"'Clock striking twelve.'

"'No. The other noise.'

"'What? That sort of shuffling scuffle?' snivelled the potboy.

"'Yes. It is skeleton feet.'

"'No. It ain't.'

"'What is it, then?'

"'Dunno.'

"'I do. It's the Sexton. The Sexton on his horse. He's ridden up the Bier-Walk. He's dismounting under the bracket. He's come to take me. But I won't be took. I won't. I say I won't.' The Hangman swung the lantern round his head and, raising the bottle with the other hand, pointed into the darkness, screaming, 'Look!'

"The pot-boy sprang out of the porch and the Hangman brought the lantern down with a crash on to his head, and then came at him with the bottle.

"The boy had a dim recollection of thrusting his hand against the madman's throat, and of gripping hard. Then the bottle came down, and he remembered no more.

"Half an hour later the Landlord and two ostlers came from the 'Chequers' to look for the pot-boy. He was lying insensible upon the pavement. They gave him brandy and brought him round, when he screamed out: 'Mister Jolt. Where's Mister Jolt?'

"They found Mister Jolt on the Bier-Walk, beneath the lantern-bracket, his arms across his face and his legs crumpled under him.

"'He has fallen from the wall,' said one of the ostlers. 'Broke his legs, by the look of it.'

"'Drunk. It will give my house a bad name,' muttered the Landlord, as he uncovered the dead man's face. When he saw it he sprang to his feet. 'Run for the Doctor. I think he's dead.'

"When the Doctor came and looked at the distorted face he said, 'Yes—he's dead. A seizure. I warned him to keep off spirits.'

"'He had none to-night at the "Chequers,"' lied the Landlord in his own defence. 'Wouldn't let him. Has to think of the "Chequers'" good name. Not a drop of hard liquor, I assure you.'

"'I dare say,' nodded the Doctor. 'He carried it with him. See.' He unclasped the dead man's fingers, which were clutching the broken neck of a bottle. It had cut deep into his hand, which was caked with congealed blood.

"'Hallo. Finger-marks on his throat. How's that?'

"The pot-boy looked at the Doctor and stammered, 'It's what he feared, sir. The Sexton's ghost come for him. It's the thirteenth of November.'

"'Nonsense,' snapped the Doctor. 'You must have seized him by the throat when he came at you.'

"'I was knocked senseless with his lantern,' answered the pot-boy stubbornly.

"'Hallo. What's this?' The Doctor had turned the dead man's head, and they all saw the mark of a great hoof on his face.

"'I couldn't have done that now, could I, sir? It's the Sexton's horse, like when Mister Quested was found here.'

"'More likely this, I think,' answered the man of science lifting a great cart-horse-shoe from the gravel. 'He was raving drunk, and he fell on this.'

"'Put it down, sir,' whispered the Landlord.

"'Horse-shoes won't harm us. They are lucky,' said the Doctor.

"'That's been dropped by the Devil's horse,' shuddered an ostler.

"The Landlord suddenly pulled the Doctor's hand from the corpse. 'Look! That proves it,' he cried, and pointed to the wall.

"From a crevice in the old stones there appeared a gigantic and glossy worm, which slithered and dropped upon the Hangman's neck and slipped in under his shirt before the Doctor could free his hand to take it.

"And so, my dear Kent, it became a local ghost-story. The general opinion was that the Sexton's horse had trampled him as it had Cephas Quested, and the Sexton's bony fingers had finished the job by throttling. Then the King Worm had come to claim him, and from that day not a soul who had been at the hanging would venture up the Bier-Walk upon November the thirteenth."

At the end of this story my host got up from his knees, for as he had described the Doctor's examination of the dead Hangman he had knelt on the carpet using the side of the chair for the Bier-Walk wall. In fact, the whole narrative had been a very subtle amalgamation of conversational style linked into movements that had been highly dramatic. The whole thing had gripped me as though I had been in a theatre, watching a great actor in some moving drama. Indeed, I thought it a pity that since he had confessed he had been on the stage at one point in his curious life, he had not continued to grace the boards, as they say.

So moved was I that I could not speak or even think of what to say until he had picked up the spade and taken it across the room to the specimen case. Then he gave me my cue, by asking, "Well, what do you think? Curious story, isn't it?"

"Well—I think I'm very glad not to be sleeping in the Chapel. I also think that if the other stories in your collection are one-half as grim, our friend Carnaby could not have given you a better title than 'Master of the Macabre.'"

"Which reminds me that I have not yet opened Carnaby's packet," he laughed. "As I told you, however, during dinner, my whole mind is at the moment occupied with our friend Porfirio, and the experiences we both had last night. It's always as well, I find, to keep to one thing at a time, and pursue it relentlessly. It gets one further in the long run."

"Then since we are, or at least I am, entirely engrossed with the story of your murderous Sexton and your Hangman," I replied, "I am entirely in agreement with your theory, and before we embark on anything else, please satisfy my curiosity on one or two points. How, for instance, did you obtain these relics of a tragedy that happened a hundred years ago?" I had picked up the pathetic little curl, found myself actually blaming young Piper for being so unromantic as to marry somebody else.

"You are quite right, my dear Kent," he replied. "We think along the same lines, and the manner in which I got possession of the poor relics is a fitting end to the whole story."

He came back to my chair and, taking the curl from my hand, gently replaced it in the shelter of the spade's handle. He then strolled over to the fire-place, put on another log, and stood facing me.

"There are still Questeds living in Aylesford, you see," he explained. "Perhaps fortunately for my collection they have no love of what they termed 'the morbids,' and were glad enough to exchange that poor little relic from their grandmother's Bible, though nothing would have induced them to part with a curl of their own brat's head of hair—and a nasty little bit of work it was. The price of our poor Kitty's curl was a particularly nasty-looking tea-service they had set their minds on. It made me feel quite hot when I went to pay for the thing."

"And the spade—was that in Aylesford too?" I asked.

He laughed. "Stolen property of the church, I'm afraid—though I was not the purloiner. And do you know, hardened as I am in horrors, I shouldn't like to dig with it. I feel its history would bring bad luck to any work it was put to. It certainly led me a dance of some thousands of miles to get hold of it. It was easy enough to get on its track. Until a few years ago it had hung in the Sexton's tool-shed at Aylesford—and then one of the present sexton's sons emigrated to Canada. Without a by-your-leave of the Vicar, he took with him any spare churchyard tools he could find, the spade amongst them. Now—I have always found that travel has been a good means of adding to my collection, so I didn't hesitate to follow the spade. One meets with queer talkers in the smoking-rooms of liners. Anyway, Hoadley and I packed up and went to Canada, where we ran our sexton's farmer-boy to earth, and with him the spade just as you see it now. He couldn't tell me who had put the horse-shoe on the handle, but he did know certain details of the old story which I had not been able to draw from the old inhabitants. These days the Aylesford people seem particularly cagey about the tragedy. The churchgoers feel that the story is somewhat a reflection against their parish.

"I must own that I was glad to find the spade still in use, and he was more than glad to hand it over for a modern tractor which he wanted for ploughing. He thought, of course, that I was making a fool bargain. A spade for a tractor—but then—I preferred the spade. By the way, there is another relic of the affair which you had overlooked. Probably didn't realize it belonged or didn't know what it was. As a matter of fact, I got it from the present Doctor of Aylesford. He found the bottle all labelled with a lot of other junk when he bought the practice some years back."

"The Hangman's brandy bottle?" I guessed.

"No. Much more grisly. Look."

He handed me over a sort of glass jam-jar containing some object in spirits. It had a label on it bearing an inscription in old-fashioned copper-plate handwriting.

"Pickled—*what?*" asked my host, smiling.

"Good God, man—how awful," I ejaculated, shuddering. Then I read the inscription out loud:

"VER REX

Taken from the deceased body of Mr. John Jolt, sometime Hangman of Her Majesty's Prison at Maidstone
and placed in spirits by me Alroy Silvester, physician
and surgeon, for exhibition at the above's inquest."

I looked up at my host as I handed him back the jar which had preserved the fat coils of the largest worm I had ever seen in England. Then counting on my fingers, I recited the following list: "*A pretty girl with hair like the harvest moon: her infatuated lover: a mad and murderous sexton: a drunken executioner: a terrified pot-boy: a hanging horse: and then the great star—KING WORM.* What a cast."

My host struck a comic attitude of an old actor, as he replied: "Aye, laddie, as you say, what a cast. And what '*props*' they had to furnish them withal." He too began counting on his fingers: *"Fire-works: human bones: a coffin rope: a bell-rope: a premature calendar: a Devil's horse-shoe: a hank of hair: a blood-stained spade: a Bier-Walk lamp-bracket: the overhanging branch of a churchyard elm: a lantern: a brandy bottle: and chimes of midnight off.* All the ingredients for a fugue macabre. And now another glass of port and so to bed."

I managed to cross the hall to the sturdy oak staircase with the aid of the crutches, and then discarded them for the stout banisters on one side and the Master's shoulder on the other, Hoadley following with the crutches. In this way by hoppings and hoistings I reached the landing.

"And now," warned my host, "you want to be careful not to slip. We take rather a pride in keeping these floors polished, eh, Hoadley?"

"I'll go careful," I said.

Looking down at the magnificent black oak beams so perfectly joined to make a solid floor, I remarked upon their width. "The upstair floors of most of the old houses I've seen have been inconveniently sloped and creaky. But here we might be walking on polished marble."

My host nodded. "The builders of this place knew what was required of them. Only the best work did for an archbishop's house privileged to entertain royal princes. They certainly didn't stint their material. During the renovation we had occasion to examine underneath this floor from the ceilings below, and we found that each plank is rounded—a complete half section of tree trunk cut to match. Each trunk runs solid the whole width of the house. You'll certainly not be kept awake up here with creaking boards. I often wonder what grim or exciting secrets lie in the thickness of these walls, especially as the rich altar treasures of the monastery can't be traced. It's known that old Islip didn't take them to Maidstone when he robbed Peter to pay Paul. It would be fun to find them. Now, my dear Kent, the Tapestry Room is that door, but *en route* come and have a look at my Spanish walls. This door opposite yours."

I followed him to the room while he switched on the lights.

"You put a fire in Mr. Kent's room, Hoadley?" he added.

"Why—yes, sir. Of course," said the old man.

"I call that rank favouritism, when you haven't got one yourself," I protested.

"Don't you worry," he laughed. "I have. You see, I'm not sleeping here to-night. Hoadley has made up the bed for me in the Chapel. I want to see if your experience of last night will be repeated on me."

"I call that exceedingly brave of you," I said, not envying him in the least.

"Not a bit," he answered lightly. "Just curious. Besides, this room hasn't been very active lately. Maybe the spooks are getting bored with me."

"More likely that they're afraid you'll terrify them with your stories. This is a splendid room," I said, looking with awe at the richly embossed leather stretched over the walls—"but," I hesitated to say what I was thinking.

"Come along, then," urged my host. "A splendid room— BUT——?"

"Well—being pretty tired and anticipating a good night, if I had to sleep here, I somehow wouldn't bet on its not being very active, as you say. P'raps I'm sensitive or something."

"It's a grand thing to be. Don't despise it." He put his hand on my shoulder and patted me with frank affection. From that moment, indeed, I knew that he and I were good friends. "I'm afraid you're going to suit this house too well for your peace of mind till you get to know it better. It may drive you at first: almost bully you into giving it your complete understanding. I've lived in queer places but never in a house so real, so alive as this. It's just like a human being with moods. You've got to humour it. You've got to understand its mind."

"Mind?" I queried. "Don't you mean its ghosts?"

He shrugged his shoulders. "Quite frankly I don't know whether I believe in ghosts or not. But I believe in dreams, and the trouble I find with this place is that you're never quite sure what you've *seen* or what you've just dreamt. But come—Hoadley has made up your fire. Come over to the tapestries and I promise you they will treat you entirely sympathetically. You may think me childish, but I have always hugged the belief that every so-called inanimate object in this world, whether beautiful or ugly according to our standards, has a being—an entity of its own. Else—why should certain stones be lucky to some people and bad for others? When you are fond of a thing—your typewriter, for instance—why shouldn't that thing be fond of you? I almost think that things can think."

Meanwhile we had slowly crossed the landing and entered the Tapestry chamber. At my first glance I turned and said, "I don't fear the ghosts in here. It wouldn't tolerate an evil one. If I may say so, Mr. Hogarth, you are a very wise man and far-seeing. You seem to know things by instinct. About me—for instance. You say quite definitely that I shall like this room before I've seen it, and I find it almost caressing me. You didn't say the same thing about the Chapel. Now—why? Was it because you knew instinctively that I should hate it in spite of its lovely architecture?"

"My dear Kent," he answered, shaking his head, "you must not give me credit that belongs to the house itself. You have heard both Hoadley and myself speak of its influences. To sensible men like ourselves that word sounds more fitting than 'ghosts,' for we have yet to prove the real existence of such things. But 'influences' we both know and feel, and so, my friend, I leave you, as you so aptly put it, to its caresses."

And with that he left me to Hoadley's administrations. I did not detain the old man long, though he delighted in showing me where he had arranged my things, and the door concealed by the tapestry which led me to the bathroom. But I could see that in spite of his kindness and thought for my comfort, he was anxious for his master.

"Indeed, sir, you will find, as the Master says, that this room is most congenial. I only regret that you did not occupy it last night. Indeed, I tried to dissuade the master from occupying that Chapel. But when he gets a notion in his head—— But there, sir, I dare say you notice how it is with him. And with all respect—the word is 'obstinate' where the Master is concerned. You will find this four-poster just as comfortable as the great one you had last night—but more intimate. You have the same system of turning on and off the lights, and the bell is here to my room just the same. One press on the button and the old Genie will pop up, if I may so describe myself. And I hope and know, sir, that you will spend a good night here."

He was almost gone, but the Dean's Verger in him made him indicate the fire-place, where it seemed the same log fire was burning. "Built in the style of the one in the Library, sir, but lacking such a congregation of figures. Only two, you will observe, sir. On that side Thomas à Becket in his martyrdom beaten to his knees by the wicked knights who are not represented, thank goodness. His poor arms raised to Heaven and the inscription '*In manus tuas commendo spiritum.*' Matching him on the other side we have King Henry the Second feelin' very ashamed of hisself, as his words convey '*Misericordia*' and the miserables is just about what he should have felt. In the centre slab, sir, the Lions of England of that time, animals to be reckoned with if the real ones was as gaily enamelled. The other achievements of arms represent all those princes of the blood who at one time or another paid a visit here and slept in that bed, for this, sir, is really called the Royal Chamber, but the Master don't like to be thought at all snobbish, though in the time of that there Henry, before he'd quarrelled with his primate, he slept here hisself. Shouldn't think he slept very well, not considering all the wickedness he had lurkin' up his sleeve. No, sir, I think you'll sleep a good deal better than he did and won't have to say no Misericordias either. And now, sir, I'll leave you to a really good night." And Hoadley followed his Master.

For a long time I kept the lights on and studied the scenes of the tapestry. I had read something of its history that afternoon in the Library. Made by the nuns of Malling Abbey by the orders of Henry the Second, it set forth the glories of St. Thomas of Canterbury from the days when he had been the King's favourite and chancellor. It was easy to follow his whole career till the final Martyrdom and Shrine, with his ascent to Heaven. It is said that the repentant and frightened king paid a great price for its execution as one of the penances imposed upon him by the Pope. It was certainly a beautiful work of art, the early scenes being gay with hunting incidents and feastings. I went on looking at the scenes with my eye but not with my mind's eye. That was focused entirely on my peculiar and fascinating host.

Was it really possible that the house had the power to tell him of the future—my own arrival, for instance. Then again were the dreams that he seemed to believe in rather than ghosts able to effect a cure for his neuritis. He had dreamt of a great hand touching his shoulders and healing him, just as I had no doubt dreamt that a hand had manipulated my bandages and taken away the pain. Certainly in waking the cure had been in both cases an accomplished fact.

And then I slipped off into sleep without even turning out the lights, for when next I woke it was to hear Hoadley turning the switch and pulling back the curtains to let the sunlight in, for it was morning, and I felt very guilty at my ruthless waste of electricity.

But Hoadley disclaimed my feeling of guilt with, "That's nothing, sir. If you'd have had a bad night the Master would have agreed that the best thing in the world was to keep your lights full on. But you didn't have a bad night, so you're all the better off, eh, sir?"

"And did the Master dream or see anything strange in the Chapel?" I asked.

"He didn't mention it, sir, but I rather gather so, since he got up early and was working on that material he brought back from Malling Abbey." Hoadley's tone was purely conversational and casual, as though a little thing like his Master seeing that horror Porfirio was the most natural thing in the world.

Hoadley went on to say that his master's mind was very obsessed by the Abbot's history as he had not yet broken the seals of Carnaby's packet, which he had placed in the Library safe.

That morning I felt so refreshed that I insisted on getting up to breakfast, which was served in the Library.

My host immediately asked me how I had passed the night, and whether I had dreamt. I thought he would be disappointed when I confessed that although conscious in my sleep that there was a tranquil spirit close to me I had seen nothing. This seemed to excite him tremendously, though he didn't say much except to ask, "What sort of *tranquil spirit*? Have you any idea of what manner of person it could have belonged to?"

"Oh, it was probably pure imagination," I replied, remembering suddenly that once I did wake up only to sleep again more peacefully than ever. "But there seemed to be a sweet perfume near my bed which conjured up a vision in my mind of a rich and beautiful young girl."

"Whom you didn't actually see?" he asked.

"I don't mind saying, 'Unfortunately, no.'"

"Never mind, you will see her. In your dreams you'll see her and be conscious of her when you're awake. My dear Kent, the material I brought to work on from Malling promises to be most interesting. I can already place the lady—the rich and beautiful young girl, for I've been translating a part of her history this morning, and shall spend the day trying to learn more."

"Won't you tell me about her?" I asked. "In case she does manage to appear I should get on much better with her if I knew something of her background."

"I've never yet told a story by halves," he replied seriously. "Perhaps you will solve this one before I can. But it seems to me that a house like this with the power to influence men like ourselves should have a good story somewhere, somehow. Keep an open mind. I know that you're a bachelor but have no idea whether you are heart-free. I wonder if that would make any difference to the lady making an appearance. No accounting for women—even their ghosts. Well—we'll see."

All that day we worked together in the Library, saying very little except when breaking off for meals. I was trying to catch up correcting proofs of a novel and he was translating the Malling papers and books. But as far as I was concerned, progress was slow, and I found myself thinking more about the house, Porfirio, and the lady's perfume than I did about my work, and it struck me that although my host seemed to be covering a lot of paper with his notes, he too found it hard to concentrate, so I think we were both relieved when after dinner the time was propitious for another macabre tale. The choice of the story came quite naturally, for I had asked whether he had ever heard of anyone else, other than himself, who had made collecting stories the be-all and the end-all of his life.

"I have known of a number of men who did it together. Not quite the same thing, of course, but they certainly gave me an item for my collection that I value especially when I had almost ruled it out because I had not been able to get a suitable relic. But by sheer good fortune—or rather let me say, fluke—I succeeded, and so was able to score it up in my specimen case. My way has always been to finish off a thing properly. Shall I tell you that one or have you a special choice that whets your curiosity?"

"Having had one sample of your collection," I said, "I am quite sure that every relic in the case has a unique tale to tell. But I think, if I have a choice and my memory does not fail me, after the spade a piece of tarnished gold cord that lies upon an old grey wig is uppermost in my mind."

"Now, don't deny that the house is influencing you," he cried out in triumph, "or is it that our ideas jump together? The cord and wig are the relics of the very story that I was referring to. Let's have them out and set them by you. I am quite sure they will make the story more true and vivid. Question me after I have finished if you wish, but if possible don't interrupt till then. Listen, then, to the Tale of the Tale-Makers. And don't forget that I can vouch for its veracity."

"The Tale of the Tale-Makers?" I repeated. "And who are these Tale-Makers? You know them, of course."

"I don't quite see how I could," he continued, laughing, "since they lived in the reign of the Merry Monarch Charles. But all the same I can prove it true, and by those relics," for by now my host had placed the wig and the cord at my elbow, so that I could touch and finger them when I wanted.

"But who are they, or rather who were they, these Tale-Makers?"

"A club, my dear fellow—a very unique club."

"The Tale-Makers, eh?"

He nodded. "Yes—a tale of the Tale-Makers' Club."

CHAPTER SEVEN

BRING OUT YOUR DEAD

"IF I were a parson and this story a sermon, my text would be: 'IN THE MIDST OF DEATH WE ARE ALIVE.' Does that sound promising for the macabre? Does its setting sound good and seasonable when I tell you it occurred during the Great Plague of London? It shows us, too, that the craze for queer clubs is no modern innovation. Queer clubs and strange societies have, of course, existed from the first page of history. Many have been invented by the fantastic brains of fiction writers like yourself. Some have been presented to us on the boards of Drama. Yet none of the diarists that give valuable illumination to the pages of history have ever told of that select community known as 'The Tale-Makers' Club,' and why?—because any notoriety would have meant the rope to more than half its members.

"The Tale-Makers used to meet in a famous old inn out Hampstead way. Most of the members used to keep their horses saddled in the spacious stables, because they were all gentlemen of fortune or misfortune one way or another, and it was reins or gallows when the game was up. Frankly, most of the members appear to have been criminals in a big way. They ranged highwaymen with their romantic swagger to bank robbers and blackmailers. The last class were aided and abetted by several members of well-known literary talent, who could word good letters for their forging colleagues to copy. Now these experts kept a journal or diary of the exploits performed by the adventurous members, and these tales were told at club meetings, and afterwards copied out so that at Christmas time votes could be taken to decide the best yarn of the year, when a purse of guineas would be given to the winner.

"On a certain windy night, when the very trees of Hampstead crouched their heads in terror of the heath and weird shadows danced and played upon the whitewashed walls of the upper room in which the Tale-Makers sat with glasses in their hands before a roaring log fire, the President of the Club, after rapping the table with the butt of a horse-pistol, called for silence while he proposed the recovered health of a gentleman who sat on his right, a member, he reminded them, who had been regrettably absent from their circle for three years. 'It is no new thing for a president of this club to welcome back members who have been away from us for that amount of time. Indeed, since I have held this dishonourable office, I refrain from telling you how many members I have welcomed back after *five* years—hard. My friend's absence had nothing to do with iron-studded doors and turnkeys, I assure you. In plain words, he has only been imprisoned in a comfortable bed somewhere in the country, where the wicked cease from troubling. He has been ill. He is now well again. His pistols are reloaded; his famous horse is saddled below; and I trust that in the immediate future many, many a fat alderman from London City will be of his money-bags by him deprived, while crossing our back-garden of Eden here—Hampstead Heath. I am hoping, too, that we shall all be his first victims, because I am going to call on him to tell us the adventure that led him to his long lie-up, and I think none of us will be able to compete with him for the annual purse of guineas for the best story of the year. That he has won the purse time and again can make us anticipate great pleasure in listening to him. I therefore call the toast—"ANTONY GABOND." '

"I cannot describe this gentleman, since my source of information is silent on the subject. Picture him, my dear fellow, how you like. I can't help you, though my own mental picture gives him height, a figure—slim but big bones, and a decided rakish manner. A strong man, of course.

"Needless to say, his fellow-members gave way to boisterous enthusiasm, which gave Gabond time, no doubt, to toss off a glass or so of brandy, for I am sure he was never above drinking his own health, and then—after running his fingers round the inside of his cravat, which I have observed is a favourite habit, even in this dreadful collar age, of most men who look to the gallows as their possible undertaker, he took snuff—no doubt very elegantly—and began.

"'Gentlemen and Tale-Makers, I am about to tell you of an episode in my life which will haunt me with unutterable disgust and loathing until I make my last speech at my farewell performance on the little lofty stage at Tyburn Fields.' (Antony Gabond, by the way, started his vagrant career as an actor in Covent Garden.) 'I see some of our members here who will remember how very hard pressed some of us were after our valiant attempt to filch the Crown Jewels. I was not even among the suspects, for some reason, and all might have gone well with me had I not in this very room accepted a wager to hold up the King's Coach in Whitehall. You all know how successfully that turned out, but, of course, it will never be known in history, because such official disgrace is wiped off its page by those in power lest public blame should fall upon their heads.

"'One of my rascals was collared though, and he eventually turned King's Evidence against me. Now, you know yourselves— at least some of you do—how very hard it is to give the authorities the slip in the broad daylight, and remember, I had had no warning that the game was up till an impertinent officer showed me a warrant with my name on it. It was neck or nothing—I could see that—so I went at him with my head down, bowed in shame, he thought, and butted the wind clean out of his stomach. My clothes—such elegant ones, too—were ripped to ribbons as I plunged through a crowd of his subordinates, and then I was out in the streets with half London running at my heels. They had successfully cut off my retreat to the stables, so I could get no help from my faithful grey stallion, and how I longed for him when I found at last that I could run no more; for I had done double-dodge through the slums and filth heaps for something like two hours all told. Twice I had been headed off and nearly caught, and once a damned soldier had struck at me with a dirk so that my shoulder was bleeding profusely. But it was to that wound that I owed my life and final escape, and you shall now hear why. The damned Plague had broken out in London, and by some instinct I had led my pursuers into the infected quarter. As I glanced over my shoulder to see what advance they were making, I remember noticing that many of the crosses upon the doors of the pest-

ridden houses were daubed roughly in the colour of blood. I kept
on thinking about this as I ran, and God—I did have to run, I tell
you. I noticed, too, that my pursuers thinned off a bit when I ran
them into the plague quarter, and those who did keep up the chase
took care to run in the middle of the road. This proved to me that
they were nervous, and well they might have been, for we continually passed houses with the doors nailed up, and naked corpses
upon the cobblestones. Fear and poverty deprived the dead of any
sort of winding sheet. I recollect one tavern that we passed where
there was quite a pile of bodies waiting for the carts to take them
to the great pit cemetery. But the man dodging with a running
noose around his neck don't stick at trifles; for anything's a trifle
compared to Jack Ketch and his craft. It was this thought that gave
birth in my mind to a desperate nightmare scheme. I put the spurt
on, about the last I had in me, I think, and shot up an alley. There
were three bodies in that alley over which I had to leap: but I rather
welcomed them as I knew that they would serve as a check to my
cowardly pursuers; for men with free lives and happy prospects do
not take long chances like adventurers whose necks are coveted by
the Newgate gang.

   "'At the end of this alley was a court and beyond that a very
respectable square. This last I found to be empty when I broke
into it well ahead now of the wolf pack. I knew that men would
not walk abroad in a square like this, if they could possibly avoid it,
as it was in the plague quarter, for I noticed a door here and there
with a cross on the outside to warn people away. Then I discovered a piece of really good fortune; a large house at the far corner,
screened from the alley I had entered by owing to laurel bushes
growing thick in the centre garden. The luck was not so much
that I had found a wealthy-looking mansion, but that its front door
was by mistake or some purpose left ajar. I paused in front of the
flight of steps to get my breath, and then heard the crowd in the
alley and court on the farther side of the square. Well—neck or
nothing—I could certainly run no more. I was dead beat. I ripped
off my neckercher, soaked it with my blood—and God, how I had
bled—and then quickly daubed a red cross upon the great oak
door. Then I pushed it open and closed it behind me. One thing

was certain—my pursuers would avoid a plague-marked house. Now the hall into which I had trespassed was of some estate—the property of some rich City merchant—no doubt a worthy alderman or burgher, anyway rich enough—for no sooner had I closed the door on my pursuers and was listening to them scampering down the turning at the side of the house, than a most important-looking serving-man in gorgeous livery entered the hall from the double-doors of the dining-room, in which I could see the large table being set out for dinner. I could see the white linen table-cloth which happened to be exactly the thing of all others that I most desired. Now for the last scene, I told myself, conjuring up my remaining strength—the fight at the curtain of the play and then applause—from myself, of course, as there would be no audience I hoped—and then a long rest—no not in my theatre dressing-room, but almost as good, the cold cobblestones outside. But I am jumping too fast ahead of your kind comprehensions. I flung myself upon the astounded serving-man who went down before me like Young Siward with Macbeth, and I quickly and most efficiently gagged him with his own wig, forcing it half down his astonished gaping gullet and securing same with a frog-cord I ripped from his fancy uniform. I then repeated this business with two other of his frog-cords torn from the scarlet coat—and with these I tied his feet and hands, before pushing him bodily into the case of a great clock that was ticking ruefully the unhappy minutes that had so suddenly descended upon the house for which it conducted time. The case had a key. I turned it on him—pulled out the key and threw it into the hall fire-place. It was a strange thing that I had often considered the possibility of a clock-case being used as a hiding in a case of emergency. The serving-man disposed of, I then went into the dining-room which was fortunately empty of any human being, and sweeping the silver plate and glasses from the table, I grabbed the white cloth, rending the costly lace from its border. I stripped off my coat and shirt, the latter being by now saturated with my blood, pulled off my boots and hose, and shame to say, my breeches. Then, covering my nakedness with my white linen table-cloth shroud, I went back into the hall.

"'My pursuers had been baffled at my disappearance, but had

come back to the square and were actually hammering at the door of the next house. This was eventually opened by someone none too pleased, for I heard high words between the officer and an angry inmate with a high-pitched female voice. The door banged-to again, and then I heard them come up the steps of the house that I was in.

"'That they were terrified of infection was plain, for none of them was willing even to touch the door on which a red cross had been newly fixed. But at last one bolder than the rest cried out stoutly that he cared not, for was there not money enough on Master Gabond's head to compensate him for any risk he ran?

"'Now I had no intention of letting him knock upon the door and arouse the inmates whom I expected to see at any minute. Besides it was possible that the prisoner in the clock might free himself sufficiently to cry out. So turning the latch, I opened the door quickly, and just sufficiently to let my body tumble out, contriving as I fell on the steps to slam it behind me as though someone had been glad to get rid of a plague corpse. As it happened, I rolled into the man who was coming up the steps to knock and, my faith, I have never seen anyone so surprised, for he lost his balance, as he cried out in terror, and down we went together upon the cruel cobbles. The mob was immediately thrown into the wildest panic, for all they had seen from below was a naked man in a shroud thrust round the door into the street.

"'I kept my eyes open all the time—I quite forgot to close them—but I believe that only served to frighten them the more, for they were out of that square like a pack of rats leaving a doomed vessel.

"'And now—would you believe it?—but I lay on those cobblestones for hours and nobody heeded me. Those who might have done, passed hurriedly by on the other side, for corpses were common enough in the streets those days.

"'I was very weak from loss of blood and my gruelling race for life, and I must have fainted, because I could remember nothing more till nightfall, and it was a strange awakening I had too, a rumble of a heavy cart and a weird wailing, impersonal voice wailing that ghastly addition to the London street cries, *"Bring out your dead! Bring out your dead!"*

"'I heard it as though in a dream till somebody kicked me over on my back, for I was in the track of the great wheels, and then I was lifted up.

"'Thank God for the darkness that had fallen, or I might have been discovered; but the dead-carriers did not linger over their grisly work in the days of the Great Plague. Besides, they could see very little by the light of their evil-smelling torches. But it was not the torches that stank, as I was soon to discover. The stench came from within the cart.

"'As I said, I had been lifted up; in fact, they were already swinging me backwards and forwards, and I was expecting my terrible plunge amidst the dead, when one of the wretches noticed the fine texture of the table-cloth. I was accordingly dumped down again in the foul gutter, while those carnivorous vultures produced dice and threw hazards for my winding-sheet. As far as I could judge, the driver won, for I saw him later wrapped up in it upon the lofty box-seat—a weird, grotesque figure—a well-selected coachman for such travellers as those who rode within the cart.

"'As *those*, do I say? I should have said as *we*, for was not I the moving spirit in that ghastly coaching party? No man, I think, can reasonably call me a coward. I have looked Death straight in the eyes a score of times and kept a firm upper lip. I have never been ashamed of my behaviour when face to face with Death; but this was more than face to face, if I may joke upon it; for here was I, thrown stark naked into a heap of corpses, the most of which were half-putrid. Just you picture for an instant the sight that I enjoyed within that cart with its tall sides. The torches stuck in the iron slots behind the driver's seat gave me a hellish light, flickering and flaring as we bumped our way over the jaunty cobblestones. Sometimes when the road was clear the driver would crack his whip and the horse would put on speed, regardless of the creaks and bumps. And as the corpses bobbed about, I knew I should go mad. Things that had been men; things that had been women and children; and now the cast-aside victims of that raging Plague; no stitch of clothing upon their rotten bodies—the carriers had seen to that—they jostled and jumped upon me at every jolting of the cart. Then we would stop at houses to take up more of the terrible passengers;

and what a nightmare it was when each new body was roughly pushed over the black sides of that beastly cart. Some were flung high up into the air and would crash down upon us, half-burying me in the horrors. This was evidently an amusement amongst the carriers, for they would laugh and clap their rough hands, when they had tossed one higher than usual. They would have done more than laugh if they had been lying on their backs amidst the crew, and watching the dead bodies rained upon them from the night sky. Sometimes a body thus treated would miss its aim and fall on the side of the cart, and then it would break on the rough splintered wood and we—I and my dead companions—would be sadly bespattered. And then their wreckage would follow, in several pieces, and join the jolting dance.

"'I cunningly contrived to keep to the edge of the cart, so that the new arrivals would slip from me as we rode; sometimes a limb coming away in the process. But sometimes the pile would mount up in the centre, and the very first jolt would avalanche them down upon me.

"'Can you fancy an avalanche of DEAD?

"'How many travelling companions were thrust upon me, I know not. By that time I must have been mad—but presently we reached the pit and the unloading began.

"'I could see this pit through a chink in the cart, and I wondered when my turn would come to be shot in. I had forgotten by that time that I was alive—I thought I was like the rest of them.

"'The back of the cart was suddenly tilted up and we slid off on to the ground, or rather the first lot fell on the ground and we fell on the top of them, whilst others in their turn fell on the top of us, and effectually covered us up.

"'And then *they began pushing us into the pit with great pronged sticks like forks.*

"'There was a leg in front of me, and until its owner was shot over the brink I could not see into the pit. But at last I did—and at the sight of that terrible hell my strength returned.

"'With a yell for battle I arose, throwing the bodies from me, and there I stood amongst the dead, facing the terrified carriers. They stared at me in horror, and I, slowly opening my mouth till

I thought the corners of my lips would split, uttered the most ghastly shriek that mortal man has surely ever heard produced. Perhaps I am wrong to call it a shriek, for it was a kind of cough, but so loud and piercing that my whole system seemed to be shaken. A medical friend has since told me that this same rending revulsion that tore its way through my physique must have saved my life by expelling in one effort all the contagion that must have seeped into me during my ride in the Plague cart.

"'The carriers, of course, fled—all save one. This creature was standing too near the slippery pit-brink, and without a cry he lost his balance and disappeared amongst the dead. I believe the force of my shout had pushed him backwards. And then I did go raving mad. I was alone on the brink with the dead. Alone save for the horse in the cart, who was used to horrors, poor beast, and didn't know what to do. Perhaps he didn't care.

"'The carrier had come to the surface and was squealing like the hog he was. I rent off limbs from the bodies I had ridden with and pelted him hard. God knows what horrors I was not guilty of—but—oh—the last horror I remember only too well. Even now when I awake in the night I scream out at the thought of it.

"'I unharnessed the horse—for I had need of him—and I pushed the heavy cart over the brink, and I heard the squelch of it cutting through the massed bodies as its great weight carried it down beneath the muddy, bloody, filth-clogged liquid, for the heavy rains had swollen the ditches in the midst of which the pit had been hastily but deeply cut.

"'Now whether it was that my brain had gone or whether it was really a fact, I know not; I only know what I saw—whether mentally or actually—and I tell you that at the noise of that mud-jellied squelch, a tide of matter—of poisonous, putrescent matter, rose rapidly to the very brink of the pit, and as it lapped and gushed over my bare feet, I saw the carrier trying to swim, but utterly unable to make any headway towards the bank. I had stuck one of the torches in the mud in order to see to the horse—the others had gone hissing down in their sockets of the cart, and it was by that weird light that the carrier's eyes met mine and realized that there was no help to be got from me.

" 'But the horror of his face made me leap on to the horse, which, God be praised, was now as frightened as I and made immediately a mad rush—a fierce gallop away from those accursed fields, for we were both in the grip of terror which pursued us with the sound of the treble gurgling of that drowning man.

" 'At any rate, we rode till I can remember no more. Oh, the thing in my memory was the silhouetted shape of Old Paul's; now, I hear, a burned-out mass. I rode till I was a squealing, gibbering idiot: where I rode I cannot say after that, except that I had galloped well into that illness from which it has taken me three years to recover.

" 'Well, gentlemen, Plague-ridden London has been destroyed by fire while I lay unconscious, and I dare swear that the warrant for my arrest was burnt with thousands of other less important documents. Well—no doubt they'll have to make out a good many fresh ones before they've done with me, but the authorities were never so near to catching me. Perhaps I should say "God bless the Plague," but no—I would rather take my bow at Tyburn than go through such an escape again. And that, gentlemen, is my story, which I believe our friend Billie Butcher is down to beat.'

" 'Master Gabond,' cried the gentleman in question and a notorious house-breaker, by the way, 'I cannot beat it and I will not try, but I can and will complete it, for you have solved for me a great mystery, which with the President's leave I will tell you instead of the personal adventure I had planned to give. God knows this mystery was personal enough, for it frightened me more than the black knocker of Newgate.

" 'One night during the Plague I was drinking with a lot of gibbering cowards in a tavern of Cheapside. I confess that I was not putting a very brave front upon things myself, and I shivered in my soul as they did when we looked through the casement at the deserted streets, that stank of foul weeds and rotting vegetables. Row upon row of plague-stricken houses. No noise but the rattle of the dead-carts, and nothing to do but pray and drink. I drank: for it was too risky to rob. Presently we hear the noise of a galloping horse. We pressed close to the window, expecting to hear an official crying out some news or announcement: for even the

City Criers rode and rode fast through the infected quarters. Gone were the days and nights of the watchman and leisurely beadle.

"'Nearer and nearer came the rider, till right outside the tavern a steed was pulled up on its haunches. A mad-looking creature it was, too, but not so terrifying as its rider, who sat bare-backed on his crazy horse, and was himself as naked as Adam before the Fall. He was a fine rider, for he spun the animal round at the window and made it crash down the glass with its pawing fore-hooves. The catch broke and the shattered casement swung in and fell at our feet. We leapt back for safety as the rider lolled over the sill and cried for drink in the Devil's name. With black terror in my heart I handed the Thing a mug of raw spirits, which he took at a gulp, hurled the mug at my head and dashed on. That was all. But I have often sought for some explanation other than just a drunkard's imagination, and I am your debtor, Master Gabond, for having given it to me.'

"Another member sprang to his feet, a timid-looking individual in spite of being the quickest and highest feed lock-picker employed by the house-breakers' community. He was rich, too, from his legal City business of locksmith.

"'You all know me, Joe Sunderland of London Wall,' he cried. 'My word is my bond, whether I undertake to build a lock or break one. And I'll be hanged, drawn and quartered if I don't give you the sequel to these two yarns.

"'I have always maintained that a good locksmith should first be apprenticed to the clock makers' trade. My family has had both trades for generations. Now in the Plague-time nothing suffered like the clocks of the City. Journeymen winders and repairers neglected their business, and the City clocks ran down. Most of the journeymen took one journey—to the country, and stayed there for their health. Then came the Fire. Clocks got burnt, same as everything else, and those that had one left took a pride in 'em, as they were at a premium. As you know, some fine houses escaped the Fire and it was to one of these in an old square that I was called in to repair the locks and oil 'em up. The rich burgher who paid me asked if I would unpick the lock of a clock-case in the hall. The key, which he said was of silver, had been stolen. He blamed one of his serving-men, who had disappeared with his wife's best linen table-cloth. He had taken the thing after wantonly ripping off the valuable lace border, which proved him a fool. He had left the costly plate and many other things of great value, and decamped, no doubt afraid of the infection, with just that one piece of property. He had also stolen his livery, but left behind the rest of his clothes.

" 'I found the livery when I opened the clock-case. It adorned his dead body. Not a pretty sight, my masters. A wig jutted out of his mouth, like an actor's beard badly put on. It was tied with a piece of gold cord. So were his feet and his hands. No—not intentional murder, I think. Shall we say manslaughter in self-defence? Anyhow, it could be brought in as committed when the assailant was not in his right mind. The mystery that concerned the householder most was not the man's death, but what he had done with the fair linen cloth. And even I with my clockwork mind could never piece that together. I thank you, Master Gabond, for having put my mind at rest.'

" 'I cannot return the compliment, Master Sunderland,' replied Gabond ruefully, 'for you have put mine ill at ease. With my record, I fear it would be a hanging business.'

" 'If it were known,' put in the locksmith.

"The President rose and looked round the room, as though summing up the honesty of those present—a somewhat doubtful task. But at last he smiled as though well satisfied and, turning to his right-hand neighbour, said with great assurance, 'You can take it from me, Master Gabond, that it never will be known outside the circle of this exclusive Club.' The name of that president was William Wycherley. Very young to be a president of any club. Only twenty-nine. That is, of course, if it happens to be our William Wycherley who wrote plays for Drury Lane."

As on the night previously, he finished the story by putting the two relics back in the specimen case.

"But how on earth did you manage to get hold of them?" I asked. "Considering the adventure happened in the days of Charles the Second, how did you begin to track down the relics?"

"By an incredible fluke, my dear fellow," he laughed. "Near

London Wall there was an old house I knew for many years. The ground floor was a shop and there were living premises above it. It was, I should think, the finest half-timbered building in the City. It is now one of my many quarrels with the Germans; for although it successfully escaped the Fire of 1666, it was utterly destroyed during the Blitz. You will appreciate the connection to my story when I tell you that the same family had lived there since Tudor days, and the emblazoned sign hanging over the narrow street bore the words *Joseph Sunderland & Sons. Instrument makers. Clocks et cetera.* All that time running the same business, and then—the whole family wiped out with their house. It was a direct hit. I was recommended to them when I wanted to buy a compass for one of my long journeys, and so made the acquaintance of the old man. Thinking his trade might be a likely hiding-place for some good stories, I confided in him the object of my proposed journey. He told me that his family records only contained one queer story, concerning the purchase by one of his ancestors, a Joe Sunderland, who lived during the Restoration, of a fine old case-clock. A regular great-grandfather, he called it. He showed it to me where it had stood since the year of the Plague—in a corner of the room behind the shop, which he used as an office. You couldn't tell the time by it in that room, because you couldn't see the face. The case was over nine feet high, and when wound up it took the great lead weights a year to reach the ground. As there had been no ceiling high enough to house it, his ancestor had cut through the floor of the upstair parlour, and there you had to go to see the face, which struck me as being somewhat ironic, that one had to look down on the floor to see the time of the tallest house-clock one was ever likely to meet. When he opened the case-door in the office, he unhooked that wig and cord beneath which a piece of parchment had been pasted, saying, 'The gag used by some person or persons unknown, who caused the death of Walter Collins, serving-man to John Wilkes, Alderman of the City. Death due to suffocation.' This, you see, proves that the Tale-Makers' Club kept Master Gabond's secret."

"Then how on earth did you piece out the rest of the story," I asked.

"Ah, that's where the incredible fluke I mentioned comes in," he answered. "He showed me the record of purchase in his records. It seems that the wife of John Wilkes could not bear to live in the sight of a clock that had such a ghastly connection with murder, so Wilkes sold it to the clock maker and locksmith of our story. Naturally, the wig and cord went with it, and Joe Sunderland, knowing as he did later the true facts, preserved the relics in the clock, taking care not to incriminate his fellow club member."

"And did the clock or compass maker that you knew give them to you?"

"I tried to buy the clock which, of course, he wouldn't sell," explained my host. "But he made a bargain in jest, which finally he had to keep, saying that if I could solve the mystery of the serving-man's death I could have the wig and cord, which, you'll agree, seemed a safe enough bet on his side. But he reckoned without the fluke, and it happened in Charing Cross Road. I have always been fascinated by beautiful print, and I happened to see in a bookshop window a very fine example in the title page of an open Bible. Two things struck me at once. The date and the super-scription. 1625—and in ink, aged brown, '*JOSEPH SUNDERLAND: HIS BOOKE. From his fonde parents to commemorate your confirmation at Olde Paul's, upon December the fifth in this year of Grace 1625.*' Thinking this would interest my instrument maker, I went in and bought it. Such a weighty volume demanded a taxi, which I took straight away to the City. Old Man Sunderland was so delighted that he offered me the wig and cord in exchange, but this I would not accept, and in any case I did not consider that these relics had earned them a place in my specimen case, for the story on the face of it was too thin for my collection.

"Late that night, however, I took another taxi to the house on London Wall. My instrument maker had telephoned to me the news that I had not only won the relics, but had also unearthed a yarn that was very odd indeed. He had found between the leaves of the Bible a folded printed broadsheet of the story as I have told it to you. It contained a footnote stating that in accordance with Rule Seven of the Tale-Makers' Club, a privately printed version of this year's winning story is thus forwarded to each member, who is reminded that this paper must on no account pass into other hands or be seen by other eyes. No doubt our friend the locksmith put his copy into the safe custody of his Bible thinking that like himself no one would take the trouble to open such a book. I imagine that that double-faced picker of his own locks must have parted with his Bible to pay for drinks when doing his time in Newgate, no doubt forgetting that he had left the incriminating story against Gabond in its leaves. Otherwise the Bible would have descended like the clock from father to son. A grim story, my dear fellow?"

"Most grim—and certainly macabre," I said. "And may I add— very well told."

"Well, the credit for that is not all mine," he answered. "I had the advantage of making a copy of that broadsheet. I will show it to you in a few minutes. It is still in typescript bound up with other stories of the past. I have not yet had time to make the printed copy. But before I get it, I want you to do me a favour which you may or may not like. Do you take snuff?"

"Not as a habit," I said, puzzled. "But I quite like it. Why?"

"I should like you to take a pinch with me—out of this gold box." He took it from his pocket and held it out.

I took a pinch, and so did he. When he had shut the lid I asked him if I could look at it.

It was small but heavy and beautifully chased.

"It's magnificent," I said. "Is it very old?"

"Yes, and no," he answered. "The box isn't old as a box, because I made it."

"You?" I cried. "Is there anything you can't do?"

"I don't know," he said lightly. "You see, I've been a lot of things in my time. I didn't do the engraving—that is very old. As a matter of fact I made the box out of the clasp that belonged to Joe Sunderland's Bible. I found it shining in the rubble of their wrecked house. I thought a snuff-box appropriate to the Restoration period. And it's useful whereas a clasp without the lock to it is not much good. You were certainly entitled to that pinch, because you are the very first person to whom I have told Antony Gabond's adventure."

He then showed me the volume from his notebooks that contained his typescript of the story. I have never seen typing look

more attractive. The lettering was quite different to the usual standard, and I asked him what machine he used.

"It's just a Remington," he answered, "only I re-cast the letters
into the old English style. I like old printing best."

We talked late that night, for old Hoadley had been sent to bed
and it was my host who played the valet to me in the Tapestry
Room. Once more he was going to sleep in the Chapel. I tried
to dissuade him, but he argued, "I intend to give Porfirio every
chance of making contact with us. When I don't know all about
a thing, it irritates me. Somehow I feel that your coming here is
going to bring things to a head. I am certainly not going to let
that old blighter disturb you till you are better, and then—well, if
you want another dose of the Chapel—you shall. But perhaps he'll
make me see what he's getting at first."

I laughed. "I'll be quite frank. I should hate to sleep in that
Chapel to-night of all things."

When he left me to the peace of the Tapestry Room and I heard
him going downstairs, alone, to that lonely Chapel, I felt heartily
sorry for him. And in the morning I found that I had had every
reason for feeling the way I did.

CHAPTER EIGHT

CONCERNING TWO NIGHTMARES AND A MYSTERIOUS
OVERCOAT

I SLEPT well. Only once was I interrupted during the night. I heard
four o'clock strike on the church clock. As I counted the strokes, I
had that instinctive feeling that I was not alone in the room. Hoadley's splendid log-fire was dying down, but I could still see every
detail of the furniture, even to the many figures on the tapestries. I
suppose I saw them by the light of the fire, or was the whole thing
just a dream? I don't know. Anyhow, this is what I saw, thought I
saw, or dreamt I saw.

Standing by the door that led on to the landing was the figure
of a young woman. At the same time I recognized that sweet per-

fume that I had experienced the night before. Her face was turned
to the door, but that didn't prevent me from knowing exactly what
she was like, and when eventually she did turn to look towards
the bed, I found that I was right. A lovely little face it was—oval
and delicate, but with an expression in her large grey eyes of
proud determination. Her figure was perfect, lithe and feminine,
though very youthful. I remember thinking how impossible it is to
describe her in words. It needs the art of a great sculptor to give
her any faithful reproduction.

Now the same instinct that made me look for her, somehow
enabled me to tell exactly what she was thinking. I knew that she
had taken a daring decision and was now eager to complete it.
Whatever it was, it had something to do with the door by which
she stood, listening. Yes—she was expecting someone to come
along and open it—someone terribly important to her, who had
the key in his pocket, and who would fit it in the lock outside. As
she waited I knew, without seeing her face, that her excited joy
was turning into a bewildered anxiety. And then the key fell behind
her with a chinking noise. She turned suddenly and saw it lying
on the oak floor. I could tell the strength of her emotion by the
rapid rising and falling of the rich tight bodice covering her youthful breasts. The tapestry moved and a cold draught came into the
room. I felt it and shivered. Yes—the tapestry was being held aside,
revealing a dark cavity in the wall behind it. The cavity was an
open door leading to a dark staircase. She looked up from the key
and saw, as I did, a hand with a great gold signet ring shining on
one of the fingers. I knew it for the Abbot's ring before Porfirio
himself glided into the room, after pulling the door close behind
him.

If I had loathed the vision of him the night he appeared in the
Chapel, my abhorrence was even greater now. It must have been
the contrasting beauty of the girl which made him the uglier.

He appeared as he was when he had scourged himself, which
in itself seemed an added offence, being in the presence of this
young and beautiful girl. There was something obscene in that
massive torso with the tiny head—that great back and chest; lacer-
ated with old wounds of scourging. In his right hand he grasped

the thick handle of the lead-loaded thongs. In her right hand she grasped the collar of a dark hooded mantle which trailed on the floor beside her. In her eyes terror had grown as she stared at the awful monk. Then he spoke, in a low, sneering tone as he watched her with his horrid animal eyes. I could see his small mouth with the lips turned up at the corners into a perpetual smile, articulating words that sounded like a purring cat. Some of his words I didn't understand, and many sentences were lost through his long habit of ecclesiastical intoning, but on the whole I gathered the evil gist of his menacing message to the girl, which ran somewhat as follows:

"So you were willing to commit deadly sin with your lover, without the consent and blessing of Holy Church. Do you realize that your mere willingness has committed the sin? For there is no difference, daughter, between the willingness and the act itself. Now learn the truth. Your lover is not here. He has never been lodged in this room. It was I who tested you—not he. I who sent that tempting message of evil which can nevertheless bring you to eventual salvation. You must not blame the pretty Sister Anna for betraying you. Like many a nun, she is a woman still—a very pretty one. She will do anything for me, who has the power to forgive her any sin. Take comfort that I can do the same for you. When Sister Anna showed you the secret way from the convent opposite, she did it because I ordered her, though the poor weak creature envies you the opportunity to-night of showing your complete devotion to the Church. You are my ward; I am your ghostly protector. I suspected you would be lavish with your beauty to gratify the pleasure of the prince's page, who brought me letters from his royal master here to-day. But he rode back. There was no thought of housing him in this royal guest-room. That was my trap to snare you. Do you suppose that I would sanction the Prince himself enjoying the most luscious fruit in my orchard? No—then how much less his page, however handsome the boy may be, however nobly born. Yet you were willing. I could lay a solemn curse upon you that would wither up your beauty of body and soul. But I am merciful. You shall abase yourself. With me you shall do penance, and then atone with me. Get ready."

Her beautiful eyes were riveted to his as in terrified submission she collapsed upon her knees before him. I thought of a beautiful rabbit fascinated by a loathsome snake. Porfirio raised his scourge—swung it round and sent the thongs hissing through the air. They licked round his body opening the old flesh wounds, and then he pointed the red, dripping implement of torture at the girl. She knew what he meant. There was no escape, and while still held by his hypnotic stare, her slender fingers fumbled with the laces of her bodice. Sadistically he waited, gripping the scourge; then as she drew the garment down from her shoulders, baring her breasts and back, he crept towards her. Then, as though from Hell itself, a flame of fire lit up the room, and in the light of it the figures vanished.

The last great log had fallen in the hearth and flickered every detail of the room. Perhaps the noise and flare of it had woken me. It died down and went out, and I lay still in darkness. I thought of groping for the light switch, but there suddenly stole over me that same sweet perfume, and in its protection, I was once more sound asleep.

All this came back to me suddenly, as I sipped my morning tea, and listened to Hoadley's account of a catastrophe which had befallen his Master.

It seemed he had dreamt of the black monk who had tried to get him out into the grounds through that door at the side of the stone altar which no longer existed; for, as Hogarth argued with himself, 'What was the use of a material body trying to follow a ghostly one through a solid wall? It was not feasible. In fact, it was nonsensical.'

This, according to Hoadley, had so angered the wicked spirit that he had pronounced a terrible curse against his Master.

"He is in great agony, sir," explained the old servant with indignation. "When I handed him his cup of tea an hour ago he couldn't hold it. Crippled he is again with what I take to be neuritis. Worse than when you first saw him, sir. The Master won't hold with my idea, that he is the victim of a Latin curse. In fact, he goes so far, does the Master, as to say that it was just ordinary neuritis givin' him pain that caused him to get a bad nightmare. Now I don't hold with that. It's a clear case of a Latin curse put on him by the malignant spirit that haunts this place. Well, we'll have to see what the Doctor has to say, though he's apt to joke too much is our local. Told me over the telephone just now that any gentleman who chooses to go to bed in a haunted chapel, with a tomb for a bath and a high altar for a dressing-table, is downright askin' for trouble."

"Perhaps he's right there, Hoadley," I suggested. "Or do you think your Master and myself should both give up the pleasant luxury of good port and old brandy before retiring?"

Hoadley looked at me keenly. "Why, sir, was you troubled in the night? Not in here, surely, sir?"

"I certainly had a nightmare, and a bad one," I confessed. "Otherwise, I'll not deny I slept very soundly. If there are ghosts, Hoadley, and I'm waiting to be convinced, there's a very beautiful one belonging to this room who counteracts evil."

I then told him of my dream, which he assured me was not one at all, but an actual vision, and off he goes downstairs to the Chapel to recount it to his Master.

When he came back to superintend my bath which I had asked him to get ready, he gave me my host's compliments and begged that, as I was feeling like getting up for breakfast, I would take it with him in the Chapel.

To this I consented willingly, for the place had no terrors for me in the daylight, and in less than an hour I was seated at a table by his bedside, making a hearty meal. He, on the other hand, was in great pain, one side of him being completely paralysed.

"But whatever the doctor says," he declared, "I shall spend the day in the Library, though I may be forced to annex your invalid chair. This Latin curse as Hoadley persists in calling it, is a damned nuisance, just as I thought I was fit again. However, I shall sleep here again to-night and see if Old Porfirio won't change his tactics. If he heals me, as he seemed to do before, I'll make a date to join him in the garden by the back door. If I believed in ghosts, like Old Hoadley, I should think he was trying to show me some long-forgotten secret that keeps him from his rest."

"Perhaps the missing treasure of Old Islip's time," I laughed.

"That would indeed be a welcome addition to my macabre museum. And while on that subject," he went on, "I had another dream last night, apart from the nightmare you have heard. Oh—quite ordinary—but I dreamt our mutual friend Carnaby came in. He was in a terrible huff because I have not yet examined the package you brought me down. So that has made me change my mind. I will not devote the whole day to Old Porfirio and the Lady of your Dreams soaked in perfume—in fact, I may give the pair of them a miss till I come back here to sleep. Instead, we'll open the packet and see what Carnaby can tell us of a problem that has irritated me since 1912."

"In what way has it irritated you?" I asked.

"Because the damned thing has all the ingredients for a very good story," he laughed, "and there isn't one in it. Just a curious preamble, a few mysterious incidents, and then—no explanation. However, Carnaby had high hopes of being able to help me, and the packet will be his answer, no doubt."

"Do you feel well enough to tell me the preamble and the incidents?" I asked. "It would make the opening of Carnaby's packet much more exciting for me."

"It was what I was going to suggest," he answered. "Then I shall have your help in examining his deductions. But I hear the Doctor's car. I'll deal with him first; but whatever he has to say about my Latin Cursitis, I'll get Hoadley to park me in the Library, and tell you there how I once was given a mysterious overcoat in India, which disappeared."

I could see that the doctor was thoroughly mystified by Hogarth's complaint, but to my relief, he had no objection to his patient being moved into the Library for the day. "I'll send in our hospital masseuse this afternoon," he said. "Till then, put on a warm dressing-gown and take it easy. You are certainly not a rheumaticky subject. Can't understand it. I've never known you indisposed before, my dear Hogarth, and if massage doesn't help you, I shall feel inclined to agree with Hoadley and Shakespeare and say that you need more the divine than the physician. That will necessitate me resigning in favour of the Rector. We'll have to get him along with holy water, bell, book and candle, and a Latin prescription to remove the curse. But seriously, my good fellow, I should move back to your old room and not try to sleep in this place. I'm a religious sort of chap in spite of a scientific training, and although I admit this bedroom is the lap of luxury in which it should be possible to sleep, there may be spiritual objections to the practice that we wot not of. I shouldn't feel right in sleeping in a consecrated building myself."

"What nonsense," laughed Hogarth. "Many's the time I've heard you snoring during the Rector's sermons."

"That's different," retorted the doctor. "At least, I'm clad in a respectable tail-coat. Pyjamas aren't respectful, whatever you may say."

And with that retort he left the Chapel.

While waiting for the Master to join me in the Library I amused myself by hobbling over to the specimen case on my crutches, to see which relic I would ask my host to tell me about after dinner. The two skulls looked promising and gruesome, and as they were set out at different ends of the case, I concluded that they each had their own adventure to tell. They certainly looked eager enough, and their grinning promised stories of grim humour. I had nearly decided on one of them when my curiosity was whetted by the pathetic and broken-winged body of the white moth. What tale had that delicate creature to tell? I think I had decided on that, when Hoadley entered with his Master's keys and opened the safe, placing the packet I had carried down from London upon the table.

In a little time he wheeled in the Master who fingered the packet as he talked.

"I'm going to tell you the whole thing just as it happened, leaving nothing out, so that you can get the full background. No doubt there will be a lot of extraneous details when you come to sum up your impressions—so forgive me if I mix trivial matter in the concoction.

"As I said, it started in India in 1912. As a youngster of twenty I was on the stage. Already I had the urge to collect stories—true ones—and I saw in the theatrical profession a chance of seeing the world. I confess that I also loved acting, and so was doubly fortunate in becoming a member of the famous Matheson Lang Company, which set out on a world tour. From South Africa we proceeded to India, the Company being the star attraction for the Durbar held by George the Fifth and Queen Mary. We played in Bombay to coincide with the King's arrival and in Calcutta for his farewell. It was in this latter city that the adventure started.

"I have been there since many times, but never have I known the place so full with sightseers from all parts of the world and so many notables taking part in the ceremonies. Bejewelled elephants with gorgeous trappings seemed to take up half the space in the streets and everywhere could be seen glittering uniforms amid the picturesque colours of the East.

"One day—the day when the adventure started—our company had been invited to play a cricket match against the Maharajah of Natore's Eleven, a famous team, many of whose players were well known on English county grounds. We were taken out in cars to the magnificent private ground, where we found ourselves confronted with these first-class cricketers. I remember one Indian gentleman whose bowling quite demoralized our scratch team. He seemed to run for a mile, leaping high into the air as he raced for the crease with his wild hair and gleaming teeth, and then delivering the ball like a cannon-shot.

"Our wickets fell to him so rapidly that we were forced to follow on, but the absurdity of this ill-matched match in no way diminished the keenness of our opponents. They might have been playing England herself, which I take it was a mark of their true hospitality, for they would not change their best bowlers for fear of giving us the inferiority complex we felt anyway. Although a lovely day, it was a tiring one, too, for the heat was as fierce as the bowling, and the magnificent refreshments forced upon us were conducive to sleep, so that by the time we had finished our night's work in the theatre, we were all eager to hurry back to our hotels.

"In those days the theatres of the Far East had been mostly served by touring musical comedies, and the rules of the stage door were lax in the extreme. We found that anyone seemed to have the right of popping back-stage whenever so disposed. Strangers would walk into our dressing-rooms and invite us to supper-parties, and then casually stroll on to the stage itself to watch the play from the wings. Naturally, this lack of theatre discipline hampered the work of staff and artists, and Mr. Lang wisely put a stop to it by forbidding anyone to come past the stage door without a written permission from the management. As a stage manager it fell to my lot to sign these papers, which were only encouraged after the fall of the final curtain.

On this particular night we had more visitors than usual, mostly people who had witnessed the day's cricket, and were no doubt curious to see if we could play a play better than a game. So it happened that I was very late before being free to leave the theatre.

"Now, going backwards and forwards across the stage while giving out calls for the next day, I noticed a gentleman in evening dress with a black overcoat over his arm. He was a smart-looking man, dark and bronzed, and had the cut of an Anglo-Indian officer. He seemed to be very interested in every man connected with the company. For the ladies he had no eyes at all: but each actor he scrutinized closely, and then seemed to find them wanting. There was nothing offensive about him. He was sober and self-contained, and I wondered whom he was waiting for.

"At last everyone had gone but Matheson Lang himself, who was entertaining a party of friends in his dressing-room. Ready to go myself and having settled everything for the next morning's rehearsal with the various members of the staff, I called in to say good night to Mr. Lang.

"One of his guests, who remarked that we were certainly better actors than cricketers, asked me what I thought of mysterious India. I replied that the fast bowler was the most eerie thing I had seen in the country so far, and he said that had I lived in India as long as he had, I would have encountered many more eerie things than that. Now, I added that I had no wish to, little knowing that I was to meet an inexplicable adventure outside that very door, for there I saw again the mysterious stranger with the coat over his arm.

"He was watching me as I crossed the stage for the last time towards the stage-door. He seemed to be sizing me up, and was subconsciously nodding his head, as though he approved of me.

This is not conceit, for he may yet have been looking for a prize booby to suit his turn.

"I could see that he was undecided whether to speak to me or not, and thinking perhaps I might have met him at the match, I walked back to him, asking if he were waiting for anyone and could I help. I told him I was stage manager, gave him my name and held out my hand. This he ignored, but seizing my left wrist, he suddenly curved my arm and placed the black coat he was carrying over it, saying solemnly, 'The coat.'

"I looked at the folded garment over my arm and asked, 'What coat?'

"He just said 'That one,' and promptly turned his back on me and walked quickly away.

"Somewhat bewildered, I followed him to the stage door, where I again asked, 'Whose is it?'

"Instead of answering, he put a rupee on to the stage door-keeper's window-ledge, growled a 'Good night,' and hurried out.

"I followed and, to my astonishment, he broke into a run. I remember running after him and calling out, 'Hi, sir. This isn't mine.'

"He only ran the faster and towards a car which was standing against the curb with its engine running. It was a large open car with four men in it—all in evening dress.

"On his reaching the car it began to move forward. He jumped on to the running-board and was pulled into the back by his companions.

"I shouted emphatically, 'This is not my coat,' which made the others laugh. But the man who had given it to me did not laugh with them. He leaned over the back of the car and, pointing at me, called back—'Wear it. Wear it.'

"There was something in the way he said these words which sounded sinister, and I was to remember that tone afterwards.

"Well—the car disappeared round a corner and I was left with the coat.

"Not wishing to carry such a heavy garment on such a hot night to the hotel, I turned back to the theatre in order to leave it in my dressing-room.

"Passing the stage door-keeper, I told him what had happened. He said he had noticed the men in the car, and that they seemed to him to be gentlemen who had been dining too well, but that the gentleman with the coat over his arm was stone cold sober, and had followed the party of Mr. Lang's friends on to the stage, so he naturally thought he was one of them. Now the coat had been neatly folded with the outside showing. The stage door-keeper remembered it perfectly and pointed out that I had signed the paper for Mr. Lang's party and that the mysterious gentleman had evidently tacked himself on to them in order to get through to the stage.

"We looked at the coat. It was made of good, heavy, black cloth with black wooden buttons. When I unfolded it to hang it in my dressing-room, I was astonished to find it lined with scarlet.

"This seemed to prove it to be what it looked like—a military officer's top-coat, but carrying no regimental buttons or badges.

"Anxious to get back to my supper, I left it hanging in my room, and walked back to my hotel, where I remember telling one of my colleagues about the adventure.

"The next morning I showed him the coat and tried it on. Had it been tailored for me I couldn't have had a better fit, and Monty—his name, you may remember, as he became later a famous Hollywood film actor, Montague Love—well, he advised me to stick to it, as it might prove a useful piece of wardrobe in some play. But being curious as to why it had been handed to me, I took it to the house manager, who had a notice pinned up in the cloakroom, asking if anyone had lost an overcoat on such-and-such a date, and that if so, provided that a correct description were given, the management would be pleased to return it to the owner.

"As we were to re-visit Calcutta after our tour in China and the Philippines, I left the coat in the manager's office, and meeting him again some months later, he told me that since no-one had claimed it, I had better keep it, with the suggestion that if I were to change the scarlet lining to black, I would have a very serviceable coat for winter in London. So I carried it to my hotel and told my bearer to pack it in the bottom of my trunk.

"He picked up the coat and looked at it, seeming to concentrate upon the red lining. Then with fear in his voice, he said, 'Pack this? No. Not this. Bad.'

"'Bad?' I repeated. 'I think it's jolly good. What makes you say "bad"? Look—it fits me perfectly.' There and then I put it on. My dignified Indian servant looked at me with horror in his eyes, and abruptly left the room. I never saw him again, which was strange, since I had not paid him his wages.

"As he had been with me on my first visit, and had, without my asking him, met me on the return journey to look after my baggage, and in all things had proved himself honest, willing and capable, I was at a loss to understand how I had offended his good sense of judgment, for until the coat episode, he had continually expressed a wish to return with me to England, and remain my servant. Such loyalty I had appreciated, and it made his sudden walking out on me the more bewildering.

"Well, I packed the coat in a spare trunk filled with presents for people at home, and thought little more about it. Some months later I returned to England from South Africa, unpacked it, and hung it in an empty wardrobe, for I had by then got into the habit of a wardrobe trunk.

"More months went by before I gave it another thought.

"You remember the play *Mr. Wu*? I was not in it, as I wanted to give up all my time to the writing of a book. My brother had taken my place in the Company and we were still living at home at father's vicarage in Westminster.

"One evening a terrific rain-storm broke out just as he was about to start off for the theatre. He had left his evening coat at the cleaners, and so borrowed mine. Later on he phoned me to join him at a supper-party. I told him it was all very fine, considering he had bagged my coat.

"His answer was, 'You've got to come. Why not put on the mysterious coat from India? If you think it looks odd, all the better. Make a point of it. Blame me, and then tell them all the story. It will give us something to talk about, and one of the party may be able to solve the great mystery.' So I changed and put it on over my evening clothes, and really worn like that it looked most distinguished, and I rather kicked myself that I had never thought of using it before. Of course, the snag was the red lining. One hates to be conspicuous, and I realized it would be noticed when I took it off in the restaurant. I had to decide whether to be eccentric or wet. Well—the rain beat me to it, and off I went in the coat.

"On arrival I found my brother's guests waiting for me in the lounge, and they all said the coat looked very smart, and asked me where I got it. My brother said I must tell its history over supper, which was all ready, so I went to park it in the cloakroom. It was there that the next curious thing happened.

"There was one other man at the cloakroom counter. In my hurry I just noticed that he had collected his own overcoat and was putting it on. He placed a sixpence in the tipping saucer and was going out, when he looked at me, watching my coat as I took it off.

"I did my best to conceal the conspicuous lining by folding it outside up, as when I had originally seen it. But I was reckoning without the attendant, who promptly unfolded it to give it a good shake as it was wet. He then placed it on a shelf with the red lining well in evidence.

"The leaving customer noticed, hurried back and stared—first at the lining—then at me. In my anxiety to hide the lining, I had paid little heed to the man, and it was only then that I saw he was a Hindu. From me he looked again at the coat, and seemed puzzled. And now the strange part begins. He glanced at his wrist-watch, and said to the attendant, 'I have more time than I thought. I am going back to my friends. Perhaps the rain will stop later.'

"He took off his coat again and re-checked it. Then he followed me into the restaurant, where he joined a party of three Indians who were sitting next to our table.

"He gave a whispered explanation of his sudden return, and by the way they kept looking at me, I gathered that I, or the coat, had had something to do with it, and it became very obvious when I was telling the story of the thing, that they were all four of them trying to overhear the conversation. We were a long time over our supper, but none of the Indians moved till I did. They got up simultaneously, and hurried past us to the cloakroom, evidently determined that we should not beat them to it.

"By this time the rain had stopped, and while we were waiting for the ladies of our party, the Indians waited too.

"We called a taxi. The Indians called another, but they did not start till we did. They were obviously trailing us and, of course, we linked it up definitely with my coat.

"When we pulled up at the girls' address in Kensington, the other taxi stopped at the next house. We left our cab ticking up and purposely went in for a final drink. We had arranged that on the way just to see what they'd do. Peeping through the blind of our friends' dining-room, we could see that the Indians were still waiting. One of them had got out and was talking to the others through the door.

"In order to see again what they would do, I went out and paid our taxi off, and then returned into the house. This did not shake them off. They waited.

"So we waited too, for about half an hour, and then walked out. As we passed the Indians, I said audibly, 'Let's walk.'

"They paid off their cab and followed us on foot.

"We walked them nearly to Westminster, refusing all cruising taxis. Then we saw two taxis on a rank and, taking one, directed him to drive us to the Tower Bridge and back. The Indians sure enough followed suit. We brought them back to the same rank and walked on home. They paid off their cab too, and when we finally let ourselves in, they parted after leaving one of them to watch from the pavement opposite our front door.

"Being now very thrilled with the adventure, we spied on the fellow. Two hours later he was relieved by one of the others, who had changed from dinner-jacket to a lounge suit. By then we thought we'd had enough, so went to bed, but in the morning we noticed that another one was watching the house before break-fast, and was relieved while we were eating. As the relieving one was chatting earnestly to his colleague, I went out and asked him point-blank why we were being watched. He said politely that I had made a mistake, and that they were waiting for a friend who lived next door. I said that as I knew the people next door very well, could I help by giving them a message? After a quick con-sultation in their own tongue, they told me it didn't matter, and walked away. I saw neither of them again, but within a quarter of an hour a turbaned Indian, one of their servants, no doubt, was watching our house from the farther side of the square gardens. This vigilance was kept up by other Indians for three whole weeks. Whenever I left the house in the coat I was followed. Without it I was left alone, except on one day when I passed them carrying a suit-case. Perhaps they thought it was inside. It was. I took it to a tailor, and had the red lining changed for black. There were no secret papers in the lining, for I watched him strip it, but we did make one discovery.

"In the small of the back, a seam had been taken in to conceal a hole, singed round the edge, which might have been made by a revolver bullet.

"During that three weeks I had to go one evening to Charing Cross and meet some girl cousins returning from school on the Continent. On the platform I noticed an elderly gentleman watching me. I was getting used to that sort of thing by this time. I was wearing the coat, and so had been followed by the Indian from Westminster. My new Nosey Parker was the typical Anglo-Indian, hard-bitten, bronzed and swagger. I put him down for a retired colonel. His penetrating stare was so offensive that I was about to ask him what he meant, when the train steamed in. A few minutes later I was escorting my young cousins through the archway, when we had to step on to the narrow pavement to make way for a private bus. Inside was the colonel and a party of little girls. He caught my eye, and banged on the window for the driver to stop. He then pulled down the back window and beckoned to me ferociously. I raised my hat and stepped towards him.

" 'That coat,' he snarled.

" 'Yes, sir?' I asked innocently.

" 'It is,' he muttered. 'But it's really not my business, and I'm damned if I'll be mixed up in it. Drive on.'

"Up went the window with a bang, and the family bus jerked on, which sent the old gentleman sprawling on top of his charges, which served him right, for having given me something fresh to puzzle over in my mystery.

"After this the square was haunted by an Indian in a white

turban, who always carried a suit-case. It was a large case, and from the easy way he handled it, I suspected it to be empty, and as you shall hear, I was probably right.

"Whenever I spoke to him, he always answered that he was waiting for his master.

"One evening some friends dropped in and told us that this Indian had come up our basement steps with his suit-case and had taken on their taxi. They had been told the story of the coat and wanted to see it.

"I went upstairs to get it, and found the wardrobe locked and the key gone. We never found the key, and finally had to get a locksmith to open the door. You no doubt guess what we found. No coat. It had gone, and so had the discarded red lining which I had kept out of interest.

"Well—there you are—we saw no more Indians and no more coat, and the only sequel was that I received a receipt for repairs to coat from the tailor. I went round and said I had not paid. He told me that an Indian servant had come into his shop and asked for my bill which he promptly paid in my name. So at least they were honest in that they did not expect me to be out of pocket for their theft. Well—I mean, I suppose they stole it, but I don't really know. Perhaps they had some claim on it. Anyway, why all that fuss for a coat? I am convinced that there was some deathly important secret somehow connected with it, but I don't mind telling you the whole damned business has irritated me for years, because nothing seemed to fit the lock of the puzzle. Let us now see what Carnaby has made of it."

Even the little energy required to break the seals made Hogarth wince with pain, and his irritation burst out with, "Confound this neuritis—paralysis—common or garden cramp, or whatever it is; but I won't let it spoil my enjoyment. No, not when I've waited for it since 1912. I *will* open this thing."

With an effort he forced his fingers to obey him, and slowly turned back the folds of the thick paper.

As he looked down into the parcel, he gave a low whistle of astonishment.

"Hallo," he cried. "So he's got it after all."

"The solution?" I asked eagerly.

"No—the red lining—and wait a minute—a card."

He lifted a calling card and looked at it closely, raising his left eyebrow and closing his right eye. Then half amused—half puzzled—he went on, "But it's not Carnaby's card. It's from—let's see——

> *The Very Reverend O. K. Preddal, B.A.,*
> The Vicarage,
>   Little Middleston,
>   Nr. Great Middleston,
>   South Riding,
>   Yorks."

He looked across at me. "And how many phoney things do you get out of that?"

"Phoney?" I echoed. "A comic address, perhaps. Who is the Reverend gentleman? Ever heard of him?"

"No more has anyone else," he answered, "outside Carnaby's bright imagination. I spotted six impossibilities. First, I'll bet you a fiver there's no such name as O. K. Preddal in Crockford's Clerical Directory. I've got an old one in my reference library, and you could see if you doubt me. Then it is extremely unlikely that a Very Reverend would still be but a Bachelor of Arts. The initials O. K. are quite ridiculous—the name Preddal is a scream. I'm sure there is no such place as Little or Great Middleston, and, of course, there is no such district as South Riding. North, East and West are the three Ridings. The very name means a Third. Old Carnaby can't bowl me out on that. He might at least explain himself."

"Could the name and address be one of Carnaby's codes?" I suggested. "Ever since I've known him he's had a mania for them. Wait a minute, though," I added, for Hogarth had moved his fingers from the back of the card and I saw some writing, "there's something written on this side."

Probably ashamed of his neglect, my host gave way to irritation again.

"So there is," he muttered. "Then why can't the damned fool be thorough and put P.T.O. under his assumed name?"

"What's it say?" I asked.

"Sounds like a Samson riddle in the Bible. Listen." And he read out slowly:

> *"The coat was made for the lining.*
> *Not the lining for the coat.*

"Now, what the devil? . . . Hallo again. I thought this was his scribbled signature, but I can see now, it's '*More Anon.*' Now why shouldn't he have been more explicit? Carnaby isn't the man to get the wind up about things. Why should he be so cagey?"

"Perhaps," I said, "it is because he's a brave man that he can be brave enough to recognize danger and respect its power. I wouldn't have been at all surprised if you had told me that those Indians who followed you about had tried over and over again to take your life. In fact, I was surprised that they made no sort of violent attempt against you."

"And his sartorial riddle then," said the Master, "in your opinion is Carnaby, not in a jocular mood, but in a careful one."

"Exactly," I agreed. "Because of some danger, perhaps to you or himself, he thinks it dangerous to be explicit. His meaning seems quite clear that it is the lining that is more important than the coat. The mystery must revolve around the red lining. Who knows— perhaps it is really a red flag of danger, and—in spite of Carnaby's caution—may be bringing a horde of Asiatics to your door."

"Or window," corrected the Master in a low whisper, and I saw that he was staring hard at something behind my back. I was about to ask him what was wrong, when he spoke again through his teeth and without moving his lips perceptibly. "Get up naturally and with your crutches cross to get a book or something. I want to know if you can see what I can see looking through the window behind you."

I did as he told me, and as I turned towards the bookcase I saw, framed behind the glass of the central window, a black beard pressing against the rimy pane and the dark turbaned swarthy face of an Indian.

CHAPTER NINE

I HAVE seldom seen anything more sinister than this apparition. He stood there rigid, staring at me through the lead-rimmed glass. At the same time the deep bell of Wrotham Church at the end of the grounds began to strike the hour. Twelve o'clock. To be truly ghostly in the accepted style it should have been twelve midnight. But it was noon—a lovely day, with a bright sun shining on the hard snow. Somehow it enhanced the frightening picture that the Indian made. Was he the first of the Asiatic horde that I had just mentioned? Behind him against the skyline stood the lofty ridge of Wrotham Hill, whose snow-covered woods looked as white as the lofty peaks of the Himalayas. Against such a background the silhouetted stranger was in his right element. Indeed, it couldn't have been more fitting had he brought his native scenery from the North-West Frontier with him to impress us further. As I gazed back at him, hypnotized by his strange wild face, an astonishing thing happened. The great red velvet curtains from each side of the window swept together and blotted him out.

For a second I could see nothing. After the dazzling sun on the snow, I seemed in complete darkness, and then a heavy hand gripped my shoulder, and the weight of a man's body fell against me. It was the Master. He had, with a superhuman effort, got from his chair and pulled the cord of the curtains which had prevented the Indian from seeing in, and I had not heard him passing my left shoulder when I was held by the vision at the window.

"Help me back to the chair," he whispered, "or I shall faint. We will then deal with the bloke outside."

"What on earth made you get up to pull the curtains?" I asked, as I assisted him back to the chair.

"In case he should pull a gun on *you*," he explained in a whisper. "Coming on the top of your warning and the talk about Carnaby, put the wind up me. Ring for Hoadley and get him to find out who this fellow is."

"Was he—'real'?" I asked.

"Listen at the other window," he answered. "I'm getting so mixed up between ghosts and dreams that I don't know whether I'm seeing or not. If he's real, he ought to be a decent sort of a bloke, because he was wearing a dark green turban, which means he is a Holy Man who has taken the great pilgrimage to Mecca. No doubt he may also be a wild fanatic where his religion is concerned, and if he thinks we are his enemies, we'd better watch out. No, perhaps we had better not let Hoadley loose on him. If he wants entry here, he'll no doubt try the front door, and he wouldn't harm a servant for admitting him. He'd be much too careful."

Well—I looked through the curtains when I could hear nothing, and the man, whoever he was—man or thing—had completely disappeared. Neither could I see from the window any footprints in the virgin snow. Of course, that convinced us both that the thing was just another of the ghosts about the house.

We rang for Hoadley and when we asked him if anyone had seen the Indian gentleman, he said "No." His Master ordered him to make inquiries in the village when he went for his glass of beer. On his return he said he'd drawn a blank. No one answering our description had been seen by the shopkeepers.

"Then all I can say," stated Hogarth, "is, that the mystery of the overcoat deepens. How long do you suppose Carnaby means by Anon?"

Well, evidently Carnaby did not mean that day, for there was nothing from him by the post, no telegram, no telephone, and no visit, and what is more, no one saw anything of an Indian. During the afternoon the masseurs came from the hospital and seemed thoroughly mystified as to any reason for my host's pain, which was just as acute till dinner-time when it eased up for a bit.

When we were more or less comfortably ensconced in the Library after our meal and were once more sipping our port, Hogarth asked if I was sick of his stories, or would care to hear another which might be the means of taking his attention from his pain.

"Certainly," I replied with enthusiasm. "I realize that I have already had a very thrilling one to-day, but when all is said and done, that is still a mystery and no complete tale at all, and if you do not give me a proper one, I shall consider myself cheated."

"And what relic appeals to you to-night?" he asked. "Have you chosen?"

I told him that I had been divided between the skulls and the moth, but that now I chose the moth because of all the relics it seemed to be the most pathetic.

"Not a bit of it," he replied. "That little creature has one of the most violent stories in my collection. Now, if you want pathos— a sad sort of horror—let me tell you the story of that little brass button, that is all bent and corroded."

When I had brought it over to my chair he lit his pipe which I had filled for him, as his hands were still cramped, and he began:

"Some years ago a ship's company and passengers, including myself, witnessed the last act of a drama which had taken ten years to work itself out to its final curtain. The chief actor in this heroic epic was a hard-bitten old sea-captain named Dawson, though during his last ten years he was always referred to as 'Old Sharks.'

"It is the tale of his vengeance which he planned and carried out to its extraordinary conclusion.

"I was lying in a deck-chair trying to keep cool beneath the awning when I first clapped eyes on him. Tall and gaunt, his white hair and beard unkempt, he walked the blistering planks of the *Palamcitta*, barefooted. His green eyes, wide open, defied the glare of the harbour buildings.

"His costume was peculiar, and hardly the sort in which to come aboard a mail boat, for it consisted merely of a blue bathing suit, faded by sea and sun, and a great leather gauntlet, ornamented with brass studs, which he wore on his right hand. As he gazed over the deep waters of Zanzibar, his gnarled, mahogany body quivering with excitement, I watched him open a paper parcel which he had placed on the bulwarks. Raw meat. He fixed a red morsel to a hook fastened to a cork and line. Then he whirled it overboard.

"Curiosity compelled me to get up and brave the sun. A shark was lazily cruising among the floating debris of vegetable mess that spreads around a ship at anchor.

"'Good morning,' I said. 'Shark?'

"He nodded without looking at me, and when all my attempts at conversation failed to get any response but a nod or shake of the head, I returned to my chair, irritated.

"I tried to read, but the old man fascinated me more than my book.

"Fishermen should be patient, but he wasn't. He kept tugging at his line, which he gripped in his gauntleted fist. It struck me that he was using up his vitality by giving way to a consuming rage. Still I watched him till the bell went for lunch.

"The first-class saloon was under the aft deck. I sat next to the chief officer and asked him about the crazy old man above. I could see that my question was resented.

"The chief frowned. 'Yes—he's crazy all right, and with good reason. Used to be skipper of this old tub. Captain Dawson; but he's known as "Old Sharks." For ten years he's been trying to kill "Great Crafty," and the quayside is pretty divided between the two of 'em. Though most of us would like to see "Old Sharks" win, there are some who hold that the harbour wouldn't be the same without "Great Crafty."'

"'Who's he?'

"'A man-eater. A great shark that haunts the harbour. I'll point him out to you. We shall be taking in cargo all day, so there'll be plenty of opportunity. We've known him for years. An uncanny brute. Seems to know when ships are coming in, and if they're favourites of his he will go miles out to meet 'em and pilot 'em in.'

"'And was it this old shark that sent Captain Dawson crazy?' I persisted, for I wanted the story naturally.

"The chief frowned again. 'I don't like the yarn, because in telling it I live it over again. You see, I was there. I saw the whole thing, and it's ten years to-day. I wonder if the old man remembers the date? I was up on the bridge with him when it happened. Four bells and a sweltering afternoon like this.

"'Dawson's wife was spending the day on board and had brought her kid daughter with her. Mrs. Dawson was the daughter of our shipping agent ashore. She was a pathetic creature with a weak heart—never been strong since the birth of her only kid. We all loved that child. The crew couldn't do enough for her. Just five, she was, and as pretty as a picture. Fair hair and a jolly little face, and sea-green eyes like her father's.

" 'I remember that the noise of the donkey engines worried the skipper, because his wife was asleep under the aft awning. He kept going half-way down the ladder to see if she was moving, and each time he came back, he muttered, "All right so far."

" 'It was on one of these little trips that it happened. I thought he'd gone mad, for he suddenly leapt down the remaining steps to the well-deck and, knocking people aside, ran for the aft ladder. Knowing something must be wrong, I followed to see, and, my God, there was the kid crawling on hands and knees on the outside ledge—the wrong side of the bulwarks. She had managed to squeeze herself through the opening of the bollard and was watching something below her in the water. She was wearing a little white coat with brass buttons, and I remember thinking what a row the kid would get into as there was a smear of black oil across her back.

" 'Just then I saw Mrs. Dawson wake up. She looked round for the kid, and then saw her husband leaping along the deck. With an awful scream she jumped up and ran too. Whether it was the scream that frightened the child or the sight of her father dashing towards her, I don't know, but she slipped and fell overboard. I can see it all now. Mrs. Dawson leaning against the bulwarks with her hand pressed to her heart, as her husband stripped off his jacket and dived overboard. In the meantime I had dashed down from the bridge and raced aft.

" 'The skipper had just risen to the surface when I got there, and then the water round him was churned into a maelstrom, and the white belly of a huge shark flashed in the sun. Up came the great tail clear of the water and then down into the depths went that dear kid to her doom.

" 'We dashed now to get the skipper aboard before the shark came up again. Only just in time, too, for as we dragged him to safety, we saw the evil black fin once more.'

"The chief paused here as though overcome with the dreadful memory. Then he went on, 'The loss of the kid was tragic in the extreme, but that was only half of the calamity, for when we turned back to the deck we found Mrs. Dawson lying dead. The death of her child and her husband's peril had been too much for that frail creature. Her heart had failed. I went ashore to break the news to her father, and when I returned I found the skipper completely changed. From a sane and healthy sea-captain, and one of the finest that had ever sailed, he had become the crazy, fierce "Old Sharks" you see on deck now.

"'The days and nights following were pretty ghastly, I can tell you. He refused to sail. He held us to his command at his revolver's point. We just obeyed. He organized shark hunts. Sixteen we caught in three long days and nights, but he was not satisfied, because when they were cut open he could find no trace of the brass buttons of the little girl's coat. At last one of the crew came forward and told him it was useless, for the shark that had taken the child was "Great Crafty," a sagacious old devil, well known to all Zanzibar. No bait would ever tempt him, the man said.

"'"We've tried him, sir, with poisoned meat, and he just laughs and sheers off. There's no poison, no hook, that will ever get 'Great Crafty.'"

"'"I'll get him," says Captain Dawson, "if I have to fish till the sea gives up its dead."

"'At the end of three days' hunt the shipping office ordered us to overpower the poor madman, bring him ashore, and then sail without him.

"'Well, we rushed him. In the scrimmage he shot one of the crew, but it was not a serious wound, and the fellow bore no resentment. You see, we all grieved for the skipper, and we do still. He comes aboard whenever we touch harbour. Lives here on a pension from the company, and spends all his time just fishing for shark. That universally hated sea race have never had such a bitter enemy as he. I couldn't tell you the indescribable horrors he inflicted on the brutes he caught during those awful huntings. He ordered us to wire them taut and to keep supplying him with red-hot irons. My God, it was horrible. But he's not allowed to torture the ones he catches now. One curious habit he has, and that is whenever he kills, he adds another brass stud to his glove. He calls it his battle gage. Well—that's his tragic yarn, and it seems only yesterday. Yet it's ten years to-day. Four bells it was, too.'

"Instinctively we both looked up at the saloon clock. Two. From the deck came the sound of 'Four Bells.'

"At that instant a wild cry came from above. ' "Great Crafty" heading straight for us. Astern!'

"There was a rush as the crew swarmed to the side. We left the table and hurried on deck.

"There were no ribald jests, no comic greetings indulged in this time by the crew, for they were all in awe of 'Old Sharks,' who stood erect and stark naked on the ledge of the aft bulwarks, immediately above the fatal bollard. His bathing dress lay on the deck behind him. His right hand, still wearing the brass-studded gauntlet, was clenched. His wild green eyes looked down into the water, as the long torpedo body of the largest shark I have ever seen slowly approached the ship.

"I watched the brute as it stopped dead opposite the cork float, beneath which hung the baited hook thrown over by 'Old Sharks.' The great body revolved, showing the dreaded whiteness of the belly.

" 'He's going to take bait at last,' whispered one of the crew.

"But 'Great Crafty' had not earned his name to be fooled by a meated hook, and he rolled over again as though the bait insulted his intelligence.

"Then it was that 'Old Sharks' still keeping his eyes upon 'Great Crafty' spoke to us all assembled on the deck. Brandishing his fist toward the hated fish, he broke his long customary silence in a voice of thunder.

" 'Do you see that evil thing beneath us? Ten years ago at "Four Bells" he was the cause of my wife's death by killing her child. For ten years I have fought his kith and kin, and for each that I have killed I have added a brass stud to my glove. But this "Great Crafty" will take no hook as other fish. Therefore, I have devised a cunning bait, and one that even his craft will not avoid. It is to be a fight to the death, and the last round I shall win.'

"Then an expression of supreme hate overshadowed his face as he addressed the shark.

"'I invite you, you damned "Great Crafty," and my enemy, to a Borgian Feast. You shall eat: I will drink.'

"Up went the gloved hand to his mouth. We saw him toss the contents of a green bottle down his throat. Then dropping the bottle into the sea, he stripped off the glove and flung it at the shark, as he hissed through his clenched teeth: 'Thus I throw down the gage.'

"The shark let the heavy glove sink after the bottle. He was crafty still.

"Although I believe we all realized that we were looking our last upon 'Old Sharks,' we had not the power to interfere. The situation was too big for us. Besides, what was the use? We knew that the bottle contained some deadly poison. We knew that the old man had heroically prepared himself as bait. Had we now the right to rob him of revenge?

"He dived straight at his enemy. One of the crew maintained that his arms gripped the shark as the white belly turned to the attack. But for my part I couldn't see. The drenching salt water blinded me as the unequal but titanic struggle was waged upon the surface.

"In a few seconds it was over.

"A furious lashing of the sea. A vicious uptilt of the great tail, and then down into the depths went 'Old Sharks' in the voracious jaws of his enemy.

"How long we stood there I don't know.

"Bareheaded, we waited in the burning sun till I thought I should faint. And then at last there floated up from the deep, the dead body of the great shark.

"The crew hauled 'Great Crafty' on deck, and when his jaws were opened they found wedged in between two teeth a blackened piece of brass. That piece—yes. Corroded with salt water but it still endured to prove the guilt of the shark. One of the buttons from that little white coat."

*   *   *   *   *

I looked from the button to my host, but for some minutes I couldn't speak.

It was Hoadley who broke the silence.

"Excuse me, sir, but I thought you should know at once. An Indian has been seen in the village. He went into the church for Evensong, and afterwards asked the Rector if a party of his countrymen could put up a camp for a while in the Fair Field."

"Camp? This time of year?" asked the Master.

"That's apparently what the Rector said, sir. But the Indian—he was wearing a dark green turban—said that they were mountain men and used to snow. He told the Rector that they were students, come to observe English life and customs. Sounds a bit fishy to me, sir."

"And a little sinister, too, eh, Kent? The Asiatic horde you conjured up are here, it seems. Pity we're both such crocks. The man we want now is Carnaby."

"And I let myself in, my dear fellow," said a voice from the door.

"A day of surprises, indeed," laughed Hogarth.

"How are you, Carnaby?" I cried. "We certainly are relieved to see you."

"You didn't seem so pleased this morning," he answered, "when I was wearing this," and he pulled from the side-pocket of his overcoat the end of an unwound green turban.

"Then it was you?" I said. "What on earth——"

"Couldn't help the fright I gave you, but it's a long story. But before I talk, please give me a drink."

CHAPTER TEN

CONCERNING A SKULL, A STIRRUP-CUP, AND A BLOOD-COLOURED ROBE

My host was a good host. He was never guilty of that sparing phrase, 'Say when.' He poured out a whole tumbler of whisky without once glancing up at his guest. "There you are. Cheers," he said as he handed it over.

"Thanks," replied Carnaby, without any polite protest that it was too much or too strong. He drank it neat and in one long swallow. "And that's good and I wanted it," he said as he put the glass down on the drinks table which was beside Hogarth's chair. "Oh—sorry, Hogarth Primus," he added with a chuckle, "forgot all about the whisky ration."

"It's all right," replied Hogarth. "What's a whisky ration when there's a whisky racket? I find you can get anything these days if you think it worth paying for in inflated price." He looked up at his guest and laughed. "You know, young Carnaby, although you must be only four years—five years?—my junior; yes, you were in the Lower Third when I was first exalted to keep a fag——"

"Yes—in the Sixth, O, swanky one. Do not be modest," put in Carnaby. "Well—what about my *six* years younger than you?"

"Only that you haven't altered a bit. Not a grey hair—and still that mischievous cunning twinkling in your eyes as when I would accuse you of bagging my marmalade."

"Bag—be damned," protested Carnaby. "That was Ancient Privilege of Fags, from time immemorial. I never broke rules like you did. Remember your midnight parties when we used to get out of our cubicle windows on to the gym roof and you used to horrify us with ghost stories?"

"And who showed us the way to climb by the gutter pipes, O escaper from prisons?" rallied his host. "If you two Carnabys had not been policemen or whatever you call yourselves in the Service, you'd have made a fine couple of cat burglars. Have another whisky?"

Much to my astonishment he answered, "Yes—thanks—I can do with another. Never remember being so cold in my life, and that's saying something. Spent the whole of last night in a snow-cave we dug out—yes—pretending to pray—Oh, I did say one prayer—and that was after planning a good way to escape from my followers, I prayed that in these lean times for the ruddy civilian, which I do realize in spite of being in the Service, you O Mine Host of a thousand hospitalities might have plenty of fire-water, with which to warm the chilly regions around my contemptible soul."

For the second time I watched Hogarth fill the tumbler, without a 'Say when,' and without a protest from his guest. Once more Carnaby drank, but this time slowly and with marked appreciation on his weather-beaten, mischievous face. Hogarth watched him with a smile. "And you're very like your great cousin—our famous Egyptologist policeman. I'm glad I saw him over there before his end."

"Yes—it's strange to think of him, lying in his rock tomb like a Pharaoh. Still, he was a man to be envied. Found what he wanted in death if not in life. I always think his is one of the great love stories of the world. I met old Mallaby—you remember, Hogarth—Colonel Deighton's famous batman in the Camel Corps? He told me about the funeral. Buried in the Elephants' Grave, which they found. A rock cavity with a great slab over them on which is written, *'Greater love hath no man.'* I came back by way of Cairo, and they told me there that not an Army wife dared say a word against him, as they certainly used to when he was alive."

"You see, Kent," explained Hogarth, "he loved a beautiful Nubian princess, and because he boasted of it, racial snobbery made him a lonely man. You must get our friend here to tell you that story."

"Old Mallaby can tell it better," said Carnaby. "He was there, and he had a great affection for both of them. He called them the other day, his Jet and Ivory Deities. I suppose I must be like him. I quite scared one of his friends at Heliopolis. Thought I'd come back from the grave."

"You can certainly carry your liquor like him too," went on Hogarth. "Never knew him tight. Never had a hangover, and yet I've seen him swallow whisky—like you did that first one—standing without a helmet under the gruelling sun of Upper Egypt. And he didn't bat an eyelid. Grand fellow."

"Wish I'd joined him now in Egypt," said Carnaby. "What one could have learnt from him. Strange how he stuck to Egypt till the end. Suppose it was the girl being there. But there you are—Asia always appealed to me; Africa to him."

The door opened and Hoadley appeared pushing a trolley laden with steaming dishes.

"Good God, what's this?" cried Carnaby. "Looks good. Smells damned good."

"Your dinner, sir," replied Hoadley respectfully. "I could see you had not eaten when you first appeared. It's temptin' Providence not to partake of the good things He provides. The Master always informed me that you were very careless over the matter of regular food. Now, sir, no more talkin' if I may so suggest till you ring for me to carry away these dishes empty."

"I second the motion," replied Hogarth. "You see, Carnaby, what a blessing the fellow is. Gives you a good meal and me a severe tick-off for lack of hospitality. However, I hope I should have thought of food in a minute or so."

"You certainly would," laughed Carnaby, "because I should have used Fag's Privilege and demanded it. Come to think of it—the whisky and the meal is the very least you can do for me after the years of fagging I've done for you out in India, over that damned overcoat problem. But if I demanded a whisky, even a single, for every mile I've travelled on your coat's behalf, even your black market store would run dry. Very well, Hoadley, I won't open my lips except to fill my mouth. The other gentlemen shall do the talking. They were always pretty good at it, especially your Master. I don't know your qualifications on the subject, Kent, but I believe I'm the only man living who can talk him down. Tell you what, while I eat, why shouldn't he tell us a yarn? The idea is very sound because we shall all be so enthralled that none of us will notice how very much I shall eat. Come on, Hogarth Primus. Do your stuff." And with Hoadley hovering round him, Carnaby sat down to soup.

"He's already told me a beauty to-night, or rather an extreme tragedy," I said on my host's behalf. "What's more, he's been suffering agonies from what Doctor Hoadley diagnoses as neuritis."

"It's a good deal easier now," said Hogarth. "But look here, Carnaby, I don't care how hungry you may be, you can't do the dirty on us like this. You said just now that you had been praying in a snow-cave with followers. What followers? I'm sorry, Hoadley, but I really must ask him to tell us."

"Well, cut your followers short, sir, whoever they are," whispered Hoadley, as he cleared away the already empty soup-plate. "Here's a couple of very fat little mornay escallops. They goes down very well after a thick soup, and is very good little heralds to announce 'game pie with a sherryed trifle to follow.' There's plenty of vegetables, sir, to have with both courses."

"Then, although quite one of the family, Hoadley," laughed Carnaby, "I am not going to hold back. Oh—but the followers. Yes—I can imagine you are curious. They're Hillmen. Belong to a sort of Sacred Brotherhood. Come all the way to have a squint at you, Hogarth. And because even a dirty little fag feels a kind of sympathy for his master's health, I thought it wise to trek along with them. You never quite know what these fanatical blokes might not do next. My dear friends, these scollops are delectable. My dear Hoadley, what? White wine on the top of all that whisky?"

"And your favourite claret, sir, if I remember right, to accompany the hot pie."

"I shall be gloriously stinking before I'm through," he said with a shrug of his shoulders. "Then you'll have to wait for me to recover from my passing out for my news. However, I will not say 'No.' For have I not faced worse dangers in my time? Hogarth, you are watching me in disgust. Forget me and tell us a story. One of your choice ones. Now let me see, which one? though I expect you've greatly added to your collection since I last saw you."

"This is my lucky night," I chuckled. "You see, Carnaby, I got crashed on Wrotham Hill in that blizzard, and ever since, your Master of Macabre has allowed me to pick my fancies from his relic cabinet."

"I can imagine nothing better to a man laid up with a cracked foot than to sit here, eat, drink, smoke and listen to our rascally host. Hoadley, you're a master too. However do you manage to knock up such a dinner after hours, and with such divine liquor?"

"In my long association with the Master, sir, I have copied his golden rule of always looking ahead. I am happy to state that the contents of the wine cellars which you will recollect are something spacious, have never been better stocked than at present; not even when the old dead and gone archbishops resided here. There is, as I dare say you have found in life, sir, ways and means for doin' anything so long as you remember to look well ahead. A maxim of the Master's, sir, as I say, which I have benefited by assimilatin'. More vegetables, sir. All of the Palace grounds."

"I don't mind telling you this," said Carnaby as he packed an assortment of pie and vegetables upon his fork for his first mouthful of the new course, "that these followers have a profound respect for me, because they consider me a 'Holy Man.' Well—don't smile, you cads—when all's said and done, *I am* a Holy Man in their eyes. I've made the pilgrimage to Mecca. I'm entitled to wear the green turban of the Prophet. And I can't help thinking it's a damned good thing for you, Hogarth, that I too looked well ahead in the old days, by realizing the use I could put Moslem knowledge to account. Holy Men are, however, put to some inconvenience, just as I have been on Wrotham Hill. Imagine feeling ravenous, but having to keep to a fast, and all bang in sight of the smoke from your kitchen chimney stack."

"You poor chap," said Hogarth. "But how did you give 'em the slip? And how, in heaven's name, did you manage to get into that tweed suit? Where did you change? And when?"

"After I'd seen the Rector about the camp," he smiled. "When he'd gone, I came back with my disciples, and knowing our padre's stunt here of keeping the church open day and night, I told them to wait in the ringing-room while I went up to the top of the tower to pray. I had already planted my civvies up there—— Oh, but I'm forgetting—most important; my beard. It is a masterpiece. It was made for me in the Khyber Pass by a make-up man from Hollywood. I was in charge of the unit's protection. It passes anywhere as real. Besides, my disciples, though they watch me, never raise their eyes to mine, as I am such a very Holy Man. Well, off went the beard and turban—I have them here—and down the belfry steps I walked, as you see me now. I had told them to rouse me from my meditations in half an hour. They would know when the time had gone, by starting up the steps when they heard the next striking of the church clock. When I passed them on my way out, five minutes later, they didn't recognize me. My reputation will be greatly improved for holiness when they do go up and find that I have been translated to another sphere. By the way—you have the package safely—the red lining? It is most valuable and must be kept in your safe, Hogarth."

My host told him that it was there now.

"Good," nodded Carnaby. "Now, not another word do you get out of me till I've finished my dinner and smoked one of your excellent cigars. Then I will tell you how the land lies in regard to the fellows in the church. Come on—we shall have a late session to-night, I think, so wake yourself up, Hogarth, by giving us a yarn. I'll not butt into your prerogative, Kent. Choose us a relic from the case."

"Well, then," I suggested, "suppose we get rid of one of the skulls."

I hobbled on my crutches towards the glass case, as Hogarth said, "You must learn to call them by their names. One is Yorick and the other Romeo. Two dead men from Shakespeare. Hold one up and I'll tell you which he is."

I did so. "That's Romeo," said Hogarth in quite matter-of-fact tones. "Put him back and bring over Yorick. Romeo's history is a long one. I can keep Yorick's short and snappy. True, they both happened to me—both stories, I mean, but the case of Yorick does not need the concentration which the telling of Romeo's tragedy demands." He lit his pipe and after telling us to help ourselves to drinks, began.

"You remember," he said, looking at me, "the story I told you about the Sexton and the Hangman?"

"The churchyard horse, the King Worm and the pretty girl?" I added. "Every detail of it. Why?"

"Because the following ghost story happened to me when I lived at home in that same village—Aylesford—a few miles from here. I'm sorry, Carnaby, but you've probably heard it before, as it was in our schooldays together. My father, as you'll remember, was Vicar of Aylesford. It was a grand old rambling house the vicarage—next to the church on the hill, and our garden looked straight down on to the Bier-Walk. Behind the vast stables and coach-houses, there was a large tithe barn, very useful in the old days, when the local farmers could pay their tax to the church in kind; but such days had gone, and with it the use and purpose of the barn. My father had

often talked of raising a fund to restore it, so that village concerts
could be held there and meetings. We children had very different
ideas on the subject, and were determined to cash in on our par-
ent's idea. You see, and you will remember, Carnaby, I had been
bitten by the acting bug already, and the old barn began to assume
in my imagination, a wonderful theatre. Behind our father's back
we children went in deputation to the Squire, who was all for keeping the parish gay and happy. We were successful. He immediately
offered to back the undertaking with material and workmen from
his estate. A stage was built, the great beams were polished with
linseed oil, and in place of the earth floor, we had wooden planking
throughout. I think you saw some of our shows, Carnaby. Yes—
of course you did, and acted in some during holidays. Anyway—it
thrived, and made a local reputation, our company being recruited
from the young people in the village. But it's about the preparation
for one production that concerns my yarn.

"They say that no actor is satisfied till he has had a cut at *Hamlet*.
I suppose I was the same, and we planned the production for the
Christmas holidays.

"While my sisters were busy with the costumes, I undertook
the props, and in this department there cropped up the question
of Yorick's skull. I tried a lot of things—whittling away at swedes
and turnips—carving a block of chalk—making an awful mess of
papier mâché—and ending up each attempt with an envious look
out of the window upon the tombs and graves of the churchyard.
Hundreds of magnificent Yoricks were there, only waiting to be
picked up.

"I was a great friend of the sexton, partly because his wife ran
the sweet-shop in the village, but chiefly because his grim calling
fascinated me. I put my problem to him. He was sympathetic, but
quite firm in one respect: no skull should be taken from consecrated ground with his consent. It would be more than his place
would be worth. I jingled pennies in my pocket. I asked him what
he would like for Christmas. I watched him at his digging. A new
grave. I saw him turn up an old skull that looked quite at a loose
end. I jingled my pennies with excitement. No good—he laid the
skull back and reverently covered it over.

"Then came a wonderful opportunity. The Maidstone Gas Company came to lay new pipes in the Bier-Walk. They dug a deep trench right against our garden wall, which was also the Bier-Walk wall. They made a find, which caused quite a stir for a day or so. Six skeletons were uncovered with one or two ancient pieces of pottery and arrow heads. The general opinion of the experts who viewed them was that they were belonging to the pre-christian period in Kent. That gave me a splendid argument. Even if they were Christian they were not quite lying in consecrated ground for they were on the wrong side of the churchyard wall. I told the sexton into whose charge my father had put them, with orders to cover them decently when the pipes were laid, that morally I was quite justified in borrowing one of the skulls to do useful service for the art of the village in the Barn Theatre.

"At last he compromised. 'Tell you what, Master Charles,' he said. 'I'm goin' to my dinner. You'll find an old empty sack in my tool-shed. I couldn't tell you how many skulls there is in that hole. Never had a head for numbers. So if so be that you took one when my back's turned, I'd be none the wiser. I'm comin' back after dinner to fill in the hole. And that's all I knows about it, see?'

"Vowing to keep his name out of it, I selected the best for my purpose, popped it in the sack, and hid it in one of the dressing-rooms built under the barn stage.

"When it was dark, I carried it to my bedroom, and hid it in a panelled cupboard which was next to the fire. Happened to be the best bedroom in the house, but fortunately for me it had the reputation of being the haunted room, so no other member of the family had seemed quite so keen on it."

"And I bet it lost nothing of its sinister reputation while you had anything to do with it," laughed Carnaby, finishing his trifle and tackling Hoadley's excellent cheese-straws.

"Can you blame me?" laughed Hogarth. "I was only a kid and I'd taken the chance of meeting whatever ghostly horrors might revisit it. I had that room for ten glorious years."

"And I bet you never saw a ghost the whole time," said Carnaby.

"Aren't I telling you a very good ghost story now about it?" he exploded.

"All right. Keep calm and go ahead," urged the other.

"That night, after the household had gone to bed, I made up the fire, put on my Hamlet costume, and opened the cupboard doors where the skull rested on a shelf. I had planned to rehearse the grave-yard scene with the new member of the cast 'Alas, poor Yorick.'

"A large open oak chest I was using for the grave itself, and I thought I had better put Yorick inside it before I started. I was crossing the room to get it when I stopped with my heart in my mouth, though refusing to believe what I thought I saw. *One of the eyes had come to life in its deathly socket.* I told myself that this was nonsense; that it was merely a trick of the light. I looked away from it to turn up the wick of my oil lamp, then looked again. It was there—no doubt about it—a living eye, for it moved. I carried the lamp to another position, and as I moved so did the pupil of the eye follow me. I went closer with the lamp, and that grinning death mask mocked me with a wink. Then I heard a noise. It was the noise of grinding teeth clenched tightly as in a rage. And there was that ugly eye. I could even see the veins in the white of it as the black pupil distended in its awful stare. I expected the rest of it to come to life too. The other eye—the flesh—the hair and the red lips. I couldn't stand it any longer. I did a thing I have always felt ashamed about. I hardly like to confess it now."

"Oh, come on," interrupted Carnaby. "I know—you had another drink."

"Don't be silly. I was only a kid. Thirteen or fourteen. No. I took the lamp and tiptoed along to the night nursery where my kid sister slept. She was always game to follow me into any adventure. Sort of flattered her for me to say how brave she was. I woke her up without disturbing the younger ones, and whispered that I had got something wonderful to show her. She was all agog to be in on it, and pulling on her dressing-gown tiptoed hand in hand with me carrying the light along the passage to my room.

" 'I've made a Yorick,' I whispered. 'Look, there it is on the shelf. Looks rather weird, doesn't it?'

" 'You *have* made it well,' she said in that gushing tone that sis-ters adopt towards their elder brothers. 'But I suppose you've only had time to make one of its eyes work so beautifully.'

"Then I knew that my fears were true. The eye *had* come to life. It wasn't just something wrong with my imagination. This kid could see it too.

" 'It's a beastly thing,' I said. 'And I didn't make it. I got it from the Bier-Walk, and it's angry about it. I'll have to get it back there.'

"That kid was a trump. Damned sight braver than I was. But then, she quite enjoyed it. Told me she felt that at last she was living in a fairy story, and that the skull was a witch. I didn't quite see it like that. I felt something dreadful was going to happen to me because I had disturbed the dead. Well—we went into conference about it, and came to the conclusion that I must make amends to the ghost of the skull by burying it in the real churchyard, where no doubt it would be better off than it was before. The best site, I thought, would be near the rubbish heap where the marks of fresh digging wouldn't show. It was, of course, impossible to do this in the pitch dark. We must wait for dawn. But to harbour it all night in my room was unthinkable. The rest of it might return to life, and I should be confronted by a severed head looking at me with two eyes. I said that we must get it as far away from our doors as possible—but I didn't like to touch it, especially as we kept hearing that subdued sound of grinding teeth.

"Finally I threw my bath-towel over it and wrapped it up. Now came the question—should we throw it out of the window? We decided against this, as the noise would wake the household— questions would be asked—and in the confusion of explaining, I might betray my friend the sexton. I didn't want to get him the sack. The thought of a new sexton while he starved was awful.

"I decided to deposit the thing as far away from our doors as possible, and the long back passage that gave access to the servants' bedrooms seemed the best spot.

"We crept out on tiptoe. I carried the horrid bundle—she carried the light. We opened the baize door which led from our landing and while she kept it back and held the candle high above her head I went on. As I advanced into the gloom I got the feeling that the thing was moving in its wrapping. I expected it to bite through the towel at any second, and couldn't bear it any longer. I bowled it, towel and all, along the floor with all my strength.

"It travelled the whole way and came up sharp at the end with a bump against the cook's door.

"Thinking someone was knocking, she called out sleepily, 'Coming—just a minute.'

"We had retreated to the safety of the baize door where we stood shivering. The cook, an awful old tartar, lit her candle and unlocked her door—saw nobody—and then looked down at her feet. The long bath-towel had unwound itself, exposing the skull. She saw it and jumped to the natural or perhaps unnatural opinion that a skeleton had come after her through the landing window from the churchyard outside.

"She gasped—banged the door and turned the key. We heard a whimpering, and were not quite sure whether it was the cook or the skull.

"Then to my horror, a deep voice echoed through the house. 'Charles? Charles?'

"'It's calling,' I whispered. 'It's calling ME.'

"'No—it's worse,' my sister whispered back. 'It's father. He sounds angry. Quick—we'll have to bunk.'

"Again came the voice. To my utter relief I found that she was right. It was my father's voice. And what a relief.

"'Aren't you in bed, Charles?'

"'I was rehearsing—that's all, Father,' I called back.

"'Much too late. It's midnight. Turn in at once, and put out your light. And no more noise.'

"'Yes, Father,' I answered meekly.

"We heard his door shut. But we didn't turn out the light. We sat till morning on my bed, whispering and wondering what the skull would do next.

"It did nothing. Waited for us to take the next step. With the first noises of dawn—that is, voices floating up from the bakehouse and the clinking of milk cans being fitted to the local chariot, we were in our clothes and ready for our final adventure.

"Along the passage we went. It was still pretty dark, but a faint light shone through the window upon the corpse-like figure. I heard the cook stirring so had to make haste. I stooped down to cover the skull with the towel again and there was the eye sure enough. It was no imagination on either of our parts. A perfect eye come back to the dead socket—but only one. And as I lifted it, I saw how I had been fooled. The whole mystery had been created by my carelessness in not having cleaned the inside of the skull, and the fact that I had put it into the warm cupboard by my fire. The heat had attracted two creatures who had lived in the mould inside that skull to creep towards the opening of that eye socket A great white slug had got there first and had curled itself around the cavity, while through it, but forbidden by the slug to pass, had come the black head of a gigantic churchyard worm. This head now gaining ground now losing it—but always prevented from escape, had given a perfect impression of a distending pupil. The movement of these creatures had displaced the small fragments of mould, which dislodging, fell upon the paper on the cupboard shelf, making the noise as of grinding teeth. On realizing my stupidity, I made a solemn vow that I would never again be frightened at anything, until I had made a careful investigation to prevent if possible the cause of fear. Well—there's nothing more to tell. I buried the skull under the rubbish heap—and that was that."

"Did you bury it or just hide it?" I asked.

"Buried it some feet deep—all decently in consecrated ground with a concentrated rubbish heap for a monument."

"Then how is it that you still have the skull?" I asked.

"Ah," sighed the Master. "My artistic temperament overcame my moral scruples. Every attempt to produce a Yorick's skull became more ludicrous. 'The play's the thing,' I said to myself and obeyed Shakespeare's order by turning resurrectionist. Yes—I confess it—I dug up the skull—everyone said it looked most life-like, which was the very worst thing to say about any skull—especially as I had seen at least one eye of it very much alive—but nothing more was said—and no questions asked, perhaps because the bookings were phenomenal, not only clearing all expenses, but making quite a bit for the Sick and Needy Fund. And since, as you see, the skull is still with me, I must have overlooked putting it back—in fact, it is the founder of the whole collection in that case—my first relic. That's the story exactly as it happened, with no embroidery, and now, Carnaby, as I see you are embarking on your second cigar, perhaps you will tell us what I am hoping will prove the most intriguing story from that case there. By the way, I suppose there is nothing against my adding the military lining of the coat to Reliquary?"

"I should think nothing at all eventually," replied Carnaby, speaking slowly and in vague tones as one who is more interested in getting an expensive smoke to burn smoothly, than in what he intended to say. "But I think at present we must make a rule that it shall never be brought out of your safe unless the three of us are together." He paused, inhaling his cigar with appreciation. Then a frown crept over his merry face. Hogarth saw that expression and asked, "There's danger in it, then?"

Carnaby nodded. "Yes—but I intend to be as unscrupulous as you were over Yorick's skull. Now let's see. Where shall I begin? You mustn't expect a story from me, Hogarth. I never had your gift of the gab—at least, not in English—though I can argue the flea off a cat's whisker in Pushtu. You raise a questioning eyebrow, O erudite Six-Former? Then learn wisdom my good Hogarth, from your one-time Marmalade-Wallah. Pushtu is the common tongue of Pathan and other Moslems inhabiting the North-West Frontier, and there are some two and a half million tricky fellows up there who take a hell of a lot of convincing about anything. But one can learn a lot from them. Certainly the investigation of your coat problem has taught me one thing. *Never take anything for granted because it seems obvious.* It prejudices your judgment from scratch. Now, from the start, both of us fell down over two major points. First—we made the coat itself the chief item of our mystery, when we should have concentrated entirely on the lining. The bloke who originally gave it to you said, as he jumped on to that running car, 'Wear it.' *It*, of course, being the coat, foxed us from the start, and it took me many a month before I realized that:

> *The coat was made for the lining*
> *Not the lining for the coat.*

"Associating the lining as merely an adjunct of the coat brought us down on our noses for the second time. The cut of the coat was definitely—military. Unit buttons displaced by wooden ones,

thereby giving no clue as for what regiment the coat had been originally designed. Not even rank badges had been left to enable us to
narrow down our search. We only knew the owner was military,
and the red lining helped to fox us. Certainly from time immemorial red has been the primary colour of fighting men—the cloak
of the matador—the thin red line—the trappings of the Roman
Legions—the emblem of blood, danger and rage. But the armies
of the world can't claim a monopoly of the colour—and that's
where we went wrong. We might have looked to the Church—
to the Law, but no—we allowed ourselves to run on a one-track
mind, meekly bowing to an accustomed association of ideas. 'As
far as men are concerned red linings are only worn in Army great-
coats.' That's what we accepted. That's exactly what those men in
Calcutta wanted us to accept. In fact—they knew we would.

"Now—let's see again—where am I? Yes—let me first finish
with the coat. The bullet hole. Yes, you were quite right there,
though you got the facts of it wrong. So did I, but then, I never saw
the coat till just before I left India, and by then I had all the facts
that created the mystery. The hole in the coat itself was faked, by
a clever piece of forged invisible mending. You see the bullet-hole
in the lining was made when the lining was not a lining at all. That
piece of woven cloth, which we thought had come from the Army
Clothing Department, had absolutely nothing to do with the
Army at all. It was the back portion of a red robe woven without
seam from the top to the bottom, and made from a sacred loom in
a monastery of Kabul. I have seen that very loom—centuries old—
built about eleven hundred or so, I calculated—anyway, it was in
full working order at the end of the twelfth century, because that
piece of red lining we are so concerned about was made when
Richard the Lion-Heart was taken prisoner in Germany—and
that—O my ignorant ones of the Sixth Form—was eleven hundred and ninety-two. Go up one, Carnaby Secundus."

Carnaby looked from Hogarth to me. "You will think, my dear
Kent, that I am now going to pose as the hero of one of your sorts
of romance, when I tell you that I am the only Englishman who
has ever been received as a long-term guest beneath the roof of
that ancient monastic house in Kabul. True—I was not accepted

there *as* an Englishman. I was disguised as an exceedingly Holy Man—which, strangely enough, however you may think to the contrary, is a role I find it very easy to get away with. But when I mentioned 'the only Englishman,' I purposely did not say 'white man' or 'European,' because, my masters, during Richard's Crusade, there was another who beat me to it, and beat me very well, considering he went without disguise and at great danger to his life. I have read the man's history from manuscripts preserved in the monastic library, and what I read amazed me. I realized that I had stumbled upon one of the most complex characters in history. He was a monk of great learning, fanatical zeal, indomitable courage and exceedingly strong physically. Spiritually—he was apparently a bit of a mixture for those days, for his habit of probing into everything that didn't concern him—such as the doctrines of Aristotle and Plato—and worse still in the eyes of the Church—a wholehearted study of Devilry. It was said of him that he seemed more interested in the fiends than the angels, considering that they had more power, and took a livelier concern towards Mankind. This made him unpopular with orthodox churchmen, but did not impair his extreme popularity with the Pope himself, so that his influence in Rome was much sought after. He set great store on bodily health; maintaining that virility was a god-like quality, and that carnal cravings should be obeyed as necessary sustenance for health. On this score he refused to fast if he didn't feel like it. He even had the courage to attack the enforced celibacy of the clergy, but soon found that he was going a bit too far airing such views as, 'the body is the material form of the spirit, so who are we, in our ignorance, to deny the body what the spirit prompts it to need?' He is reputed to have said that to the Pope himself.

"He certainly never allowed fastings or penance to interfere with his health, but rather used them, when he felt like it, of course, as a means of hardening his body to fresh exertion. Such a turbulent fellow soon found that work in Rome began to pall. He wanted change and adventure. To satisfy this longing in his favourite, the Pope would send him on foreign missions, and it was in this capacity that he came to England on business concerned with the Third Crusade, where he managed to impress Prince John very much in his favour. That fact becomes important in his subsequent history, for the Regent saw the advantage of having this Italian priest, so popular with the Pope, as his secret agent, especially when the monk told him it was his intention to follow the Crusaders to Palestine. This priest would be just the man who would appeal to his brother the King, who admired physical strength, just as he, John, liked unscrupulous characters. So our Italian was given letters of recommendation to the King, and a promise of as much gold as his activities required from the Prince. And so he goes to Palestine, where his influence was soon felt. He not only became popular with the King because of his feats of strength and bravery in battle, but retained, by letters and messengers, the full confidence of John, who to do him credit, never forgot his services, and rewarded him suitably when he became King. Apparently our friend didn't think much of the Crusades. Despised the petty quarrels in the armed forces of Christendom. He admired Richard himself, for his almost stupid honesty but more for his strength and chivalry. The French and German princes he laughed at, and was not sorry when he was taken prisoner by Saladin himself. Here was a man after his own heart, and when the great leader offered him his freedom, he begged that he might stay amongst the Moslems and learn what he could of that religion. After much consultations Saladin declared that he and those around him could teach the monk no more, but since he wished to master the full Eastern understanding of the six thousand Koran verses, this generous Sultan of Egypt and Mesopotamia furnished him with an escort, so that he could travel through Persia with introductions to the most learned of the Moslems. Eventually we hear that he crossed into the wild country of Afghanistan, coming to rest in a mountain monastery near Kabul. In this quiet retreat he studied, being shown every consideration by the old Sheik of the Mosque; and here he stayed for two whole years, becoming a Moslem in order that he could visit Mecca on his way back to Rome. I should say, from what I've read of him, that this act of conversion to a heathen creed, as it was looked upon, had its root in a curiosity to penetrate the mysteries of Mecca before any other European, and certainly not from any spiritual conviction. He was, of course, fully aware that Rome would condemn him as a heretic, but he comforted himself with the thought that everything would pan out all right. Why should anyone know anything about it? If he found that a too severe attitude would be raised against such an experience, he could keep his mouth shut. And even if anyone did find out—he could fall back on his personal friendship with the Pope—for he never lost the power of dominating, even fascinating people—and was there not England and Prince John? He could always retire there and find good employment. It was only by his persistent begging to make the sacred pilgrimage to Mecca, that the Sheik bloke would allow him to go away; and even then our friend had to swear on the Prophet's beard that he would return, and pass the rest of his days in their retreat.

"Obviously the Italian scamp had no intention of doing any such thing, since he eventually committed a direct abuse in return for their kindness and hospitality.

"He stole one of the greatest treasures of the Moslem Faith. This priceless relic was a solid gold goblet, heavily encrusted with a band of huge diamonds and rubies. It was reputed to have been the stirrup-cup of Mahomet into which he dropped a pebble as the signal to mount for his historic ride from Medina to conquer Mecca. This is an ancient custom of the desert still practised by many tribes calling the troop to horse. My cousin always used the phrase before setting out on a journey. 'The stone is in the Cup,' he used to say. 'To Horse.' Let's get cracking, in fact.

"Now the goblet was only brought out of its reliquary for the Feast following the Fast of Ramadan. It was then locked away till the following year.

"When the wily Italian first cast his eyes on it he thought, 'There is a fine present to give as a bribe to the Pope. There is not such a chalice in any sacred vessel-chest in Rome.' Determined to get it, he postponed his departure for Mecca, until Ramadan had passed, knowing that the goblet would not be missed till the following year. For the same safety-first reason he declined the offer of an escort, piously maintaining that a poor pilgrim should not ride like a prince, when he had but recently taken the Koran. This enabled him to take his own route, which he had carefully studied, and thereby avoiding any pursuit, should the theft be discovered sooner than he had anticipated.

"It is said that the Prophet had grasped the cup in his left hand when he had leapt on the back of his golden-coated horse, Al Borak—the Lightning. With his right hand he waved Dhu'l Fakar, his trenchant scimitar, and pointing towards Mecca, cried out that he would fill the cup with the blood of their enemies.

"The Italian's departure was not so dramatic. He rode away slowly upon a mule—slowly because the chalice was very uncomfortable lashed against his stomach beneath his flowing robes.

"For a whole year the blessings of the monastery followed him, until upon the feast day they were changed to curses. It was upon that first anniversary of his possession that he made up his mind not to give the chalice to the Pope. He had become quite attached to it himself, and he found that the Pope rather bored him. Besides, the Holy Father had no job to offer him—at least, no job that was sufficiently exciting. He therefore decided for England and John, now King.

"Here he did well—was extremely popular with the King's friends, and eventually beneficed to an Abbey.

"But now—what happens behind his back in Kabul? And the answer is—— This is where Hogarth begins to sit up and take interest."

"My dear fellow," said Hogarth eagerly, "you mustn't jump out of the picture. Go on. Go on. I'm absorbed by your mule-riding cup-snatcher."

"Behind his back," went on Carnaby, "our Afghan Sheik let fly his most powerful curses after his departed and light-fingered guest. Then he took a number of oaths as to what he would do. The first name he swore by was Fadda, because that was the name of Mahomet's pet mule. Then the ten wives of the Prophet were cited, each by name, followed by the fifteen concubines—but as he could only remember one of their names, he lumped them together in a good round oath. He swore by Bajura, the Moslem Standard and by Mahomet's Banner, Sanjaksherif. By Catum, his bow—Fadha, his cuirass (not to be confused with Fadda the Mule)—by Adha, his camel—and Hoia the Cave, in which Gabriel

appeared to him from God. I have read an account of this show of
temper. It was written down by a scribe who overheard. He found
it easy enough to vow what he intended to do—namely, recover
the relic and slay the thief—but very difficult to find any practical
way of doing it.

"He certainly knew the apostate's name, but had no idea of his
address. Useless to expect help and redress from the Pope, who
had no truck with Turks, infidels and heretics. In the darkness only
one little ray of light appeared to save him from despair. He had
gleaned it from a casual conversation he had indulged in with the
convert.

"Following his pilgrimage to Mecca, the Italian had told him
he would have to visit his patron, the King of England, before
he would be free to return to Kabul. He remembered the exact
words, 'Other than passing my remaining years in peace with you,
I should have chosen to retire from the world as Abbot of a certain
monastic community I know in England: that is, of course, were I
still in the persuasion of the Christian Faith. This Abbot's seat lies
in a beautiful part of the country, on a road known as the Pilgrim's
Way to the English Mecca of Canterbury. This delectable palace
belongs to the Archbishop who is seldom there, so that a respon-
sible Head is appointed to look after the routine of the place in
his absence and to welcome his Grace when he returns. It would
have been a pleasant life, directing the brethren in their tasks—the
gardeners, the masons, the sculptors, and above all the librarians
ever at work upon fair illuminations.'

"All this the Sheik had caused to be written down in case he
awoke to find he had forgotten it. And that is how I am now able
to tell you the story. But I see, my dear Kent, that our host is
frowning at my digression, so—to continue. Now the Sheik had
been curious to know in what way the monastic buildings of England differed from those of the Mosque in which he served, and
the Italian, saying that the archbishop's palace he had mentioned
was the only one whose ground-plan he could remember with
any certainty, drafted the lay-out of grounds and buildings on a
large roll of goat-skin. And this plan, taken in conjunction with
what the monk had told him, was the ray of light in the Sheik's

despair. After much prayer and meditation, he decides that a trusted member of his community should be sent to England on the trail of the impious thief. This messenger should be given the title 'Avenger,' and he must wear an under-robe of red, signifying the blood he was sent out to shed. Somehow he must reach England—find the Pilgrim's Way, and locate the buildings drafted on the goat-skin.

"He then realized that in order to avoid any suspicion of the messenger's purpose, the monk's drawing must be left behind, and another plan made which he could carry with him, and refer to when necessary. This must be concealed from all eyes, except those of the Avenger.

"How he solved that extremely knotty problem, I will now show you."

Carnaby suddenly got up, stretched himself, helped himself to another cigar, and then said, "As we are all three present, we'll have a look at that mysterious red lining. Let me save you getting up, my dear Hogarth. Can you give me the key of your safe?"

Hogarth detached the ring of keys from his chain and indicated two of them. "That's the one to open the panel and that's the safe. The panel's in the centre of those built-in bookcases. The keyhole's in the mouth of that carved monk's head."

"Ingenious fellow—our host—eh, Kent," and laughing, he opened the panel and then the safe, bringing out the package which held the red cloth. He unwrapped it on the table and carried it to the fire-place, shaking it out of its creases.

"Have you examined this carefully, Hogarth?" he asked, turning towards us with his back to the fire.

Hogarth nodded.

"And you saw nothing odd about it?"

Hogarth shook his head.

"Very well, then. Let me go back to our sheik, and see what he does. He sends a messenger, accredited to be on the Prophet's business, into Kashmir, to summon a distant member of his family who was the first shawl-maker in that country of shawl-makers, who used only the short hairs growing beneath the bristles of the Tibetan goat.

"His relative obeys the summons and journeys to Kabul, where he and the Sheik, his kinsman, put their heads together. A special loom is set up under his instruction. It is solemnly dedicated to the service of Mahomet, and the shawl-maker gets to work, weaving the red robe for the Avenger. When it was finished—without seam, which was a sign of great honour—it carried the secret of the monk's plan, but in such a way that only the Avenger himself—a young son of the Sheik—could see it. Any other, as we did, could spend months without discovering anything unusual. Now, I want you both to look at it close to the light."

He came over, standing between us, with the red cloth in his hand. "Can you see any irregularity in the weaving?" he asked.

We both shook our heads, for it looked entirely smooth.

"And yet," went on Carnaby, "the Avenger, wearing this, mind you and wishing to remind himself of any detail connected with the plan, had only to pull the tunic over his head, and look through it towards the sun. To illustrate what I mean, let us take this strong reading lamp for the sun. Now—look through it." He held the cloth against the light, and as we looked closely, we both saw an elaborate architectural and surveyor's plan staring at us.

Each square or oblong had an Arabic letter in its centre; and beneath the plan in small characters, each of the letters was explained: such as—an A might mean an orchard; B a stable; K a chapel; and other letters a cow-house, pig-sty, banqueting hall, refectory, sleeping rooms, kitchens, larders, etc., down to the smallest details.

"I told you just now," said Carnaby, "that I have recently examined that sacred loom, and I gathered that this drawing was made by a system of tighter weaving—by a variable touch of the weaver, now heavy—now lightly, when operating the comb, or whatever that bar is called that keeps going up and down—I forget."

Hogarth smiled. "Hoadley accuses me of having a smattering of most things, and I think you will find that your bar is called the lay, the lathe or the batten."

"Move up one, O erudite youngster," said Carnaby. "Well—there you have it—the main mystery of your coat—and before I go on to explain your own connection with the case, and how I managed to solve it in the ordinary way of police routine—I'd like to know your reactions if any. Hogarth?"

"A number of things are whizzing in my head," replied our host, "but quite frankly, only two facts which are connected with you and Kent appear to me clearly out of the fog."

"Me?" I asked astonished. "Why me? How do I come into it?"

"Because you are the only writer—or shall I say 'professional writer'—who is in on this; and I insist that Carnaby allows you to write the history of that unscrupulous Italian."

"Funny," I said, "because I was about to ask Carnaby if he would have any objections to my doing so. I'll dedicate it to you, Carnaby, and give you a share of the royalties. I must say it appeals to me. What about it? Any objection?"

"Certainly not—if you don't object to a test," he answered. "Your qualifications as a biographer combined with your genius as a thriller writer, recommend you strongly for the job. But I don't want you to be influenced by the demands of your reading public into making a grave error of truth, so do you mind first telling me how your imagination would describe your hero, the monk? Consider your clues; his cunning, his height and his strength. That's all I've told you so far."

"Yes——" I considered. "His cunning appealed to Prince John—his stature and strength to King Richard. That's obvious. But he seemed to fascinate all with whom he came in contact. The Pope—Saladin—the Sheik of Kabul—and from his ideas about women—I should imagine he dominated the ladies too. Therefore, with that in mind, I picture him as a very fine-looking man."

"In fact," suggested Carnaby, "a sort of Cœur de Lion of monks, eh? Handsome? A fine head to match his frame? A great pity his profession called for a tonsure, thereby depriving his mirror of such beautiful curly hair?"

"Something like that," I nodded.

"And how wrong you'd be," replied Carnaby. "Mind you, I'm not trying to be clever. Far from it: for in actual fact I was very careless just now when describing him. I quite forgot to mention the most striking point of his description. According to the evidence which I have read in the Sheik's journal, he was all that you agree to—a splendid masculine figure, et cetera, et cetera. But his head was *not* fine. It utterly contradicted his stature. *He had a tiny little head, with huge eyes and a small mouth that turned up at the corners.*"

"What?" In our astonishment we literally shouted, and quite forgetting we were crocks, both sprang from our chairs, staring at one another. Then Hogarth turned to Carnaby and added, "You forgot to mention something else, too, old man. Or don't you know it?"

"What?" repeated Carnaby in a loud voice, imitating us.

"Why, the monk's name," said Hogarth, who was now wincing with pain and steadying himself against the table.

"Didn't I?" asked Carnaby. "Sit down, you two cripples, and I'll go on. I warned you I was a rotten story-teller—but I can tell you his name."

"You don't have to," replied Hogarth, easing himself back into his chair. "His name was——"

"Porfirio!!"—and to Carnaby's astonishment we both said it together.

"Yes—that's right," admitted Carnaby, "but how the devil did *you* know?"

So there was nothing for it—since Carnaby became insistent, but for us to interrupt his story with what we knew about the monk. We thought he would laugh when we told him of Hoadley's conviction that we had been made crocks through Porfirio's evil power; but to our surprise he agreed with it, saying it was a theory believed and practised in the East, and that Porfirio no doubt learned it there.

Before Carnaby would take up the threads of his story, he had another condition to make, which was that he should be allowed to sleep that night in the Abbot's Chapel. Hogarth agreed, and gave Hoadley the necessary orders before urging Carnaby to tell us more.

"The rest is soon told," said Carnaby, "because it is just a succession of bare facts that I proved during the exercise of my police duties, so you will both find me very much more precise. But you mentioned just now, Hogarth, that this Palace was partly demolished in Islip's day. Porfirio was here before that, so the map on our red cloth is Wrotham Palace in all its glory. Does it tally with the plan you said you had drawn from the ruins?"

"There it is," said Hogarth, pointing to an illuminated map in a frame which hung on the panelling between two of the windows. "Take it down and compare it. I can tell you straight away that the main features as I traced them out from bits of paving and broken walls, agree with Porfirio's. So I think we can say his is the authentic plan in all its details."

We must have presented a queer group to an onlooker. Hogarth, seated in his high-backed chair, with his black quilted dressing-gown and white cambric stock, looking like some eighteenth-century character in a play; Carnaby—in his rough tweeds, kneeling, with the framed map in both hands, and comparing it with the secret draftsmanship in the red cloth which Hogarth, being nearest to the reading lamp, held out against the light; and I—leaning on my crutches above them, and peering down over their shoulders.

From the red design I could see that Hogarth's work—so artistically done—was accurate in the main features, as he had said. It was only in minor description that he was wrong—for instance—he had called one narrow chamber *Still-room*, which Porfirio gave as *Wash-house*, and another mistake, I remember, was a large hall off the kitchen, which he had marked *Scullery*, but should have been, according to our monk—*Carpenter's Shop*.

Now, interesting as all this was—I was far more curious to hear the rest of Carnaby's story—and I wondered how long I could keep patient without bringing him back to earth—for he was in a brown study, gazing at Hogarth's work. I looked at Hogarth, and as I did so, I had that curious instinct that someone or something was behind me—something antagonistic.

I didn't move for some little time, as my crutches were firmly embedded in the thick pile carpet, and it needed energy to shift them. But I watched Hogarth's eyes. Their pupils had extended as though focusing themselves upon something surprising—something which he could see immediately behind my back.

Then I turned and nearly cried out in my astonishment—for in the shadows there stood an onlooker—and a most alarming one—a tall Indian, grey-bearded, with white robes showing beneath an old European overcoat.

I have said 'alarming,' because in his right hand was a levelled Army revolver, while grasped in his left, with the fire-light playing upon it, was an ugly blue blade of a long knife.

CHAPTER ELEVEN

"WHERE IS THE BODY?"

THE deathly silence was broken by Hogarth. "Well?" he asked, and I could see him nudging Carnaby surreptitiously, who, strange to say, took no notice, except to raise the frame against the light, so that it hid the red cloth.

"What do you want?" demanded Hogarth, slowly. He had put the red cloth on his knees, and Carnaby covered it with the frame.

Thinking that Carnaby would not wish to be seen by the Indian, Hogarth took command. "Can you speak—English?"

The native shook his head—and then Carnaby slowly got to his feet and turned—but it was somehow a different Carnaby. He had rumpled his hair over his forehead, and his right eye wore an unrimmed, unribboned eye-glass. His left eye was closed, giving the impression of a very short-sighted man, and he stood with a scholarly stoop which made him appear quite ridiculous, and in utter contrast to the alert and dapper Carnaby we both knew.

"I rather think I can help, my dear Hogarth," he said in a high, feeble and hesitating voice. "In my tea-planting days I studied various Indian dialects. I shall endeavour to tell him who I am, and try to persuade him not to look so very fierce. Yes—I think that is the best thing, because he seems to be labouring under a crisis. And there's no harm in giving him my name, I think. It might do good. It can't do harm. You see, I travelled for Wilkie's the tea people, and do you know all sorts of people knew 'Ramsbottom Sahib,' and I think they liked me because they said I had a funny way with me. 'Ramsbottom Sahib'—that's what they all called me. Sounds silly, I know—I much prefer 'Mr. Ramsbottom,' but there you are, and not a soul in India ever called me Nick or even Nicholas."

All this nonsense we knew to be for our benefit—just to warn us that he was putting on an act. "He's a Hillman, I think, so, come along, Nicholas Ramsbottom—we'll try him in Pushtu."

Screwing his face into a thousand perplexing puckers—the newly-born Nicholas Ramsbottom began to speak. And what a contrast in voice and manner to the fierce, deep replies of the Hillman.

They talked for some minutes—Carnaby ranging from diffidence to petty irritation, while the grizzled warrior spoke with powerful conviction.

After their first bout of argument—Carnaby turned to us and interpreted. "Yes—he's a Hillman all right. Ramsbottom Sahib doesn't often make a mistake"—and he gave us just the suspicion of a wink with his half-closed eye. "But, I say, Hogarth, I think we should really do something about your butler-wallah. As far as I can gather, this fellow has had him lashed up and put under guard. I've told him, very definitely, that he'll get no help from Ramsbottom Sahib, if any harm happens to the old man. He may be in a bit of a stew, though, and that's why I suggest we should do something. Just a minute."

They spoke together again and it certainly seemed that the Hillman was becoming mollified, for he thrust his revolver into his coat pocket and sheathed the knife.

Carnaby interpreted. "Apparently they got through a window in the long corridor and met Old Hoadley coming from the Abbot's Chapel. They gagged him and two of them are guarding him with knives. He's in the pantry as far as I can make out. I'd better go and see, while you fellows wait here and have a chat. I'll take this awkward-looking bloke with me."

"I'll come with you," I said. "I'm only groggy on one foot, and I'll borrow this, Hogarth, in case of accidents," and I slipped a heavy glass paper-weight into my jacket pocket.

"If one crock's going, so's the other," replied Hogarth. He did not follow my lead with another paper-weight, but I saw him slip the red cloth into his pocket. No doubt this was wise.

We must have looked a very odd procession crossing the Hall.

The dignified Indian led the way, followed by Carnaby as the stooping Ramsbottom, me on crutches and Hogarth, wincing, swearing and groaning as he dragged himself after us.

The pantry was right. Sure enough we found two Indians staring at Hoadley, and gripping their knives in readiness. Hoadley, gagged but not bound, was at the sink, washing the dinner glasses. If it hadn't been for the old man's obvious discomfort, I should have laughed outright. The fact that he *would* go on with his work, though he was in reach of those deadly knives, was most droll.

Carnaby said something to our guide, who evidently ordered his men to untie Hoadley's gag, which had been executed with two tray-cloths.

"Thankee, Cap'n Carnaby," he said. "Didn't stop me workin' but I always likes to hum tunes when I'm washin' up the Master's best glass. Keeps me calm, does hummin'. But you can't hum with a tray-cloth down your throat. Well, sir" (turning to his Master), "as I often said to you when we was in India—I can't abide the Indians, and I certainly ain't changed my mind to-night."

"That's all right, Hoadley," said Carnaby, "but you can't get your own back in English, because they don't understand a word you say. Now, you help your master back to the Library and I'll deal with these fellows in the Hall."

So we hobbled back, while Carnaby jabbered away to the three natives by the front door.

While we awaited his return, Hogarth, who in spite of his pain, said he felt better for his walk, insisted on Hoadley joining us in a stiff glass of brandy.

Presently we heard the front door shut and Carnaby joined us, walking briskly and once more his old self.

"Where the body is—the vultures, you know——" he laughed, "and where there's treasure—crooks."

"But what are they here for?" asked Hogarth, bringing out the red cloth from his pocket. "This?"

"I'm glad to say we hid it most effectively," said Carnaby.

"But what good could it do them?" I asked. "And what was that sentence he kept repeating to you? I noticed the other fellows in the pantry said it too."

"Your ear is quick on the uptake," replied Carnaby. "Was it this you spotted?"—and he repeated the curious sentence, at which I nodded. "That just means '*Where is the Body?*' And you're quite right. They kept on asking it."

"Whose body—yours?" asked Hogarth.

Carnaby shook his head. "Oh, no. They're not terribly concerned about *me* as the Holy Man. They are convinced that the Green Turbaned One has been translated. Whether I have gone to Mahomet and Allah for good, they are not quite sure, but they firmly believe that I used the top of the tower as a stepping-stone to Heaven. Oh—incidentally—I give you fellows full marks for your calm behaviour. You too, my good Hoadley—splendid. I believe you'd all make good policemen."

"And we'll give you full marks too, eh, Kent?" said Hogarth. "Your performance of Nicholas Ramsbottom 'left nothing to be desired,' as the critic says in "The Stage." Without a rehearsal, too."

Carnaby shook his head, "I've imitated him before, though I can't think why he suddenly popped up in my mind. I knew him well in India. I realized, as I saw you did, that if I was recognized as a phoney Holy Man, my number was up, though maybe Kent would have got in first with the paper-weight. '*Where is the Body?*' eh? No—that meant 'Where is Old Porfirio buried?' They think he may have taken the sacred stirrup-cup with him to the grave as a bribe to the Prophet. I have told them quite flat that Porfirio, being a son of the Devil, would have been buried without the honours of God, and that no man knoweth of his sepulchre, and I've made them believe that he would never have been allowed to take such a treasure with him. And that raises the point: '*What did he do with it?*'"

"Well—what the devil would any of us do with it if we found it?" I asked. "I suppose it would come under Treasure Trove; but if it was 'findings keepings,' what would you do with it?" I put this question to Hogarth.

"I should keep mum while I had it. I shouldn't want the world to know I was housing such a thing. I don't know. Give it to Westminster Abbey for use at Coronations or something respectable, though I presume it should go back to the mosque."

"Certainly not," contradicted Carnaby. "They should have looked after it better when they had it. British Museum would be the best place."

"But we'd make Hoadley fill it with the best in Wrotham cellars before we let it go," I said. "But seriously, wouldn't the Rector here have some claim to it?"

"Now, I'll tell you what I would *really* do with it——" began Carnaby.

"Oh, no, you won't," cried Hogarth. "You'll now tell us something else—those bare facts of police routine you spoke about."

"Then if you'll excuse me, gentlemen," said Hoadley, "I'll go and resume my hummin' where I had to leave it off."

"What was the tune?" asked Carnaby.

"A pretty little anthem, sir. '*Why rage fiercely the Heathen?*' and it goes on about people meditatin' strange things."

"Strange things, eh?" repeated Hogarth, as the old man made a very good exit on his line. "Come on, Carnaby, he's given you your cue. Strange things. I believe I'm going to get my best story out of all this."

Carnaby yawned. "Can't I tell you in the morning? I'm dog-tired."

"You don't get out of it as easily as that, does he, Kent? But I'll meet you half-way, and catechize you like I used to do in my study when you stole my marmalade. Now—what induces these natives to start looking for the thing after all these years?"

Carnaby sighed, then grinned, as he lit another cigar. "Because the legend has stuck in a lot of people's imagination. Besides, most legends are founded on fact—some sort of fact—and this one happens to be history. The cup must be somewhere. In the old days it was pretty difficult to play 'hunt the thimble' from the Himalayas to Wrotham Hill, but it's easy to get about the world these days. You only want money and these rascals have oodles. Next, please."

"The man who gave me the coat in 1912—who was he and why me?"

"That's two questions. First—he isn't anyone now. He's a number. He's doing time. Life sentence he got. One of a gang of five. Clever crooks in a big way. Took me all I knew to break 'em up. Secondly—when it became known that they had stolen the sacred robe, they found themselves most unpleasantly 'on the spot.' You see, they found out all about it when they heard the legend. They knew the value of that red robe, and that it was still kept in the reliquary originally dedicated to Mahomet's cup. But whereas Porfirio had to do a job of crib-cracking to get at the cup, they found things harder, for locks were child's play to them. The doors were always kept open and guarded by a watchful custodian who never let that red robe out of his sight. There it hung for any of the Faithful to see. Well—it was the last thing that custodian saw. They killed him and made it look like robbery of the poor-box which they wrenched open. To all intents and purposes the robe was still there, because they didn't steal the whole thing. They cut out the back portion and left the front hanging—then your friend, Hogarth, who was posing as an English officer, tacked it over the red lining of his military coat. It was never noticed because it was so obvious. Well—they got away with the plan and the next thing was to find what house tallied with it. All that they knew from the record was that it lay upon the Pilgrim's Way, somewhere between Canterbury and Winchester, and it is this part of it that makes me laugh. Unable to leave India themselves for a reason I'll tell you in a minute, they got an agent to work making plans of every Archiepiscopalean palace adjacent to the Way, and to override the natural objection of landlords and tenants to having their property surveyed by unauthorized strangers, they hired a helicopter and hovered over places for days at a time, drafting bird's-eye views. Of course, the joke is that they were not up in medieval Church history, or they would have rumbled that Old Islip had beaten them to it by removing most of the palace that mattered. Mind you— and I say this for them in their favour—they realized the thing was a long gamble, for no-one knew where the cup was or is, and it happened that they had something much more concrete to work upon, which was King George's Durbar of 1912. They cleared up a packet there, robbing the Indian Princes of priceless jewels.

"They were carrying out this wonderful programme when Moslem agents got on to their trail about the red robe, and sinister things began to happen, which very soon gave the gang the jitters—a disease very inconvenient for jewel thieves to suffer from. Your friend, Hogarth, who gave you the coat, confessed the whole thing to me when I questioned him after arrest. They realized their only chance of escaping the vengeance of the Moslems was to get that coat out of India. Along comes their chance with a company of English actors, and amongst them that attractive young man, Charles Hogarth. Thinking that the stage manager would be a permanent member of a star's company, they picked on him. They even knew your London address, my dear fellow, for actors keep nothing secret from the public, and your biography and background was printed with other prominent members of that company upon the theatre programmes. Money being no object, or rather being their whole object, and that's why they had such a lot, they had you watched in Town, and where as you've told us they eventually got back their precious coat. That's really all, I think. Any questions?"

"Yes," said Hogarth. "How did you get it—the red lining?"

"On its way back from England. I was waiting for it. Then, there it was—coat and all—toiling up through the Khyber Pass. It was being worn by the one rogue in the gang we hadn't been able to catch. He was on his way to sell back the lining to the Sheik from whom he and his colleagues had stolen it. He was the cleverest of the lot, but he didn't happen to know that his enemy Carnaby of the Secret Police had got his length, and had been staying for weeks as a holy guest with the very Sheik for whom he was bound. I had no fear of his seeing through my disguise, for I had fooled the Sheik and the people at Kabul. But he was very thorough. Spoke the language perfectly. He was, of course, my senior in age and India. I invited him to share my supper, for we were camped for the night on opposite sides of the ravine.

How surprised he would have been had he known that my four followers were an armed escort provided by the Sheik to guard me to England and back. You see, I haven't come to England just to see you two fellows. I'm on a holy mission to search for Mahomet's stirrup-cup. But I certainly thought about you, Hogarth, that night in the Pass, for I had to decide which I would do; arrest this rascal I wanted badly, which would, of course, have given me away, or bring you the red lining for your specimen case. You won—and that night, when my gangster was out from a drug I had given him, I cut away the lining from the coat and tacked in another which I had all ready for the purpose. I should like to have seen his face when he eventually discovered how he had been fooled, and I hope he has lived, so that one day I can tell him that I was the Holy Man who played the tailor while he slept. Well—there now—you've got all the dope too."

"There's one thing more," said Hogarth. "The bullet hole in the lining, which you said had been made before it was a lining. How did that happen."

"In 1700 on the very spot where I camped in the Khyber Pass one of the many Avengers who had donned the robe in search of the Moslem Holy Grail was shot through the back by a robber. But the murderer was caught and the robe restored. I learnt that too, in Kabul. And that is the last question I shall answer—so there. But I'll give you all a drink."

"Give *me* a chance," said I. "I want to know what's going to happen to your disciples? You can't just leave murderous-looking rascals like that about a respectable place."

Carnaby went to the window and pulled back the curtains. "There they are, you see. Their camp fire burns brightly by the hill-side. I don't think they will trouble us to-night. And to-morrow I will get two brilliant friends of mine to deal with them. First— little Ramsbottom Sahib and later in the day our Holy Man from Kabul shall reappear as the Muezzin upon the top-most minaret of Wrotham Church. I shall give them a message from Allah to depart to their own homes and then ascend once more to dwell with my good friend Mahomet."

Saying which, he pulled the curtain close again, shutting out the weird figures sitting huddled against the distant flame. He then filled up our glasses and proposed his own health which he said he would be in need of at night-fall to-morrow.

"And now, my good host," he said to Hogarth, "having thoroughly woken me up, you will kindly make me sleep again. I demand the story of the other skull, and no heel-taps."

Hogarth smiled. "Sleepy? I'll make you scared. Then we'll leave you to the Haunted Chapel with what courage you have left. Listen!"

CHAPTER TWELVE

A BAKER'S DOZEN

"In my search for grim stories I've found myself doing all sorts of queer jobs in odd places of the world. The story I am going to tell you now took me to the oddest place on the queerest job, and the results were certainly most grim.

"The offer came through an uncle of mine who was a professor of Biology attached to the South Kensington Museum. One day he telephoned me to come round immediately to what he called the Dead Zoo, as he was in a position to put me on to something which he thought would appeal to me. It was a well-paid job, he said, and it needed somebody with guts and the power of keeping mum about it.

"Round I went and found him in the board-room. He was in the chair presiding over a committee meeting of—I suppose—some dozen old gentlemen. When I had sat down in a chair they all indicated at once, my uncle introduced me.

"'This is my nephew, gentlemen, Charles Hogarth, who, I am sure, will attempt to carry through our requirements with a good deal of spirit. I don't mind saying in front of his face, that he has plenty of courage, and from schooldays has proved a good linguist.'

"He then turned to me and rapped out, 'How is your Patagonian? Fluent or rusty?'

"It was such an odd question that I couldn't think of anything to say except to repeat, 'Patagonian'?

"'Yes—would you say that you can speak it fluently?'

"I told him No, and that I had never met anyone who could, but that if he would show me a good reason for doing so, I would undertake to speak it fluently as soon as anyone else.'

"'He is evidently a young fellow who doesn't intend sticking because of a few difficulties,' said a very learned old gentleman looking at me over a pair of thick-lensed glasses.

" 'But is Patagonian going to help him much?' queried my uncle. 'From what I've gathered, it means about as much to the Tierra Del Fuegian, as the Cornish dialect to the Highlander.'

" 'I'm only going by what the Captain tells us,' answered the other. 'It seems to me that your nephew had better meet him and chat over the possibilities. I will give him the card. Here, Mr. Hogarth, is the card,' and he handed me a very dirty visiting card, which had been lying before him on the table.

"The name 'Captain Smith' was printed on it, and beneath in pencil, P.T.O. was scrawled.

"I obeyed to find an address scribbled in pencil.

" 'I think you are right, Doctor Knocker,' nodded my uncle at the old gentleman, and then turning to me, went on, 'Yes, Charles, before refusing or accepting the offer we are going to make to you, you had better go along and see what this fellow has to say. The Captain has been twice wrecked on Cape Horn Island, and once on the larger island of Tierra Del Fuego, and on that occasion crossed the island on foot, and saw something of the interior about which very little was known before.'

" 'Then I take it, sir,' I interrupted, 'that you propose sending me to the Cape Horn district?'

" 'Yes—of course—to Tierra Del Fuego—didn't we tell you?' My uncle was a strange mixture of the vague and the abrupt. 'To Tierra Del Fuego, in order to procure, if possible, twelve specimens of aboriginal Fuegian skulls. The details of the expedition are all arranged, and we should require you to set off next autumn at the latest. We will discuss terms after you have seen the Captain. But when I tell you that the whole expense is borne by the Darwin Trust Fund, and Doctor Knocker is the Darwin Trust Fund, you will know that no quarrel as to money will arise. To procure these skulls must be your chief aim, but if in the meantime you are able to procure zoological or botanical specimens, I am sure a welcome place will be found for them in the other departments of the Museums.'

"I pointed out that as far as zoology was concerned it could prove a profitable expedition. It is a good whaling ground, but I knew that the land animals were not interesting. As to botany, I kept my mouth shut, for I was then an ignoramus of the science, though I have picked up something of it since.

"Now in spite of all their flattering remarks about my courage, I am bound to confess that I was not at all attracted to the venture, and I doubt if I should have undertaken it, had not my uncle promised me a trip to the Congo on my return. So I sought out Captain Smith. He lived in a dilapidated quarter of Pimlico—amongst houses that had seen better days. In one of these seedy ex-genteel buildings, he occupied the top floor. I went up two flights of stairs, disliking the house and the smell of it intensely. It was musty. The dirty windows were obviously never opened. One of the bedroom doors was ajar, and although it was lunch-time, the bed was not yet made, and I could see that the breakfast tray upon it was not cleared. I wondered what sort of a captain it was who could live with such a piggery beneath him.

"I very soon came to the conclusion that whatever he might be, he was at least a fellow to reckon with, for the top flight was barred by an old pair of braces, lashed across the banisters from which hung a cardboard notice with—'If you don't want Hell, don't bother me,' written in large ink capitals.

"'Hello!' I yelled, for there was nothing to ring or knock.

"'Hell!' came the answer. A tremendous voice. I heard a door shut quickly downstairs.

"'Where's Captain Smith?' I demanded.

"'Hell!' repeated the great voice.

"'I dare say,' I laughed. 'And I believe this is the way.'

"'Do I know you?'

"'No,' I bawled back.

"'Then I take it someone sent you. Who?'

"'Doctor Knocker of the Darwin Trust, and my uncle Ray Hogarth of the South Kensington Museum. Shall I come up?'

"'No,' roared the voice. 'Stay below decks. Who the hell are you, anyway?'

"'If you keep me waiting, I'm the devil,' I shouted. 'Come and look.'

" 'What the thunder do you want to see Captain Smith about?'

" 'Tierra Del Fuego,' I replied.

" 'What?' bellowed the Captain; for although invisible, I knew he must be the man I wanted.

" 'Tierra Del Fuego,' I repeated. 'The Land of Fire.'

"Then I heard another voice: a most peculiar voice. It didn't say a word—at least, not that I could catch, but it made a noise that I can only describe as starting with a croon of pleasure and then rising into a full-throated call like the triumphant crow of a cock.

" 'Keep your mouth shut, Romeo,' ordered the Captain in a quieter tone. There followed a subdued muttering—then a sharp sound as if a sword had been drawn from its scabbard.

" 'Shall I come up?' I called. 'Time's precious with me.'

" 'Yes,' answered the Captain. 'But I warn you if you are here to make trouble, think better of it, and get away before I make it first.'

" 'If there is any trouble, it will not be of my making,' I replied as I walked on up the stairs. 'But if you insist on it, you will find I am not the one to shirk looking after myself, and when the occasion calls, you'll find me pretty tough. I've given you fair warning.' I didn't see why he should get it all his own way.

"As you both know, I have experienced all kinds of surprises in my life, but never so many in the space of a few seconds as I got going up those stairs.

"To begin with, the atmosphere of that house entirely changed after I had stepped over the pair of braces that held the notice—for the stairs took a sudden turn, and I saw that the top flat was a picture of neatness.

"The walls were hung with weapons from all parts of the globe, and the metal work danced in the sunbeams that poured through the sky-light.

"On the wall facing the stair-head there was the largest head of a bison that I have ever seen. A magnificent trophy. I noticed that there were other heads all round the landing—lions, a fine tiger, wild cat and antelope. But it was the inside architecture of the flat that struck me most, for I seemed to be boarding some sturdy ocean-going craft. This idea was heightened by the ship's

wheel that was fixed to the banisters and worked a windlass, used
to lower buckets of coal or refuse. Telephone, speaking-tube and
electric bells were handy to the wheel, so that it looked as though
the owner of the top flat directed the house from this bridge. The
furniture was fixed to the floor by iron clamps, as if the top of the
house was expecting dirty weather. I discovered this when I tried
to move a chair. You see, the Captain was particular about a place
for everything and everything exactly in that place. Then I saw the
little brown man whom I afterwards knew as Romeo."

At this both Carnaby and I looked apprehensively at the grinning skull, but Hogarth went on.

"He was dressed in a clean suit of blue canvas—breeches and
blouse. He put me in mind of an oak root. His head, neck, forearms
and bare ankles were gnarled like that ancient wood, and although
stunted, he gave me the impression of enormous strength.

"I suppose he was a dwarf, for I afterwards heard many people
allude to him as such, but I always thought him a compressed
giant. His form was only small, because it was so concentrated.
Well—there he stood, having popped out from nowhere, grinning on the landing—stock still at attention, with a drawn cutlass
at the salute. I nearly fell backwards. It was so unexpected—so
utterly ridiculous. I must have stopped still for sheer amazement,
for the great voice of the Captain roared, 'Now then, boarding
party, tumble up. And no complaints because I mount a guard of
honour for you. And it's not all in compliment to you. It's precau-
tion for me, and serves as protection to the ship. Income tax and
Hoover men fly from Romeo's blade like the land rabbits they are.
And as for the Gas Light and Coke Company and those Central
London Electricities—panic is the word. I sometimes sing like an
old psalmist—"When Romeo draws his sword the host of little
merchants flee discomfited. Ha! Ha!"'

"Then I caught my first glimpse of him. The Captain was
looking at me through the glass ventilator over one of the doors
which was shut to the landing. I imagined that he was standing
on a chair inside the room, in order to be able to have a look at
me. I was wrong. He suddenly opened the door, and I saw that he
was standing on the floor. His great height would have been suf-

ficiently forbidding without the heavy revolver which he grasped
in his right hand. His huge face which strangely resembled the
hairy bison, turned from a scowl to what was meant for a humor-
ous smile of welcome. He stooped under the doorway, put up his
revolver, and came towards the stairs, giving an order to the brown
sentry in some foreign tongue I didn't get. This caused the fellow
to sheathe his cutlass, and to disappear into a little kitchen which
was fitted up on the lines of a ship's galley. The Captain held out a
huge paw—seized my hand and dragged me on to the landing.

"'Well—in spite of those old fusty professors who sent you,'
he laughed, 'you look all right, and if you are all right and a friend
of Ray Hogarth's as well as being his nephew, you are welcome
aboard. Old Ray is none so bad. He knows the rig of an animal's
skeleton better than most. A clever old piece, he is, and he's your
uncle, eh? I don't hold it against you, and you can tell him I said so.
He always owns I'm generous. Come into the Round House, and
I'll show you that I can be hospitable as well as uncivil. If you knew
as much about me as I happen to, you would not be surprised that
I take a good many precautions before receiving visitors aboard.'

"He had by this time dragged me across the spacious landing
which he called—'between decks,' and motioned me to ascend a
ladder which led through a man-trap on to the roof. This seemed
a ridiculous way of showing hospitality. Ushering guests you have
never met before through a ceiling is not usually done, but there
was something about the Captain which called for obedience. As I
went up, he called to the brown man in English, 'Rum and milk—
twice.' He took it for granted that I should like rum and milk. As
a matter of fact, I didn't, but I was perfectly aware that I should
drink it when it came because it seemed to fit in with the whole
adventure.

"I have told you the landing was like a ship, but this illusion
was more real upon the roof. It bristled with gadgets which he
explained as meteorological instruments.

"'Can't be too careful, can one?' he chuckled.

"'I should think not, indeed,' I replied, though I had not the
vaguest idea what he had to be careful about.

"In the observatory, which he called the Round House, was a

powerful telescope, round which ran a very comfortable divan. I must say that my opinion of the Captain went up when I realized the skill with which he had produced his own atmosphere in spite of the drab squalor beneath him. He must have read my thoughts as I stood gazing at the London sky from the Cabin window.

"'Might be riding into some great port, mightn't we? No doubt you wonder why I chose this quarter of the town for the building of my make-believe ship? Well—you see—I didn't. This blarsted house was left me, so I made the best of a bad job. No rent to pay. No—the scum downstairs pay me. I pay the rates—but one has to pay harbour dues in any port. The tenants were left to me as well, and a mighty poor lot they are, too, but I don't get rid of them, as it amuses me to bully them. I was born a bully, and I don't mind owning I like being one. Anything else to ask?'

"As I hadn't asked a thing—I thought it was about time I did, and got on to the business. 'I expect, Captain Smith, that you are wondering still why I am thrusting myself upon you.'

"He interrupted with a wave of his great paw. 'Nothing of the sort. I know now. At least I've guessed. But bless you, there's no hurry about that yet. You may not know it, but you are here for the day.'

"I began to expostulate that I had many other appointments.

"'Cut them,' he roared. 'There's a telephone here. All you have to do is to get on and say "Can't make it—too busy," and then cut 'em off. Most appointments can be dealt with like that. That's what I do with most of mine. Cut 'em off and I wish I could do the same with the silly people's heads too. I suppose you realize young man, that we've got a hell of a lot to thrash out. The whole thing boils down to this. What we are asked to do is certainly going to affect our whole lives, or end 'em, like that,' and he snapped his fingers. 'First, we'll get to know each other a little better. I know more of you than you of me. Your uncle is an old friend. He has recently told me about you. Don't suppose he's told you anything about me, because he's an honest man, and he doesn't know anything much to tell. So, my lad, this being the situation, you'd better let me do the talking for a bit. I'll explain—but here comes our rum and milk.'

"The little brown man he called Romeo brought in two silver goblets on a tray. I took one and drank the Captain's health. I must say it was the first time I had ever liked rum and milk. Romeo knew how to mix it. Plenty of nutmeg.

"'Two for lunch, Romeo,' he roared. 'And what are you giving us? Where's the bill of fare? Something decent, I hope?'

"His queer servant disappeared and returned again smartly with a menu card, which was neatly written in French. The Captain took it—glanced through it quickly, then handed it to me.

"'Not bad,' he muttered. 'Hope it will be to your liking, Mr. Hogarth.'

"It promised to be a most excellent meal, and I told him so.

"'Very well then, Romeo. In half an hour's time in the saloon. In twenty-five minutes, two mint juleps in here. Go.'

"Strange drinks for a strange man, I thought, and then he began to talk.

"'I regret that I cannot claim to be a real Smith. I took the name on my twenty-first birthday, because it was my favourite name. My real name was Ackstart. Hans Ackstart. I followed the sea because I liked it. I followed shady business on the seas, because it gave me a chance to bully shady people. I cannot tell you all my history. Not that I'm ashamed of it. Far from it—though you might be if it had been yours. I just cannot tell it because it is too long. You have handled a Bible? My history, for bulk, would make it look like a two-leaved programme at a ship's concert. A bully history, mine is. I must have bullied more people than any man that has ever lived. Some have tried to bully me. I'll never forget one skipper, God rest his soul in hell, and he's there all right—a great fellow as big as me with a crew of dirty dogs who helped him like a pack of rats. I was mate, and we'd agreed to do the underwriters one in the eye, and pile up the old whaler *Albatross* in the Straits of Magellan. For that voyage we had taken on a wheel in place of the old whale-bone tiller. So fearful was I that my good seamanship would stand me in bad stead before the smash came, for you see, I was going to get my own back in the way of bullying, and put that whole crew where they belonged in hell along of the ship—where was I? Ah, yes. To avoid failure, I lashed myself to the wheel, when I'd fixed it to the required destruction point. I knew I was asking for death, but I didn't care, and I was better off than the rest. They had no chance in the hereafter like I had. You see, I was never really dirty as they were. In fact, I'd done so much good one way and another that I remember feeling a bit ashamed of myself. Made me feel priggish. But there wasn't much time to think. It was blowing half a gale which at the mouth of the Straits is some gale. Before the crash came I shouted, "Every man for himself," just to hear 'em squeal. Half an hour later I came to myself on a rock, with that wheel still lashed to my chest. I was the sole survivor. That was when I crossed the Land of Fire. The wheel saved my life. The natives took it for a halo. If I pointed the spokes at them they shivered. It's the wheel down below by the banisters. Romeo fears it yet.'

"'But what on earth made you carry a ship's wheel across the island? Not just gratitude because it had saved your life, I take it?'

"'No—just common sense,' he answered. 'It was a material proof that I had hold of the wheel when she went down crash. I belied the damned owners, who when things went against them with the underwriters, fastened the blame on me. I walked in with the wheel. The simple-hearted skipper willing to risk his life by carrying out orders. They lapped up as much of that bunk as I cared to dish 'em out. I got heavy damages against them. But as far as their firm went, I was done, and they influenced others for a time.'

"'And they didn't give you another chance?' I asked.

"'Didn't give them one,' he laughed. 'The blighters died. I wiped out that firm as quick as I had sent their foul crew to the bottom. I just mention this so that you'll have confidence in me. I'm not the fellow to run foul of. That trip did another good turn for me. It was on that occasion when I crossed Tierra Del Fuego and kidnapped that servant of mine I call Romeo.'

"'Kidnapped him?' I repeated.

"'Had to,' answered the Captain. 'You may not credit it, but that ugly little devil is an ardent lover. He didn't want to come with me, when I got rescued, because of a girl he was in love with. He still hankers to go back because he's afraid someone else may run off with her.'

" 'Perhaps you would let him go with me when I visit the place,'
I suggested. 'I don't know what you feel about it, but I expect I
shall go with you or someone else as skipper. Anyway, my uncle
told me you were the only man who could give me any practical
advice and perhaps help.'

" 'Neither your uncle nor that old dead-bone setter, Knocker,
know the difficulties. I'll tell you some of them after lunch, when
you'll feel better able to cope with them. Go and get skulls, eh?
Sounds all right—but it's going to be hell. Do you know that
Tierra Del Fuego is the one spot on this earth which makes me
afraid. It's a place that gives you the staggers. If I refuse to go,
you'd better sheer off too. That's my advice. As to help—well, I
don't think I could lend you Romeo. He'd never come back. Oh,
hell—and it means leaving this ship here all so snug.' He suddenly
got up, took a turn or two outside the Round House, then crashed
back through the door, his face contorted with rage.

" 'All right, then, damn you. I'll go with you, Mr. Hogarth. I'll
call you Charles. You call me Smith. I've dropped the Hans. But in
front of the crew, mind, it'll be Cap'n and Mr. Hogarth. That's for
discipline.'

" 'But I don't know that it's as easy and as quick as all that. You
say you don't want to go and the next second you change your
mind. I know this—I have by no means decided.'

"He then astonished me more than ever. He came over to me
and in the most fatherly manner he patted my shoulder, while a
most seraphic smile spread over his huge face. He looked like a
benign patriarch.

" 'There, there, you are not the sort to go back on me,' he said
quietly. 'No one else in God's earth could have swung me over as
you have. I'll look forward to being a sailing companion to you.
Charles, from now on we're friends. We'll get those skulls and,
damn it, we'll find Romeo's Juliet for him too. Here are the juleps.
Come, let's drink to our enterprise.'

"He was a most bewildering man. I didn't know whether I was
standing on my head or my heels. I had never been so rushed into
anything in my life.

" 'Mind you,' he added as we went below to the dining-room,

which certainly looked much more like a ship's dining-saloon, 'If I hadn't liked the trim of your sails, I should have refused point blank to follow you on this mad trip. But since I do, Smith is with Charles and Mr. Hogarth's with the Cap'n. I'll get your skulls for you if I have to sacrifice mine own, just as we'll get Romeo's Juliet for him, though she be married to twenty Parises. Oh, yes, Mr. Hogarth, I know my Shakespeare.'

"After an admirable meal he told me something of the country we were being sent to, and I found that he could be practical and business-like when it suited him. At least I had found a companion who promised to help me to a good story for my collection.

"The very next day we gave our signatures to the undertaking, and with Romeo for my coach I started in to learn the lingo. Meantime, the Captain saw to the necessary equipment, while I continued my studies, and he put his house into the hands of a caretaker, an ex-seaman friend of his, who promised to bully the tenants in his absence.

"In one respect old Professor Knocker was too much for the Captain, who wanted to fit out a ship in London Docks. The Doctor pointed out that this would be altogether too expensive, and would curtail our own expense money. In this latter, however, he was prepared to be more than generous, and partly for my sake the Captain knuckled under and agreed that the three of us would sail as passengers on whatever boats were convenient, and when my uncle promised the Captain the next command of any expeditionary boat that the Museum authorities sent anywhere, he cheered up and we left England in high spirits.

"On our voyage to Rio, we discussed all sorts of voyages the Museum might sponsor for us, and if it had not been for Romeo, I fear we should not have talked much about Tierra Del Fuego. But Romeo could think of nothing else. He delighted in the present trip. He was inspired. I have never seen anyone so hopelessly affected by the devastating disease called Love. He couldn't do enough for us, especially when the Captain made him understand that he would be able to bring his wife with us on our next voyage.

"'Where go with my wife? What land?' he asked eagerly.

"'We shall go to buy her gifts in many places,' the giant rogue

said solemnly with a wink behind his back. 'We shall ride drom-
edaries along the road to Samarkand. We shall get her Persian rugs
there. We shall sail on many ships amongst the Spice Islands. There
we shall buy her nutmegs. Then to India for jewels. She must have
jewels. Then if we have time we'll slip over to the Ivory Coast and
get her a parrot who can talk.'

"'And then?' asked Romeo greedily lapping up the fairy tale.

"'I'll think out a lot more places, and a lot more things to buy,'
he said.

"'Tell me, please, one more place and one more thing,' pleaded
the love-sick one.

"'Well——' hesitated the rascal, rather stumped, as he was getting bored with the subject. 'Certainly to the Arctic to get her a
stylish seal coat.'

"When I expostulated with him, he merely said, 'Well, it's not
so impossible. Besides, if he brings a wife in tow we'll get an extra
servant for nothing, shan't we?'

"I suggested that all this depended very largely on whether the
Fuegian Juliet would be willing in the first place to leave her island
home, and secondly to take Romeo for better or for worse.

"He dismissed this with a laugh. 'You don't know these people.
They're not like Romeo. I've bullied him into being a good and
faithful servant. The Fuegians are a lousy, ill-moraled gang. Their
women do what the stronger man tells them. It will be a case of
finding Juliet's present husband, if he hasn't strangled her, for she's
bound to have a husband you know, and then he and Romeo will
have to fight for her. With us to back him up, Romeo will win,
although let me tell you, our task is not going to be too easy. If we
get away with our twelve skulls and our blushing bride, we shall be
some pirates.'

"We reached Rio better for the voyage. The Captain proved a
good and amusing companion at sea, though it was irksome to
him lounging in a deck-chair when he was itching to be up and
doing on the Captain's bridge.

"We had to spend a few weeks in Rio, waiting to get a passage
on a south-bound vessel. At last we were fixed up to the Captain's
satisfaction.

"The *Stevedore* was an old tramp of miscellaneous lading that traded with Chile. Her owners agreed to have us landed on a point opposite Staten Island. Our plans were all settled. We should use the landing-point as our base, and erect a high flagpole for signalling ships. The *Stevedore* would read our signal on her return trip, while her sister ship, the *Lascar*, would do us the same service. In the event of our non-appearance at the signal station for three months, a rescue party would be organized to find us.

"By the horror with which the crew of the *Stevedore* viewed the place, I saw that it would be difficult for a rescue party to be formed.

"However, the money had all been deposited by the Darwin Trust and the owners had assured us of their full collaboration. I strongly suspected, however, in spite of all the Captain's optimism, that if we did not return from the interior on our quest for skulls, that the ship owners would but shrug their shoulders and leave us to our fate.

"Now, Romeo had persuaded us to bring along the wheel of the *Albatross*, and it was agreed that the mighty Smith should strap it to his back and once more play the 'god' before the ignorant natives.

"Our main goal was to be a certain mountain known to Romeo as very sacred, in which existed an ancient cave temple, guarded and greatly revered by the island medicine men, or whatever their holy devils were called.

"In this place were collected hundreds of skulls of bygone Fuegians, which were worshipped, apparently, as devil-gods. We agreed that we would somehow beg, borrow or steal our round dozen skulls from this cheerful depository.

"We were also to call upon Juliet's father. He was a freelance whaler, and inhabited a cave not far from our proposed landing-place. We could learn from him the whereabouts of Juliet.

"We had all three of us by this time definitely decided that Romeo's sweetheart was married. Even Romeo thought it by now highly probable in spite of his attractions, for he was very vain.

"He kept explaining to us how the fight would be arranged. There would be no unpleasantness between the husband and himself, until they met with knives and settled their domestic difficulties by the death of one. I must mention that by this time I had well mastered the Fuegian lingo, and now that I am playing Carnaby's trick of coming out of the picture in my narrative, let me say, too, that were I given the chance of living my life all over again, I should refuse it on account of those dreadful weeks spent upon Tierra Del Fuego.

"They say that Magalhaens, the Portuguese navigator who discovered the Straits, gave it that name by reason of the numerous fires he saw on the coast during the night; but that rugged hell never meant 'The Land of Fire' to me. For 'Fire' read 'Mist' and you've got it. As far as I was concerned the whole adventure might have happened upon a rockery in any London Square garden during a fog, for though I climbed for miles over those dreadful rocks, I never saw farther than a radius of five yards the whole time.

"The sailors who rowed us and our supplies ashore, helped us to erect our flag-staff, but fearing that the weather would continue to be misty, they thoughtfully added a case of rockets and flares.

"But in spite of the kind consideration the officers showed us, I could see that the men who had sailed there before held the place in dread by the alacrity with which they landed our stuff, and I confess that when the last of them pulled away for the ship, I would have given anything to have gone with them. A dreadful feeling of loneliness seized me, and I cursed the day on which I had signed on for the crazy adventure.

"Right from the start of setting up our base camp, the obscurity of our whereabouts became scaring. We were always losing sight of each other in the mist, and I know that I never got a clear idea of what the lay of the land looked like.

"We soon discovered that when we moved from our flag-staff, we had to chalk arrows on the rocks in order to find our way back again. Wherever we went, we went on tiptoe. Whatever we said, we whispered, for that eternal mist, and the fear of what it hid, made us painfully cautious.

"There was another thing which helped to demoralize our nerves. We would hear whisperings when none of us was talking.

Sometimes these sounds seemed to come from one or two people unseen, but very often at dusk it seemed to be the whisperings of a vast crowd. This went on for over a week, whisperings all round one; and when it sounded like a crowd I can't tell you the trapped feeling I had.

"Yes—it was well over a week and in all that time we never saw a soul—only heard. It was quite a relief when we saw our first native. It chanced to be Juliet's father. I believe he had been watching us for days—creeping behind boulders on the fringe of the mist wall. When he first appeared I happened to be alone cooking the dinner. It was the first time I had that experience, for much as Romeo assured us that he could find his family caves about a mile away and be back within the hour, the Captain wouldn't let him out of his sight. No—we must all stick together, he said. I once heard him telling Romeo that if he attempted to break away into the mist in search of his damned Juliet, he would be shot in the back as a traitor. Romeo was very afraid of him, and I began to think that it had been more fear than devotion which had made him stick to his master for so long.

"On this particular occasion the Captain had agreed that he would let Romeo try to find his home, but insisted on going with him. He asked if I minded staying behind to guard the camp and I told him no, not from any heroic zest of doing my duty, but for a private reason of my own—a plan I wished to carry out behind the Captain's back.

"You see, I had noticed that ever since the ship had sailed he was deteriorating. His nerves were more on the jump than ours. Romeo was nervy through wanting to learn about Juliet. That you can understand. I was nervy through sheer damned dread of the mist and the invisible circles behind it. But our Captain, who had been such a gay companion on the voyage, was nothing more than a bundle of ill-tempered nerves, and I suspected that the cause of it was drink.

"He had himself suggested to me that neither of us should touch our stock of spirits unless through necessity—illness or the like. I applauded the plan as we couldn't possibly know how long we should be marooned, and although we had plenty of cases both of brandy and whisky with us, it would not last for ever. We had agreed to limit ourselves to a tot each at nightfall. That small amount to a hardened old sinner like the Captain could not have made him thick in his speech and somewhat unsteady on his pins when he would wake me to take my turn at the watch. Therefore, to satisfy myself, the first thing I did when they had disappeared beyond the curtain of white was to unlock the chest we had already drawn three bottles from. It seemed at first sight that I had wronged him, for the bottles were unopened and untouched. However, since my suspicions could not rest at that, I opened one of our spare cases, and already nearly half the packing slots were empty. This enraged me, not that I grudged the old man having a binge in secret, but that he should have been so cunning as to help himself to the reserves which he knew I might not look at for weeks, and heaven only knew what might not happen before then. It was the deceit and unfairness, and worst of all a sort of fear of me that made me know his nerves were driving him to cowardice, and I resolved to tax him with it at the first opportunity.

"In the meantime I kept to my promise which was to prepare a good supper against their return. And that brings me back to the native—Romeo's father-in-law to be, we hoped. I had raised my head from the stew-pot, expecting, as usual, to see nothing but the mist, when he stood there with a primitive harpoon in his hand. I must have cried out in my astonishment, for he sprang towards me, but stopped suddenly when I gave him a salutation in his own tongue, and incidentally pushed my revolver in his face.

"He asked me if I were a white servant of the great white god with the wheel, who had been blown back to the island on the wind. I told him 'Nothing of the sort.' I didn't see why the Captain should get away with it as far as I was concerned. I wasn't going to be labelled as a servant of that ridiculous wheel. He had lashed it to his back before starting off with Romeo and I thought how stupid he looked. I think what annoyed me most about it was that he had lost his sense of humour and really began to believe in the wheel as a symbol of godhead. At first, like any sane person, he had kicked at having to wear the thing at all, but since he had been drinking, he developed a sanctimonious pride in putting it on, and one day he had spoken with tears in his eyes of Christ bearing His Cross for sinners, at which I lost my temper and told him not to be a blasphemous ass.

"Well—I got talking to Juliet's father, and was glad to get first innings behind the Captain's back. I told him that I was altogether a superior god to my servant with the wheel, and because I saw that I had gone down in his estimation by reason of my menial task, I added that I, and I only, knew the magic way to make the food of the highest heaven. A lot of bilge, but it sounded all right to him, especially when I finished up by playing him a lively tune on a tin whistle, and then presented him with a pocket mirror, for we had brought plenty of gaudy knick-knacks with which to pro-pitiate the natives. By that time he was showing me the greatest respect.

"I said that if he did everything I told him, he should have a magic pipe for himself, which threw him into an ecstasy, and so I thought it the right time to announce why the white gods had come to his contemptible island.

"From him I gleaned that Juliet was married at the moment. Her husband was a whaler, but that as he happened to be away for a few days, Romeo might go to Juliet's cave and love her. This gross piece of advice shocked me beyond words. When the whal-ing husband returned a fight could be arranged, he informed me, and his daughter would abide by the decision of strength. He seemed quite easy in his mind on that score, but what he wasn't so sure about was the possibility of getting the dozen skulls from the temple in the mountain. Of course, I told him that if he didn't get them there would be trouble for someone, and that someone would also be the loser of much silver and many trinkets.

"He promised to return and discuss the matter after sunset, so at that I gave him a whistle pipe, with the warning that should he break faith, the voice inside the whistle pipe would take shape and rend him, which alarmed him very much. Now, as luck would have it, Romeo and the Captain had discovered his cave while he was talking to me, and Romeo had chalked a sign which ordered the old fellow to visit our camp secretly and alone that evening.

"Finding this further command from me, as he thought, made

the old rascal think that I had repeated my command by magic writing, and from that moment I became a full-blown god in his estimation.

"That night, when we were huddled round our cheerful camp fire, the old whaler crawled towards us. The Captain was for giving him plenty to drink, but I told him not to be a fool, and added that in future when he wanted a drink himself he must come and ask me for it, as, for our own security, I had hidden the keys of the chests. He flew into a peevish rage at this, but as he spoke in English, Juliet's father was none the wiser. It annoyed the Captain still more to notice how I had somehow stolen the thunder of his god-head, for Juliet's father, though even respectful to Romeo, paid me all the homage which the Captain thought should be his perks. He certainly didn't like Romeo and himself being lumped together as 'the favoured of the god'—meaning me. The Captain took not the least interest in my plans for procuring the skulls, though he was enthusiastic about the arrangements for Romeo's fight, and he kept making Juliet's father shake hands with his excellent son-in-law to be. The whole thing was becoming just damned silly, except that I found myself becoming more and more sorry for Juliet's present husband, who, as far as I could see, was not going to get a dog's chance of his life. I had no quarrel with Romeo. I liked the little man—but I was not going to sit back and see murder done. That, I knew, would be the Captain's way of it, for when they discussed the possibility of Romeo losing, he told them not to worry on that score, as he would have a knife ready himself. After which they all three took the absent whaler's extermination as a settled thing. As to Juliet's feelings on the subject—well, they just didn't exist as far as that trio were concerned, and I determined to contact her myself and get at the truth of what she thought.

"On this point, however, I was quickly disillusioned, for she made her first appearance that same night.

"I never had such a shock about anyone in my life. So entirely different was she from the Juliet of my imagination, for I had naturally taken everything Romeo had said about her with a grain of salt.

"By what I had read of the native women, and indeed from what the Captain had told me in his sensible moments, I was quite justified in seeing her as a weather-beaten, mahogany-coloured girl, attractive, perhaps, to Romeo, but positively lousy and repellent to a white man.

"Not a bit of it.

"Juliet—for we always called her that, though her own name which meant Maid of the Mist was more descriptive—Juliet was a glamorous minx. She certainly owed her good looks to her mother's lack of morals, and I could see that her father, far from being the ugly old scamp squatting by our fire, had been some handsome white sailor, shipwrecked on the coast. How else could she have come by her auburn curls? In the light of our flickering fire, her complexion appeared to be olive, and seemed to be reasonably clean. I dare say she was quite grubby really. However—her eyes were distinctly blue, and her well-developed young figure was lithe. In fact, the little frippet was damnably alive and mischievous. I wouldn't have trusted her a yard.

"She wore a sort of jerkin made from an old sail, but it was lined with white fox, and she carried a tough staff whittled sharp at one end. I don't know what she did with that. Spiked fish, perhaps—or rivals.

"Without a word she sat herself down between the whaler and me and for some reason, best known to herself, gazed across the flames at the Captain.

"Romeo had risen when she entered the circle, and although he drew his knife to show he was ready to do battle for her, I suppose, his sheepish glances made him look quite ridiculous. He had what Shakespeare calls—'the very quotidian of love upon him.'

"To my frayed nerves what followed was just about the limit. The Captain's eyes were devouring her, and she was deliberately leading him up the garden. I have never witnessed such a flagrant flirtation, and I began to see that as far as our mission was concerned, the burden would fall on me. I suspected too that all the time the Captain had been using us for his own ends. Or couldn't he have been quite such a fool? Had he met the girl before when he had wandered through the island with his damned ship's wheel? Had he come back to get her? If so, poor Romeo's life wasn't worth much. I didn't think it was, anyway.

"All this time the whaler talked of the arrangements for the great fight, and of the impossibility of getting away with the sacred skulls.

"After a long time of this sort of thing, the girl stood up, and for the first time looked at Romeo. I can only describe it as the look of a queen dismissing a favourite who had fallen from grace.

"Poor Romeo was stunned. It was quite shocking to see.

"Then looking at the Captain, who, by the way, was still wearing his wheel, she slowly backed towards the mist.

"Like a mesmerized animal he got to his feet. Then with a laugh—she ran, and before I could stop him, he leapt after her, and just as he disappeared, I caught sight of the unsealed neck of a whisky bottle. The swine!

"I heard him cry out and her distant laugh—and then silence and nothing to see but the mist. And the whaler went on talking as though nothing unusual had happened. Then in sheer rage I got up and ordered him to get out.

"He slouched off, mumbling that he dared not get the skulls, but that Romeo was welcome to fight for his daughter. I thought we were rid of him, but not quite, for he came back, just a vague shadow in the mist to add with a devilish grin at Romeo, 'Seems, son, you'll have two to kill now.' Then he sprang away to avoid my clenched fists.

"Poor Romeo. I vented my rage on him. He was far stronger than I was, but these events had beaten him, so that I was able to shake him like a rat. Then I flung him to the ground and, as he lay there whimpering, ordered him to go at once to Juliet's cave and to tell his master the Captain, that failing to return to camp immediately, I would make his name stink in every port where the red ensign flew.

"I thought he would refuse point-blank, but no—I had another surprise, and at that moment I own I found it a pleasant one.

"'I will give him your order, Mister Charles,' he said quietly, as he got to his feet, 'and if he does not obey you on the instant, then they shall all see what the Land of the Gods and Devils is like.'

"He turned and strode away with a great show of dignity, and I liked the way his powerful hand took a firm grip on the handle of his knife.

'So I was left again, but with the hope that Romeo would play the man and give the three devils, girl and all, their passports back to hell.

"I listened for some time but could hear nothing, and, of course there was nothing to see. When I turned back to the fire I saw a man warming himself by it and grinning.

"This enraged me, too, and I said rather stupidly in English, 'And what the hell are you thinking funny?'

"He answered in grave Spanish, explaining that he was the Juliet's husband, and had listened to our conversation or rather to the talk of the old whaler, and he wanted to bargain with me concerning the skulls, before tackling his rivals, Romeo and the Captain.

"He explained that he was the only foreign trader upon the island; that he did business with the Argentine ports, with Uruguay and Brazil, and that he was the only one who was free from the superstitions of the island: in short, that he was the only hope I had of getting the twelve skulls, about which he had heard us talking.

"The upshot was that he agreed to procure the specimens for one pound sterling a brace.

"He refused my offer to accompany him, on the plea that my presence would add to his own danger.

"He asked me for a drink. I gave him a hot rum. He drank to my good health, which he said would be kept in better condition if I would remain where I was until his return.

"He thought it would take him a week to get to the temple in the mountain, a day or so in which to plan and execute the theft, and a little less than a week for his return, which would be easier as the land sloped down from the high plateau to the coast.

"'I will execute your business for you, señor, with the greatest despatch,' he said politely, 'and it is a pleasure to have dealing with a foreign gentleman like yourself, who can speak my Spanish tongue so well.'

"I thanked him for the compliment and then asked him what I should do if by some unlucky chance he should fall in the fight.

"He made light of that, and said that he was well used to the duel of the knife, and that I need not worry. Whereupon I told my new ally that he would not be facing a duel, but attempted murder and foul play. Whereupon my Spaniard grinned again, showing his white teeth.

"'I am a good Catholic, señor, and educated. I know that you English are famous for tact—and it must have been your blessed English saint and archbishop who first taught it to you. Before he was sent to England by Pope Gregory, he said to his blessed mother, Santa Monica, "When I am in Milan, I do as they do at Milan; but when I go to Rome, I do as Rome does." So, señor, with me. When I talk to the clean, I talk—clean—as with you. But I act dirtier than the dirtiest when dealing with the dirty.' He spat in the fire and jerked his thumb in the direction taken by the others, adding, 'I will speedily deal with my domestic affairs, but I go now to get skulls.'

"Then began my awful solitude, the like of which I never wish to experience again. I must have spent three weeks by that flag-pole. A certain amount of exercise I took by tying the end of a ball of twine to it, and then walking out into the mist with this life-line in my hand to guide me back, for my great dread was that of losing the camp.

"Otherwise I ate a little, drank a little more, allowing myself the extra tot forfeited by the Captain, and sleeping only when I couldn't help myself. Of course, the whole time I was listening and trying to see beyond the mist. But I saw nothing and all I heard was the wind, the seas, and the massed whisperings after dusk.

"No news of Juliet or her two ill-assorted lovers.

"At last I could stand it no longer, and made up my mind to go into the mist and look for them.

"I filled a fat flask, packed up some food, put a supply of chalk in my pocket, and started off one morning along the lifeline. This I soon had to say good-bye to, creeping on away from it and care-fully, oh, how carefully, chalking the rocks as I went. How cautious I was never to get out of sight of my last mark until I had chalked another.

"I found myself tired out with watching and anxiety, and when I had gone not much more than a mile in this tedious fashion, I was quite done. So I sat down, had a snack and a smoke, and then dozed off.

Was I wet? Was I soaking wet? Yes—for I awoke to find a dreadful rain storm raging. How long I had slept in it, I had no means of telling, as my watch had stopped. The mist had grown thicker, and had closed in upon me. To my horror I found that the chalk marks I had made upon the stone against which I had been leaning had been completely obliterated by the rain.

"I crawled back the way I had come. Not a chalk mark could I find.

"I started walking, at first slowly and then faster, till I broke into a run.

"That finished me.

"I lost my head. I began to shout. This somehow developed into a continual screaming. Still I ran. I tried but I could not pull myself together. Over clay-slate, green-stone and granite I stumbled on, and when night fell I still ran. I know that I fell exhausted once and slept. When I awoke, I ate what was left of my rain-sodden food and set off to run again. I felt that I must reach somewhere soon. But it was all the same. Just boulders, stones, pebbles.

"All that day I ran, and again far into the second night. Then I fell, striking my head against a rock and I remembered no more.

"When I came to myself I imagined I was still dreaming. But I soon discovered that I was awake, and I could not believe it. What I saw didn't make sense.

"I had fallen close to the edge of the cliffs. The sun was shining on the sea far beneath me, and upon it rode a sturdy man-of-war. Yes—they were called that in those days, you youngsters.

"She must have been a mile off shore, but what thrilled me was the fact that I could plainly see the white ensign flying from her stern. I went mad. I sprang to my feet on the very lip of that precipice and shouted. As I did so, something caught in my boots and nearly threw me down. It was my life-line entangled round my feet.

"Now although the sea was clear, the infernal mist still clung over the island.

"Indeed, as I ran back with my fingers burning along the life-line for very friction, and sped to find the flag-pole, I was swallowed up in it once more.

Quickly I set the rockets and fired them off—rapid fire it was— and then ran back to the cliff edge with one of our flags, which I waved frantically. Oh, but the suspense was ghastly, for I could not make out whether the rockets had been seen, and I'm bothered if the mist didn't thicken again and shut out the sea.

"I yelled myself hoarse and fired my revolver till my ammunition was exhausted.

"Then I stood quite still and listened. Nothing. Not even whisperings.

"Then, just as I was despairing, I heard the most wonderful sound of oars getting nearer, for the wind had dropped, and by their rhythmic regularity, I thought the rowers could be none other than British sailors pulling towards shore. I clambered down to the shingle. I knew the quickest way, for how often had I planned this heavenly moment? I shouted and kept on shouting, and at last my shouts were answered by the heartening voices of British bluejackets. H.M.S. *Reputation* had visited the Falkland Islands, and was bound for British Columbia. So was I saved.

"I confided my story to Captain Harker, who was not only most sympathetic, but very angry on my behalf.

"How he railed against my employers for having sent me on such a hopeless quest, which even had it been successful, he maintained was totally unnecessary. Who wanted to look at Fuegian skulls, anyway? he asked.

"For Captain Smith he had no sympathy at all. Had he not sold his friend a pup? Had he not deceived his servant? Had he not done that unspeakable act of running off with a native's wife? And when I repeated that the native was to me a Spanish gentleman, he answered, 'Anyone who is not British is just a native. I know, my lad. I'm older than you.

"'The blackguard Smith, for I will not keep hearing you refer to him as "Captain," has generally lowered the prestige of the white man, and deserved all the trouble that he asked for.' He stoutly refused to let me land again in search for him, and would not countenance risking the lives of his men by sending a search party. In fact, he stated emphatically that he had not got the power to do so. He had no wish for his interference to plunge him into any international complications. And yet much as I hated Smith for what he had done to me, I could not bring myself to abandon him to his fate without an effort. But with Captain Harker, all my efforts were of no avail. All he would consent to do was to stand by for twenty-four hours after firing a warning gun to bring Smith aboard.

"And yet he was not a man devoid of the common humanities, for hard as he was upon Smith, he was kindness itself to me, giving me a berth on the chart-room table and inviting me to feed in his cabin.

"Well—the mist cleared a good deal during the day, and when the sun blazed out, I could see through his spy-glass every detail of our camp, and I watched it zealously all day. But there was no sign of life.

"When I had told the details of the venture over and over again the Captain's rage against Smith increased.

" 'I'll spike that fellow's guns for him, anyway,' he said. I didn't quite see how, any more than I understood why he should break his vow and send another boat-load of his men ashore. I discovered later that they went to bring the chests of drink aboard. 'No more drink for Smith,' he said. At sunset we fired another gun. But no sign from the camp. Just as we were finishing dinner, the Quartermaster came to the Captain's cabin and reported that a boat was being paddled towards the ship.

"We went on deck. It was now dark, but sure enough I could see a canoe in the glare of the searchlight. As it got near ship I could recognize the navigator as Juliet's husband, my Spanish friend.

"What at first I took to be another person in the stern, only proved to be a large sack, and I realized that my specimens had been procured. Captain Harker agreed for my sake to have them taken aboard, on the understanding that I did not open the sack or speak of it before the men.

" 'For I don't approve of this official skull running,' he said. 'But I certainly agree that you, Mr. Hogarth, have suffered too much at the hands of the Museum authorities for me to let you go back a failure. Take the Quartermaster into your confidence. You can rely on him. He will smuggle away your precious relics. But the less I know about them, the better my conscience will be pleased.'

"Accordingly, I explained the whole situation to the Quartermaster, and handed him six pounds for the purchase, which he manipulated alongside. I had told him to count the specimens by sense of touch and not to open the sack, explaining that this would be in accordance with my bargain with his captain. 'You needn't object if the dozen is a bit short,' I said.

" 'I'm shippin' 'em as fresh loaves of bread for the Cap'n's table, sir,' he answered with a respectful wink. 'When I buys bread I don't pay for short weight. No more will you, sir. Specially with a dago of a Fuegian Spaniard. What a mixture, sir.'

"That was the Quartermaster. He was tough but he had a sense of humour.

"I watched him jump nimbly into the canoe and he began feeling the skulls through the sacking. I heard him counting aloud.

" 'Thirteen?' he queried. 'Good man. You've made it a baker's dozen, have you?'

"The Spaniard guessed what he meant and I heard him answer in Spanish, 'Ah, yes, señor—one more—for luck.'

"I called out in Spanish, ordering him to find Captain Smith and to see that he was aboard by sunrise, but Captain Harker took me by the arm and led me to his cabin, telling me to leave things to the Quartermaster in order not to attract too much attention.

"So we settled down to our coffee and cigars.

"Presently I noticed that the Quartermaster was trying to catch my eye through the open door. He was standing outside on the deck, but out of the Captain's eye-line.

"I made some excuse and joined him.

" 'I've got 'em stowed below in my cabin, sir,' he said. 'But if you've no objection, I should like to take 'em out of that sack. The carpenter's fixin' me up a tin-lined box. Also, sir, I understood you to say as how you was after ancient skulls, and if so, I has a suspicion that that there dago has gone and done the dirty on you.'

"We reached his cabin. 'Let me go in first, sir, and if you don't mind we'll fasten the door before turnin' on the lights. Only mind how you go, sir as I've a barrel of quick-lime, which ain't healthy stuff to get on your shore-goin' togs. Now, sir,' he went on, 'I'll turn on the lights.' He did so and he was looking straight at me with a very serious expression. 'I didn't like the feel of them skulls when I counted 'em in that canoe, and now that I've got 'em here, I don't like the look of that red stain on the sack: so, if you've no objection, we'll turn 'em out on the floor, and have a look at 'em.' He cut the cord at the sack's mouth and, to my unspeakable horror, upset on to the cabin floor a heap of newly severed heads. Yes—freshly killed. Flesh and hair complete. I know I turned sick with the shock. But the Quartermaster appeared utterly unmoved. He went on calmly, 'This ain't no time to be squeamish, sir. It ain't our funeral, thank God, but THEIRS. You wants skulls—not heads—and you're goin' to have what you wants—skulls.'

"Whereupon he began lifting them one by one, and lowering them by their long hair into the lime barrel.

"We were now rolling a good deal, which kept the heads in motion upon the floor. They looked horribly life-like. The deck of the neat cabin was now becoming unpleasantly slippery, when one of them slithered with the ship's roll, and bumped against my foot. I looked down and—oh, God—*I met the glassy stare of Captain Smith!*

"I looked at the others, and there sure enough, on the floor, rolling about with the few that were left, waiting their turn at the lime-barrel, was the face of the hideous love-sick Romeo.

"'That was our servant,' I gasped as the Quartermaster put it into the quick-lime.

"He then lifted the head that was wedged against my boot. He held it by the strong red beard, because the hair of the Captain's head was cropped.

"'Don't put that in,' I shuddered. 'It's the head of the white man we are waiting ship for.'

"The Quartermaster didn't turn a hair. 'He ain't eligible, then, for the Museum. We'll give him a separate burial.' He climbed on to his bunk, unscrewed the port-hole, and thrust the great head of Hans Ackstart, alias Captain Smith, out into the night of spray, wind and waves.

"'When them in the barrel are done to a turn,' he went on,

'which in this case is lookin' sufficiently ancient, I'll fish 'em out and pack 'em. You've nothin' to worry about, sir.' He then put a lid over the lime barrel. 'I'll just swab up a bit, sir, for I likes a clean and tidy cabin, and then take you back to the bridge. The old man will be up there now, sir, and a bit of a blow will do you good. But I was forgettin' something—most important. Here you are, sir. I owe you this,' and he handed me a five-pound note. I looked puzzled, but he explained. 'Your change, sir.'

" 'Change?' I queried.

" 'Yes, sir. You see, sir, I only give the dago a quid, and I thought that was overdoin' it. But seein' as how it were twelve murders, I don't think one and eight a go will break you. I says twelve and not thirteen, sir, because I'm a very nervous bloke when it comes to thirteen anything. Judas money, I thinks, and so never calculates in thirteens. Rather lose, I would. And it might be as well, sir,' he added in a confidential tone, when I had refused the change, and he had pocketed it, 'not to mention any of this head business to the Captain. Keep 'em skulls, sir, if you must talk of it. I ain't at all sure that he might not class this business as amongst the many things which accordin' to his way of looking, lowers the white man's preesteege. He's potty on that, sir. We all has our red rags. Preesteege is his.'

"The next morning I was awakened from sleep by the shaking of gun-fire. I pulled on my overcoat and went on deck.

" 'Did it wake you up, Mr. Hogarth?' laughed one of the officers just relieved from the bridge who was drinking coffee outside the galley. 'They've been warning your friend to come aboard with live-shot. The old man wanted that flag-pole down. Said it attracted too much attention, and would delay other shipping. First shot went wide. Second blew up your camp baggage, and the third just pushed over the pole—a lovely shot.'

"I looked through his glasses and could see no signs of the camp. It had vanished like the nasty dream it was.

"During breakfast my friend the Quartermaster brought some paper to the cabin, and I remember the Captain telling him that we should stand by for Mr. Smith to come aboard until noon and then sail.

"The Quartermaster so far forgot himself as to give me a knowing wink. He was an extraordinary card. A very solemn face by reason of a scar on his right cheek which drew his lip down. I felt an awful hypocrite, looking anxiously for some sign of life where the camp had been, but as the Quartermaster said, 'It's no use upsettin' the Old Man's ideas of preesteege.'

"There—that's the yarn, and there's one incident to add. Just as the mists of Tierra Del Fuego were vanishing into the horizon, we caught up a piece of wreckage that was floating south. The Quartermaster threw a hooked line and brought it aboard, very neatly. It was the ship's wheel of the whaler *Albatross* that I'd first seen in Captain Smith's flat, and when it was presented to me by the old sailor, I couldn't help thinking that now was the time when Hans Ackstart needed his halo.

"And now for a side-line on the story.

"One afternoon about two years ago, I was in Town and at a loose end between two appointments, and happening to stroll by the Museum, I went in to kill time.

"I was thinking of the days when my uncle was alive, and my mind went back to that first interview I had with him and Doctor Knocker in the boardroom.

"Suddenly I found myself in front of a case containing skulls of various aborigines. Yes—and there were two marked *Tierra Del Fuego*.

"Back came the mist circle, and the Captain leaping after that infernal girl. I looked at the skulls closely, and wondered if by any chance either of them could be Juliet's father. I knew that neither could lay claim to be Romeo in spite of their conceited grinning, for his skull, which the Quartermaster had given to me separately, had rested ever since in that specimen case.

"A very old attendant in uniform sauntered over to me and asked, 'Know anything about skulls, sir?'

"I told him no, not much, but thinking very vividly of those severed heads. How they rolled and slithered on that slippery cabin floor.

"'Well, them two you're lookin' at is very ancient indeed,' explained the official, obviously angling for a tip. 'If I was to say thousands of years old, you might think as how I was takin' the liberty of pullin' your leg, sir. But if I was to say a million—or not to exaggerate—let's say half a million, I guess I should be nearer the mark.'

"Appreciating the grim humour of my own knowledge against the outrageous invention of the old man, I turned to him as though incredulous with a 'No—really?'

"'Ah—wants a bit of stomachin', don't it, sir?' he chuckled. I longed to say, 'It *did* want a lot of stomaching when I saw those two with eleven others, rolling about a cabin and making the place stink with congealing black blood.'

"And then—well, I *did* say it—but not before I had fished out my wallet and handed him a crisp five-pound note.

"'Anything wrong with it?' he asked.

"'There was nothing wrong with the last one I gave you, was there?'

"'When was that, sir?' demanded the astonished old fellow.

"'Thy cheek betrayeth you,' I quoted; for I had noticed a scar upon his right cheek which drew down his lip in a most solemn expression.

"'It was when those two fellows—there,' and I pointed to the skulls, 'yes, those two, with hair and flesh upon them like the rest, wanted a bit of stomaching, as they danced a Devil's Roll between our feet. Yes—it was just after you had dropped the last skull into the barrel of quick-lime. But don't be alarmed. You and I are the only people who know the truth.'

"The one-time Quartermaster scratched his head, looking hard at me, and then nodding. 'Shall I take you up on deck, sir?' he grinned. 'Bit of a blow will do you good. But not a word to the Old Man.'

"'Captain Harker?' I shook my head solemnly. 'No—he's too potty on *preesteege*.'"

CHAPTER THIRTEEN

THE WHITE MOTH

For a long time none of us moved. Hogarth's recital had mesmerized us. We both stared at him, waiting for some comment, but he didn't say anything. He sat there upright in his tall-backed chair, smiling with appreciation at his own story.

I broke the silence with, "I don't know whether we ought to thank you for such a horror, but I'm sure we do."

Carnaby, who had been smoking a pipe, got up and knocked it out against a log, which he then kicked up into a blaze. "I suppose you know you've thoroughly debunked my respect for museums," he said solemnly. "I shall never believe any more in what their catalogues tell us. I suppose the nine other skulls went to other museums, eh?"

"Oh, yes," replied Hogarth. "The committee had promised several a share in the spoils. I've seen one myself in Budapest, and I'm told that there's another in Vienna, and two in Berlin, or were. The rest are in various collections in the U.K. And now, my good Carnaby, are you more sleepy than scared?"

"I'm afraid I shall be boring company now, for any ghost that may wish to be matey in the Chapel," he answered.

"Splendid," said Hogarth. "They want someone to be tough with them. Kent and I have been too sympathetic with them, and that's flat. And talking of stirrup-cups, what about a brandy night-cap, or would anyone prefer a rum and milk in honour of Captain Smith? I'm afraid I can't do you a mint julep, though I'm sure Hoadley could, if he was up."

But we'd both had enough and told him we were ready for bed.

"Then I'll endeavour to pilot you along, Carnaby. Are you still set on sleeping in the Chapel? I can put you elsewhere."

Carnaby was still set on it, and told Hogarth that he could easily find his own way. "Hoadley told me it was the gothic door at the end of the long corridor. I know."

I am sure just to encourage us to change our minds, Hogarth poured himself out a brandy. "Mentality's a strange thing," he said. "When I was telling you that long yarn, I never had a twinge of this curse, but Old Porfirio's got me properly now. Perhaps the remedy is to go on telling you more."

"Don't tempt us to humour you," I laughed.

"Nothing else would keep me awake," said Carnaby.

"Don't be too sure," replied our host. "The monk hasn't started on you yet. Wait till you get acquainted. We may find you a crock to-morrow."

There was a discreet tap on the Library door. "There you are," whispered Hogarth. "He's come to show you the way." The door opened and Hoadley appeared in his black clothes but with a white muffler round his neck.

"I heard you stirring, sir," he said diffidently, "and I thought it might be a help to Cap'n Carnaby if I piloted you to your rooms."

"I admit I've drunk a lot, Hoadley," said Carnaby, "but I assure you I'm perfectly steady. We thought you were in bed."

"Oh, I have been sir, and asleep, thank you, but even in my room the Monk has been very aggravating. Woke me up time and again, wanting me to go out into the garden. When I conveyed to him that I wasn't havin' any, he flew into one of his tantrums, and I regret to say has been destructive in the Captain's bedroom. I think it would be best if I made you up a bed elsewhere, sir. It would only be a matter of a few minutes."

"Certainly not, at this time of night," exploded Carnaby. "Never heard anything so ridiculous. But how do you mean—destructive?"

"Sweepin' everything portable from the dressin'-table to the floor, sir. I heard the noise of it comin' from the Chapel, and when I goes in to see if by chance we had had another gate-crashin' from them Indians, the hand-mirror seems to jump by itself from the other wreckage on the floor and come hurtlin' through the air— just missin' my left ear by inches. That's destructive—and that's what I means by destructive."

"Mirror broken again?" asked Hogarth.

Hoadley nodded. "And I regret to state past repair this time.

Don't see why ghosts should get away with that sort of thing when humans ain't allowed to."

"Ghosts?" repeated Carnaby.

"You might call 'em influences if you prefers it, sir. But exist in this house they does. And as I often says to the Master, perhaps bein' old-fashioned and brought up in religion, they takes offence at the old stone altar bein' used as a secular dressin'-table for the laity."

"There may be something in what you say," replied Carnaby gravely. "Come along—I can't get to that Chapel quick enough. I'm on your side, Hoadley, and your ghosts will get no change out of me."

Of course we all went along to the Chapel. I had not been in it since I had been moved to the Tapestry Room, but to me there certainly seemed to be something evil about it. But Carnaby appeared to be quite chirpy about being left, and at length we consented on the promise that should anything unusual arise, he would ring the bell for Hoadley who would come and wake us.

I suppose that owing to the uncanny stories I had heard, even the gorgeous Tapestry Room did not appear quite so friendly as usual. I know that when Hoadley left me I felt myself longing for my own matter-of-fact bedroom overlooking the Chelsea Embankment, where at least one could see the lights of living ships upon the river, and the comforting beat of the policeman on duty. The thought of those Indians sitting round the fire in the snow-covered field gave me no cheer. I could not even be sorry for them. Serve them right, I thought.

Again I experienced after turning out the lights that uncertainty of whether I was awake or asleep. I was watching the gay colours in the tapestry by the light of the flickering fire, I know that, and don't remember closing my eyes. Then there occurred the change which so astonished me. The gay colours faded into a dull grey background, and it was not long before I realized that I was not in the Tapestry Room at all, but in the Abbot's Chapel. At my side stood Carnaby, and I could see by his grave expression that we were about to witness something very terrible. In front of the altar which was lighted with three candles, stood Porfirio, wearing his

Abbot's Cope and Mitre, both red and encrusted with jewels. He was facing the door with his back to the altar. Only we three were there.

Then I heard the door open and two masked monks entered, beckoning to someone outside, and along the corridor came the sound of silk rustling, till through the door came the beautiful girl I had seen in the Tapestry Room. She was very pale, as though suffering great emotion, but her step was firm and her eyes determined, while the poise of her head was most proud. The masked monks closed the door and shot the bolts. Then with hands folded on their breasts and heads bowed, they moved towards a dark shadow on the wall which looked like a door. As they passed me I saw that each clutched a trowel in his hands.

I wondered if once again I was to be a witness of her doing penance, but in her glorious carriage there was nothing of the penitent about her, for she walked defiantly towards the Abbot who was muttering Latin prayers in a low monotone. Suddenly he stopped and stared at her, his eyes growing large and hypnotic. It was then that she seemed to weaken and slowly knelt down before him. He then handed her a chalice from the altar, and she drank the contents to the dregs. I glanced at Carnaby beside me. His eyes were closed tightly as though in agony, and in spite of the awful fascination, I found my eyes were closing too, but not before I saw her slender fingers loosening her bodice at her shoulders. I could hear the Abbot mumbling prayers again, and then my eyes opened once more.

She was walking naked towards the black shadow where the monks stood, and the hideous Porfirio, stepping down upon the heap of her discarded finery, followed her with the empty chalice in his hands.

Knowing a hellish deed was about to be completed, I cried out to Carnaby and seized his wrist. Immediately the Chapel walls vanished, and I was back in the Tapestry Room, but still grasping Carnaby's wrist as he stood beside my bed.

"Sorry if I startled you," he said quietly, "I rang the bell as I promised, but I think Hoadley must be asleep, poor old chap, and Hogarth isn't in his room, so I came to you. Can you manage to get down with me to the Chapel? There's something going on there, I don't understand. It's a sound. The kind of sound silk makes being rustled. I want you to tell me it's not just my imagination. I'm sure it's not. Anyway, I'm not imaginative. I'm convinced that the noise whatever it is is purely physical—not psychic. Do come."

I pulled on a dressing-gown, and with his help and the crutches got downstairs into the hall. Here we saw Hoadley coming out of the Library door, who told us that his master had been in such pain for the last two hours that he had given up trying to sleep and had come downstairs. "He feels more comfortable in the Library, gentlemen. You see, the influences ain't so strong there. Was they very bad in your rooms?"

Telling him that we would join his Master in a few moments, we hurried along the corridor to the Chapel door.

Carnaby switched on the lights and we went to the fire, leaning against the mantel-piece and listening.

Sure enough the sound was not only as Carnaby had described it, but exactly like the noise of that glorious girl's silk robes. Only it was far more distinct than in my dream, which I then began to describe.

"Now that's an idea," he said, as though thinking aloud.

"A medieval monastery—an unscrupulous Abbot and a pretty girl. As you suggest—some hellish deed—those two monks. Were they masked to prevent carnal thoughts or because they were executioners? The trowels they carried suggest the practice, common enough in those cruel days, of bricking up alive. But that sound's no ghost—it's real. Listen. We must ask Hogarth if he has tested these walls beneath the plaster. It sounds from over there, and that's the outside wall."

Sleep being now out of the question, we decided on a conference right away, and went back to the Library, where we found Hogarth feeling, as he said, considerably better for his upright chair. He would not own to believing in Hoadley's theory of influences, but I had a strong feeling that he did. But to Carnaby's query about likely hollows in the Chapel's outside wall, he was very definite. "It's a strange thing on the face of it," he explained, "that a house like this, possessing such amazingly thick walls even for that period, should have a comparative shell to protect the Chapel. One theory puts the blame upon Islip, who is known to have robbed Peter to pay Paul on many occasions. He certainly took a large proportion of the masonry and woodwork for his River Palace, but he left plenty of good faced stone behind. No—my notion is that the original builders found that more seating space was required for the monks than they had estimated, and so rather than widen the outside of the wall, which would have spoiled the symmetry from the courtyard, they sliced several feet away from the inside. You couldn't brick up a body in a wall barely two feet deep. In this room, though, you could brick up a cathedral chapter."

I could see, however, that Carnaby was not satisfied, and was only waiting for daylight to examine it himself.

Hoadley brought in coffee and suggested breakfast, but we all felt it was too early for that, so the inevitable happened—and our Master of the Macabre was urged to take all our minds from our lack of sleep by producing another relic from the case.

"Very well, then," says the Master. "I believe Kent favours the white moth with the broken wing. What was it you said, pathetic? No, my dear fellow, the influence of that harmless little beast gave birth to a homicidal maniac and a long succession of unsolved brutal murders.

"When I was about nineteen and was beginning to organize my eccentric hobby that was to become my life's work, into some sort of coherent system, I drew up a list of what I considered to be peculiar professions and trades, ranging from steeplejacks to stockbrokers, with the resolve that just as soon as possible I would make myself acquainted with at least one member of each calling, in the hopes that I might collect some stories that were unusual. I mention this because in looking over that old list I find included— Keeper of Lunatic Asylum. This item I had marked with a star as being very hopeful.

"It was in Westmorland that I succeeded in making this necessary acquaintance. I was staying with cousins for my summer holiday, and through them I contacted a Doctor Godden, who was not only a well-known psycho-analyst, but was the resident consulting principal of a mental home, situated in a thickly wooded estate opposite my cousin's house.

"He was a stocky little man of fifty-eight, with bushy black eyebrows and mass of grey hair which he wore very long, because he hated going to the barber's. A strong face, but kindly when he smiled. You couldn't help liking him, though when he got irritable he was rather alarming. Perhaps that was his only fault—irritability. He hated stupid people, and sometimes I thought it a pity that he couldn't take a rest cure in his own establishment. In many cases he was as mad as his patients. He had a passion for old melodramas of the blood and thunder type, and kept a large bookcase full of them. These he loved to read to people, which he would do with great gusto when lucky enough to find anyone willing to listen, and that was how I came into his picture. I became his voluntary victim, incidentally picking up many an interesting yarn about lunatics he had treated. Every evening after dinner I would go in for a chat, which always terminated with some thrilling five-act drama. But I quite enjoyed watching the old boy 'tearing a passion to tatters,' and twirling an imaginary moustache to plant the reading of the Heavy Man.

"There was a sort of tame Hoadley about the place, called Robertson, who used to beat very hasty retreats from the study when he saw a play-book in his master's hand, and he never interrupted unless there was the most urgent reason. That was an unwritten law.

"Upon the evening which was to end with that poor old butler's sudden death, Doctor Godden was in one of his most enthusiastic moods.

"'Great treat for you to-night, Charles, my boy,' he cried, as I was shown in by Robertson. 'An absolute corker from the top shelf which I've never read to you. "Simon Lee," or "The Vicissitudes of a Serving Maid." I warn you we shall be bathed in tears at the last scene. If you interrupt us, Robertson, you shall share the scaffold with poor Simon.'

"'Simon, sir?' asked the bewildered old man. 'Do I know him?'

"'You will, if you disturb me,' replied the Doctor sharply. Which unspeakable crime Robertson committed at about half-past ten, just when his master was well embarked on the last act.

He came creeping in, holding out a silver tray with a visiting card on it.

"With a yowl of agony, which the butler took to be genuine, Godden picked up the card and glanced at it, then flung it back on the tray.

"'What on earth are you about, Robertson?' he cried testily. 'I have never heard of Nathaniel Skinner.'

"'So I understand, sir, but the young man says you will see him.'

"'Nonsense. Find out his business. If important—ten sharp to-morrow morning—and add—the fee will be two guineas a minute. That'll teach him to interrupt Simon Lee. And here's another interruption. I'm reading this play from a spare copy. You must have mine, Charles. The end leaves haven't been cut. Pass me the paper-knife, will you?'

"Robertson left the room to find out the visitor's business and I handed Godden the knife from his desk. It was a real dagger with a very sharp blade. Godden began to cut the leaves, saying irritably, 'Nathaniel Skinner, indeed—of course I shan't see him.'

"'Oh, yes, you will.'

"We both turned towards the door, and saw the young man who spoke in a high staccato voice.

"The Doctor raised his bushy eyebrows and said in a reproving tone, 'Really!'

"'And you need not worry about money for your fees and my keep,' went on the queer figure. He was an albino of, say, twenty-five—very thin-faced—and one of his red eyes had a cast in it. 'I have plenty of money, for all my relations are now dead, and each one left me better off. Now, I come to you, Doctor Godden, because you are the Principal of this mental home, and what is a mental home? Merely a polite modern term for what used to be called honestly—a madhouse. Now you have got to be as honest with me as I am with you—for it is essential that I should be placed in a madhouse without delay. No time like the present, eh?'

"'You consider yourself to be insane?' asked the bewildered Godden, for only the previous evening he had told me that real lunatics always imagined they were sane.

"'To-night? Yes. But unless you lock me up at once I shall be worse than insane. I shall be——' He broke off to chuckle. 'I shall be following my fate, doing my proper job and being—oh, a genius at it. You'll hear and read about me then, I can tell you. Now, are you going to lock me up? I cannot be honest with you for long.'

"I could see that Doctor Godden was forgetting Simon Lee, because his professional interest was caught. He motioned the visitor to take one of the easy chairs. But Skinner shook his head and brought an upright one from just inside the door to the side of the desk. Here he sat—stiff as a poker—hands on knees and staring straight at the Doctor. Godden offered him a cigarette.

"'I neither drink nor smoke,' was the answer.

"'Your case becomes more interesting then,' said Godden. 'I think you had better tell me all about yourself.'

"I made a gesture to go, but he stopped me by telling his patient that he could speak freely before me—that I was a young man in his confidence who was studying mental analysis under him. Well—I suppose I was really.

"Immediately the Albino plunged into a torrent of words—rapidly telling the story of his life. I will not go into the full details of this narration, for it has little to do with what followed. His earlier life was not very interesting. Let me just tell you that he was alone in the world with plenty of money—that he had tried his hand at all sorts of professions, but given them up because he felt they were not the thing for him. He finished with the words, 'Yes, sir—a failure—but not now—not since last night—not since my great discovery—if you go on long enough any one can succeed in doing anything—I succeeded last night in discovering my star—and I know now the one course to take which will lead me to success. Why then should this little thread of decency no stronger than the thread of a spider guide me to here to you who can put a stop to my doing what I want to do? I cannot answer that piece of idiocy.'

"'Perhaps I can,' returned the Doctor. 'Tell us briefly what it is you want to do.'

"Then he began that part of his history which held us, and which you must hear, and it had started only a few days before.

"'However well you may know this part of the country, gentlemen, it is more than likely that you have never heard of Golt Hollow. There is but one house there—Golt Farm. It is a forgotten place—deep down—and hidden—a mere socket—a rounded cavity into which the sun can never penetrate, for it is cupped around with rugged, formidable hills. Don't ask me why I have bought an option on such a detestable old place, which the house agent's office call an "Ancient and desirable residence." My only satisfaction is that I can now make the agents suffer—unless, of course, you think otherwise. As to ever setting foot upon my property again, why—I would rather do—well—almost anything. Suppose you had the power to take me back, shall I tell you what I would do? I would stab you to the heart with this paper-knife,' and his fingers closed round the handle of the dagger which lay before him on the desk. 'But you wouldn't take me back—not when I tell you why Golt Farm is so abominable. At first sight of it, I said to myself, "This house is charged from cellars to garrets with some loathsome influence, the poisonous vapours of which ooze into every room and down all those innumerable passages." There you get the mental effect it had on me. Now let me try to tell you some of the physical causes which nourished and fed those germs of fear that I had developed into my system at the first unlocking of the front door. To begin with—the grounds that surrounded it—if the extensive garden had ever been cared for, it must have been centuries ago—for there was not one pretty thing—no—not so much as a wild flower to relieve the abominable ugliness of that weedy entanglement of dank undergrowth.

" 'Over the sometime flower-beds lopped the most unhealthy vegetation—vegetation of the most pestilential order, the damnable corruption of which contaminated the very atmosphere which was tepidly clammy and altogether poisonous. Myriads of mosquitoes—disgusting dragon-flies and glossy slugs thrived the live-long day in that accursed garden, and when night set in, they in their turn were prey to the bat, the toad and the owl. But these did not disgust me so much as that debauched host of blowfly that crawled lazily upon the ground and gorged upon the puffy fungi accumulated within that rotten wilderness of mildewed plants.

" 'The utter abhorrence that I bore towards the grounds kept

me a compulsory prisoner within the house, where, indeed, I was
in no better plight, for the floorings and walls, especially those of
the ground floor, were overrun with the most detestable of house
vermin. Beetles scuttled everywhere—rats fed noisily upon the
dry-rot beneath the floors, and cut catacombs behind the oak panelling. I was not master in my own house—the vermin had the
whip hand of me. But let me tell you what it was that drove me to
abandon utterly the ground floor and hide myself day and night
in my bedroom. It was during the first evening that I was there,
and already suffering from a ghastly loneliness, for there were no
servants—a morose-looking woman in the pay of the agents who
had promised to come in and cook my dinners, took one look at
me and fled. She had never seen an albino before, evidently. There
was no one else I could get. The nearest village was six miles away,
over the moors. I ate chocolate and nothing else. Oh, yes—a few
biscuits—but I gave up that, as you can guess it was fatal to drop
any crumbs. They disappeared so quickly. Things would come out
for them, right under my feet. They say Hunger drives out Fear.
With them it did—but not with me. Well, I was sitting there in the
library of mildewed books, with the door ajar—for its hinges were
corroded and it would not shut—when I saw a black object run
past the door. I tried to deceive myself that it was but a shadow—
some illusion of the eye, for I was tired out with my journey and
disappointment, but I was convinced in my own mind that what
I had seen was assuredly some thief-prowling rat. I arose to shut
the door, forgetful for the moment of the faulty hinges. My hand
had barely touched the broken handle when another black object,
seemingly larger than the first, raced across the shaft of light that
shot from the room across the passage.

"'Now, whatever the first object may have been, I would have
staked my life that this was no rat. *Its run was more rhythmic—more
mechanical even than that of a rat.* A curiosity that I had every reason
to regret overpowered me. I *would* satisfy myself as to the nature
of these evil-looking, black, cadaverous creatures that made themselves so damnably at home in my house. I picked up the large oil
lamp that stood upon the library table, making up my mind to
trace these two venomous things that were running somewhere in

the passage, and destroy them, thus striking the first blow towards the purification of the pest-ridden house. I passed out of the door and took five paces down the passage, then stopped dead—for in my way lay a large bat. By the convulsive beating of one of its wings, I knew it to be alive—but upon it, assiduously gorging the unwholesome, yet quick flesh, stood three enormous spiders— black—carnivorous. I knew that England could never breed such specimens in the normal way, and my mind went back to a clumsy-looking incubator with a broken glass that I had seen on a shelf in one of the hot-houses, and I remembered something said at the agent's about a former tenant—an entomologist—who had made a moonlight flit, without paying his rent. I had noticed a book he had written on tropical spiders, which he had left behind in the library. I am convinced that these creatures were some that he had bred in that horrid machine and that they had escaped and driven him out.

"'I believe that the horror of that spectacle would have chained me to the spot for as long as that feast had lasted, but quite suddenly something happened that re-awakened all my sense of terror and caused me to rush blindly for the safety of my bedroom. Ah. You wait till you hear.

"'You see, I was standing with the lamp high above my head, with the heat consequently driving up against the ceiling, which was, as the floor and walls, overrun with vermin. I cannot say what, but something, evidently overpowered by the heat of the lamp, lost its hold and fell—horrible—fell right into the chimney of the lamp, which for a second flared up, and then with a smell of singeing, went out, leaving me in the dark amidst that moving host.

"'I shrieked once with terror, and dashing the lamp to the ground, surely upon the very spot where gorged those voracious spiders, I leapt through the darkness—a maniac. Across the hall I rushed—dashed up the old oak stairway, and as I ran, tore off my collar and tie, and last of all my smoking-jacket—for my very clothes seemed alive and repugnant to me.

"'But as soon as I had gained my room I remembered that I had placed my matches in the pocket of my smoking-jacket, and having no mind to spend the night in the dark, it was essential to recover them. However, it took me a considerable time before I could rouse up sufficient courage, but at last I set out, groping my way to the head of the stairs.

"'Down I went—stair by stair, stepping heavily in order to scare away the vermin. I was nearing the bottom when my foot-step sounded muffled. I had trodden upon the coat, for I heard the rattle of the match-box. As I stooped to pick it up, something ran over my hand. I kicked out in terror, and in so doing, crunched the match-box, which with a smell of sulphur, spluttered flame, and in a second I realized the jacket was on fire. I kicked it clear of the oak stairs into the centre of the hall flag-stones, and ran upstairs to get a jug of water. When I returned to the banisters the flames were leaping high, and by this weird light I could see all manner of dark creatures scuttling away into the shadows. I was about to empty the water-jug on the flames when I remembered my bed-room candle. I got it from my room, rushed down the stairs, and lit it from the fire. At least I should not now have to pass the night in the dark.

"'When I had deposited this precious light within my room, I emptied carefully the ewer of water upon the now smoulder-ing coat, and then returned towards my room, but as I passed the head of the stairs I heard the pattering of innumerable feet below, and I knew that the boldest of the creatures were investigating the remains of my jacket.

"'Now in one respect the agents had acted fairly. They had carried out to the letter the decorations I had ordered for my bedroom. White furniture from London. White linoleum. Every-thing white and shining. Not a crack or blemish anywhere. How thankful I was for this fastidiousness, I need hardly say. A white enamelled oil stove too, with a kettle. The casements were new and close fitting, so I knew that despite the moths' continual tat-tooing upon the panes, they could not effect an entrance, which so pleased me that I went close to the window and made jeering faces at the brutes, just as though they would understand. Perhaps they did, for they butted away with renewed energy and a bat came to join their flutterings.

" 'I pulled the casement curtains close and laughed.

" 'Indeed—I tried not to stop laughing, for when I did, I found myself listening to the hellish noises that came from the house. And then without warning and from beneath the door, there sprang into the room a great white moth.

" 'I leapt from the bed—dragged off the counterpane with an oath, and blocked the bottom of the door, for, you see, my first instinct was to prevent other and viler creatures from entering by the same breach.

" 'The moth settled at the base of my candlestick—and I at once perceived that it was too big to catch beneath my tooth glass. Besides, nothing on earth would make me open either the door or window, and I did not intend to have anything living in my room, my fortress, during the night. And now, Doctor Godden—listen well—that you may be able to make up your mind the quicker.

" 'There suddenly came over me a damnable delight—and you must guess what it was. Why—the lust for killing—an impulse stronger than fear. Yes—I had only now the lust for blood. Were that delicate white moth, matching the whiteness of the room, to have been turned into a human being, it would still have made no difference. I would have killed just the same, for never in my life had I felt such a diabolical enthusiasm, such a glow of cunning anticipation, as when I knotted my face-towel at the end and said calmly, "You shall die for this, you fool."

" 'And now Doctor Godden, you know my trouble. Now you can see for yourself what my vocation in the world is. For, as I struck that sideways whistling blow with the towel—as I heard the feeble fluttered thud upon the linoleum, I knew that I was a dis-ciple of Cain—a life-taker.

" 'All that night and for the long nights and days to come, my mind ran havoc. I drafted out a programme of blood. Diabolical crimes—despicable orgies. Yes—I had found my profession. So by the way I used to look at things, isn't it expedient that you should put me away? What is your decision?'

"Somehow the weakness in his peculiar face had given place to a fierce determination, and thinking that here was a very ugly young

man to be reckoned with, I was the more surprised at Doctor Godden's summing-up.

"'My dear Nathaniel Skinner,' he said kindly, 'I have an objection to people wasting their money—especially young people. My
rooms here, as it happens, are all full, and with the best will in the
world I could not take in another patient, and there will be no
vacancy for over a month. But even had I room to spare, I should
not persuade you to take it, because I dislike the money-making
side of my profession, and do my best to avoid excessive profit. Oh,
I am not saying that I couldn't treat you so that you would be more
than satisfied. But a home of this class is naturally more expensive
than the best hotel. I have to cater for a large and experienced staff,
and the likes and dislikes of my patients are often embarrassing.
I have King John of England staying here at the moment. He is
really an auctioneer, but he flies into most kingly rages if lampreys
and peaches are not served at every meal, and his Sunday joint
must always be a peacock. Well—he has to be humoured, since
bad tempers are bad for his very high blood-pressure. But there
is no need to humour you at all. I should be cheating you, as I do
not attach the least importance to these presentiments of yours.
My advice is—take a holiday—anywhere attractive—from place to
place would be best—stay at hotels where you will see plenty of
people, and don't buy any more bogey houses. And at the back
of your mind—without forcing it—think out seriously what you
would like to become. From your extraordinary flow of words
and powers of description, why not try writing? And don't bother
your head about tendencies and that kind of thing. I assure you
there's nothing radically wrong with your mind, if you develop
your sense of humour. Now, I see by your card,' and he picked it
up from the tray which the bewildered Robertson had left on the
table, 'that you are staying at the Hydro, and have given me that
number to ring in case I was out when you called. Well—go back
there and have a good night, which no doubt you will need after
your unpleasant stay at Golt Farm. If you feel like it come in and
see me again. Not as a consultant but a friend.'

"'Ah—yes—consultation,' replied the Albino. 'What do I owe
you for this one?'"

"'Under the circumstances—nothing at all. You've told us a good bed-time story. I should like to go and hunt up those spiders myself. There's a short cut to your hotel through my woods—only a step or two that way—but it's dark. I'll get Robertson to show you the way with his lantern. He'll be going your way to post my letters, while Mr. Hogarth hare takes the opposite direction. Good night, Nathaniel Skinner.'

"Well, I was for home, too, and not in the mood for any more last act of Simon Lee, which we agreed to tackle the next night, for I was grateful to the Doctor for letting me stay to hear such a peculiar story. I stayed for a minute or so, chatting to the Doctor at his front door. He was going back to the study to cut the pages of a new volume received that day from his London booksellers—it was entitled, *Adelphi Dramas*, which as he said, promised him a real treat. So I left him just as the last swing of Robertson's lantern disappeared into the darkness of the woods. And now comes a curious part of the story which will interest you, my dear Kent. You remember two concurrences of events which heralded your arrival here the other day. Every night for a whole month you were summoned in your dreams by two—shall we call them *ghosts*? And although they were not able to convey to you exactly what they wanted you to do for them, they did compel you to drive towards the coast. On the road they succeeded in commanding the powerful elements of storm to arrest your passage violently at the nearest spot on the high road to this house, where they are earthbound. At the same time they had been warning me, through the same medium of dreams, to expect you, and to give you stranger's welcome at these gates. I even knew that there would be an accident, and that you would need crutches. I was so certain of your subsequent arrival that I spent the best part of a day putting that deck-chair you are using on to hospital wheels.

"The easiest way of explaining all this is to accept the fact that there are such things as *ghosts*. So was it in this case of Doctor Godden. In less than an hour after watching Robertson's lantern light, I was sound asleep at my cousins'. And I had a vivid dream. I was back in Godden's study. He didn't know I was there. He was reading *Adelphi Dramas*. As he tried to turn over a page, he found that it was uncut. He stretched out his hand for the dagger paper-knife, and found it wasn't there. He got up and walked about the room looking for it. It was obvious that he couldn't see me. I was invisible. But I had the power to know exactly what he was thinking. He remembered like I did that Nathaniel Skinner had picked it up during his recital, and must have absent-mindedly put it in his overcoat pocket. Godden felt irritated. That knife had for years been one of his household gods. He comforted himself with the thought that the Albino would either return it personally or put it in the post. He became more irritated when it dawned upon him that he would have to go and borrow a knife from the pantry because he was very careful over his books and wanted a sharp knife. He rang the bell in case Robertson had not gone to bed. Then he remembered that he had not heard the old butler come back. He glanced at the clock. It was half-past eleven. 'Nonsense,' thought he, 'I was so engrossed in my book that I didn't hear him.'

"But it was always Robertson's custom to bid his master good night before retiring. 'The old boy's in a huff, because I flashed out at him. He's gone to bed in the sulks. I'll make it all right in the morning.' Then he went to the pantry and found a steel knife, but instead of settling down to read in his study arm-chair, he decided to take knife and book up to bed.

"The next thing in my dream I was standing outside the study in the dark hall, when there came a violent knocking at the front door. This went on—louder and louder, till the staircase lights were switched on and a very irritated Doctor Godden came hurrying down in his dressing-gown.

"He was thinking—'If this row goes on, I shall have all the patients awake.' He opened the front door. It was the Albino. 'Can't keep away, you see,' he said, smiling, as he brushed past the Doctor and took his stand by the light switch.

"'I suppose you've come to return my paper-knife,' said the Doctor. 'You could have waited till the morning.'

"'I'm not waiting,' was the answer. 'I'm going away.'

"'Well, there's a post, at least——' protested the Doctor.

"'Post?' queried the Albino mildly. 'We shouldn't send ugly things through the post.'

"'Oh—give me the knife and be off,' demanded the Doctor in a growing fury.

"'Seen Robertson?' asked the other. 'If so, how do you think he's looking?'

"'Robertson?' repeated the Doctor. 'Asleep, I suppose.'

"'Suppose? Hadn't you better find out?'

"'What do you mean?'

"'I have come to the conclusion that your judgment is not very sound, Doctor Godden. You made the last mistake of your life when you sent me away from this madhouse.'

"'For heaven's sake—go,' cried the Doctor. 'Come along, give me the knife!'

"'Certainly. With great delight.' And the Albino switched off the light and in the darkness I heard a gasp.

"In the dark I followed him as he closed the front door behind him. He strode through the wood, chuckling aloud, 'Two in one night—and with a paper-knife. I have found my profession.'

"Suddenly he turned at right angles—left the beaten track and plunged into the undergrowth, and I knew he was not returning to the Hydro. Then I saw the light of a lantern. I hurried towards it and found it was a death-candle burning by the side of Robertson's blood-soaked body.

"I stared at the candle to avoid the look in the old man's eyes, and presently the candle began to move towards me, and my shoulder was gripped by strong fingers.

"I awoke with a cry and found it was the local sergeant of police holding a candle in one hand and shaking me with the other. Behind him in the shadows, wrapped in dressing-gowns, stood the full complement of grown-up cousins. It was only four o'clock, but the double murder was already discovered, owing to the screams of one of the patients.

"They did not have to tell me what had happened—for I had seen it in my dream. But I had plenty to tell them, for with the exception of the murderer, I was the last to see the unfortunate victims alive.

"Nathaniel Skinner had never returned to the Hydro. He had gone—no one knew where—and left his luggage behind. But as principal witness I was with the police when they motored to Golt Hollow, where we found the farm just as he had described it, even to the incubator.

"We saw no spiders there—I mean, no monsters as he had seen—but in the hall, close to a burnt-out jacket on the flagstones, lay the decapitated body of a cat, still bleeding, which the police said must have been the recent work of rats. But I knew better, for certainly on the table in the library was the book on tropical spiders, and I knew the Albino had told Doctor Godden the hideous truth.

"There was the bedroom too—all white, and as the police did not attach any importance to the little body of a white moth with a broken wing, I slipped it into an empty match-box. And there it is. The police never caught Nathaniel Skinner, though he was wanted for seven other brutal murders, including the death by stabbing of the agent who had the letting of the Golt Hollow property. Neither did they find the dagger. Both man and weapon disappeared completely. A long time ago—that series of unsolved crimes."

"Any comments?" added Hogarth after a long pause.

"Yes——" said Carnaby with a grim smile. "I think it was damned lucky for you that your cousins' house was in the opposite direction to the Hydro, or you would have copped it instead of Robertson."

Hogarth nodded. "I shouldn't have liked you to read on my tombstone—*Murdered by an Albino*. Curious people, Albinos. Not normal, of course. Generally rather simple—weak-minded—though I met one the last time I was in America who bore the strongest character. He was a preacher. Oh, a great orator. I heard of him in Pasadena, and went on a pilgrimage to his village in the mountains. He ran a church there for a community of Albinos. He had a following of some hundreds from all parts of the States. Did no end of good. I stayed at his house for a few days, and I can honestly say that in him I met one of the holiest men I have ever known. His sermons too were inspired. They all worshipped him—and I don't wonder. We had many an interesting talk. I remember one discussion on dreams, in which he confessed that when he was overworked he often suffered from the same nightmare—that he was looking down from a staircase into an old stone-paved hall, and in the centre of it was a fire round which ran huge black spiders. He asked me if I could interpret such a curious dream, and I told him 'No.' On parting, he said he would like to make me a present as a memento of his little community. Was there any little thing I would like to take with me? Well, I just picked up a paper-knife from his desk and said I would value it very much. He was delighted. It's lying in the specimen case there now. Next to the moth. You see, I had recognized it as Doctor Godden's dagger. That's all."

"And he was *the* Albino?" I asked.

"And you didn't tell the police?" echoed Carnaby.

"I don't think even Doctor Godden or Robertson would have liked me to disturb the saintly atmosphere he had created amongst those happy people. He had suffered much with some nervous malady, and when he recovered he tried to help others, and certainly succeeded. He had found the work he was fitted for and was utterly unconscious of ever having committed the smallest unkindness to any human creature. Oh, yes—he is a well-beloved man. Known everywhere as the White Prophet. No one calls him by his proper name—Nat Tanner. And it's odd, isn't it, that a tanner is a sort of skinner?"

Carnaby nodded as he examined the dagger. "You are quite right, Hogarth," he said. "Even the policeman in me agrees that you could only have acted as you did."

Then Hoadley came in and announced that breakfast was served in the morning-room.

CHAPTER FOURTEEN

"LET ME OUT! LET ME OUT!"

DURING breakfast I asked Carnaby what was going to happen to the Indians, whom I could see cooking at their camp-fire.

"Don't worry about them," he said casually. "They'll hang about for a bit after what I told them, just in case they get a communication from their Holy Man, which by Jove, they are going to get to-night. But I'll pop over and speak to them after breakfast. Or rather Nicholas Ramsbottom will. Then I am going to solve the mystery of the silk skirt in the Chapel. You two crocks can come and sit there and watch me at work."

It was certainly droll to watch him with the Indians. We watched him from the window, crossing the snow-covered field, with his scholarly stoop very marked, especially when climbing over the fence. He appeared to talk for about a quarter of an hour, and then came shuffling back, followed by the respectful salaams of the Hillmen.

"That's all right," he said. "They will wait till to-morrow before striking camp. And now for the Chapel."

Although Hoadley had banked up a great fire, we both sat with rugs over our knees, as Carnaby insisted on keeping a window open so that he could slip outside every few minutes. He was busy measuring with a carpenter's rule. But he was very thorough, for whenever he was outside he stooped in case the Indians were watching. Soon I found myself getting very sleepy. The heat of the fire and the glare of the sun on the snow, combined with our night's vigil, quite overcame me, and I was fast asleep; and once more I saw quite plainly the huge frame of the monk with the tiny head. He was listening at the wall opposite to me, and as he listened he was grinning in a most devilish manner. And I knew what he was listening to. It was her voice. The beautiful girl's voice, calling desperately from inside the wall, "Let me out!" Over and over again she called, and I knew then what had happened. He had bricked her up alive. In my rage I sprang forward, crying out, only to find what a fool I was, for it was not the monk but Carnaby who stood listening at the wall opposite.

"Hello, old chap," he said. "Not nightmares in the sunshine. That's all wrong."

"It's not," I answered. "I know now why they've haunted me. She's there—in the wall."

Carnaby whispered back. "I believe you're right. And you're right too, Hogarth. The wall is too thin to hide a skeleton, but you've forgotten something. Exactly outside here is the buttress which supports the wall. I've examined the ivy outside which covers it, and with the help of a saw which I found in the tool-shed, I've uncovered a little hole, just big enough for a hand to go through. It's a hollow buttress, Hogarth, and we're going to disfigure this beautiful plastering in the cause of historical research. I'll respect the carpet. I'll get Hoadley's help with dust-sheets and a pick." Between them he and Hoadley made quick work of it. They spread dust-sheets and then Carnaby cracked the plaster with a blow and began chipping it away with an entrenching tool. Once he stopped and said, "Listen."

Yes—there was a noise that we had heard before. *It was like the rustling of silk.* "But it's not silk," said Carnaby, "it's dead leaves stirred by the breeze that comes through the little cavity outside."

Then he lifted the pickaxe and attacked the wall. Very soon he had dislodged some of the big stones, and we could see through the dust that rose about him, a hollow formed by the buttress. He worked feverishly—till his heavy blows weakened the inserted wall, and with a crash down it came into a rubbled heap. And as the dust cloud cleared we saw a skeleton swaying towards us. It fell—and down the rubble heap there rolled a tiny skull. Carnaby alone appeared to take no notice of it. He was lying on the piled-up stones peering into the hole. Then in a choked voice of triumph he cried out, "God."

We saw his arm stretch down into the hole, and then he scrambled to his feet, swaying and stumbling, as he tried to stand upright amidst the ruin. "It's true, you chaps. It's true." And over his head we saw something flashing in the sunlight, and heard him say in a hysterical giggle, "It's the cup—Mahomet's cup—his stirrup-cup. The whole blarsted thing is true. We've worked it to a finish."

I can hardly remember what followed, except that we all went mad. I saw Carnaby and Hoadley clutching each other in a sort of war-dance, while Hogarth was conducting them like a jazz band leader with a trenching tool in his hand, but between each gesture crying out that his cursed neuritis was giving him hell. For my part, I had fallen off my chair and was holding tenderly the poor skull of the lovely woman of my dreams. It was all that was left of her. The bones had crumbled into dust. Then we were all huddled in a circle on the floor, gazing at the stirrup-cup.

Carnaby recovered first and sent Hoadley to the cellar for the best bottle of anything he could find, and before long we were passing the cup round and drinking from it. At last Hogarth took command, and told Hoadley to brush himself and fetch the Rector and the Doctor, and at last we had left and locked the Chapel, with the curtains drawn tight, and were met in conference round the Library table, with the wonderful cup locked up in Hogarth's safe.

For the rest of that day—well, I know we had meals and I know we slept, and that the Doctor and the Rector neglected their duties to be with us in all our consultations. We all agreed, however, that for the present we would keep the whole thing to ourselves, until we decided on the right course to take, for there was no doubt as to the value of our find.

I know we were all calm enough at nightfall when Carnaby set off to deal with his Indians. He was very mysterious about it, and a very long time away too. We began to be anxious about him, though his orders had been to stay put, till his return. We were anxious, too, about something else. He had insisted on taking the precious cup with him, wrapped up in his Indian clothes. We felt, however, that whatever he did would be right and wise, and so it proved.

At last through the open window facing the church we heard the strains of his voice. He was intoning from the top of the tower, but we couldn't see anything. It was too dark. I don't know how long we waited. Close on an hour it must have been—before a surprising thing happened. The side of the tower was suddenly illuminated, as though in a flood-light.

Hogarth whispered, "That's nothing to do with Carnaby. It's the lights of a powerful car that has pulled up on the hill by the Bull Hotel."

Then we saw something white climbing down the face of the tower, and we realized it was our agile Carnaby. We could see his whole passage down the side till the trees hid him. Now the lights of the Library where we stood were out, so that we could see better, and presently we made out four tall figures on the top of

the tower with their arms in supplication to the sky. Then someone turned out the lights of the car and we could see nothing. But
we heard a chuckling behind us and turning saw a ghostly figure
appear in the darkness. It was Carnaby dressed as the Holy Man,
in beard and turban, and an uncanny light played upon the rich
jewels of the stirrup-cup he held in his right hand.

"Convincing, eh?" he laughed. Then he disappeared. For a few
seconds there was darkness, then the room was lighted up, and we
saw him standing by the switches.

"I'd like to throttle the owners of that damned car," he said. "I
thought they would debunk my miracle. But all's well. Our Indians will be off at sunrise. You see, they had taken the advice of
Nicholas Ramsbottom, and had gone to pray in the belfry. Then
they heard the muezzin, which differed a bit from the orthodox
one, because I was up there first and I called them to me by name.
They didn't know that the unearthly illumination about me was a
torch. All they could see was their Holy Man holding the cup, and
I told them not to covet it as the Prophet had need of it in Heaven,
and had sent me to show it as a sign that I was now his cup-bearer.
They swallowed it and grovelled as I bade them farewell. Then I
vanished. In other words—I turned off the torch. In a split second
I was over the ledge of the tower and had begun my get-away, a
very perilous journey, especially when those lights blazed at me.
It's all right, Rector. I'll go up again later and put things tidy. You
see, I had pulled up one of the bell-ropes, and dropped it through
the sounding slats of the bell-chamber. It took me within a foot
or two of the ground. Now, my good Hoadley," he went on as he
removed his beard and turban, "I suggest drink, then dinner. After
which, in order to dispel the memories of this nightmarish day,
our good host shall tell us one of his jolliest little horrors."

"Well, you've certainly the right to command here," says Hogarth, and I believe a merrier party had never assembled even in the
days of its glory, as that historic palace saw that night.

When we were once more settled in the Library, and Hogarth
was pressed for his story, he insisted on choosing his own subject.

"We have had a historic day," he said. "Very well then, I will
close it with a historic tale of the medieval times," and he lifted

from the specimen case the cushion with the handsome key upon it. Then he began.

CHAPTER FIFTEEN

A DODGE OF DEATH AND THE END

"I AM only going to make one reservation in telling you this fragment of medieval history; and that is that I must not divulge the name of the town where it happened, nor, for the same reason, that of the village on the hill outside it. Both these places I must re-christen, for that was the bargain I had to make with the town clerk ten years ago, before he would let me walk off with this relic—the ancient key of the town gate.

"A crafty old fellow he was. Wouldn't take a tip—oh, no—but he certainly encouraged me to leave a bundle of notes behind me on the table, for he was awkwardly in debt, and cared for nothing but to clear himself.

"Well—he was quite satisfied, poor devil, and so indeed was I, wanting this key for my collection. I admit I was conniving in a civil theft, but as he put it, 'Who is going to miss an old key that now has no lock in which to fit it?'

"Imagine, then, this fair town of—Grizzelstein, I'll call it—a rich gem set in Central Europe, and visualize a sunny morning upon a market day. But I want you to observe that there are no tradings taking place in the crowded market square. No—the people are only busy—whispering—whispering rumours of news beyond the walls, such as——

"'There is no doubt about it, Gossip, that another city has fallen to this plundering Outlaw. He has utterly destroyed it—cathedral and all—for he has no respect for religion. Ours is the next city on his line of march. Ours is the next.'

"The Mayor hastily summoned his confederates to the Council Hall.

"'Gentlemen,' he said, addressing his eight aldermen, 'we are an independent city, and in the present crisis we cannot look for any succour from neighbouring states. We have no standing army. The few men who could fight seem to have lost all heart since our Prince played the traitor, and left us in the lurch. His cowardice, as you know, has demoralized the guard, and the one cry of the city seems to be that we should sue for peace and escape with our lives. I very much doubt whether we shall even succeed in doing that, for this Outlaw is a bloody-minded scoundrel, and has shown no quarter up to the present. However, we must do the best we can, which is very little short of suicide.' And the fat little Mayor sighed, for he had been very happy as a mayor.

"All that day terrified villagers hastened into the town for safety and spread the panic. They told of the mighty army of robbers that was now but a few hours' march away, and they spoke of the rumoured blood path that was left behind them, and rehearsed the horrors that would soon be theirs. And with one voice the population cursed the Prince, for although he had ruled them during the days of peace with a wise and tactful hand, yet as soon as he perceived his city to be in the conqueror's march he had turned and fled, God knew whither. That afternoon the advancing army surrounded the town, and the conquering Outlaw chose for himself as headquarters the church of the village of Hanech. This village was on high ground, and from the tower of the church the conqueror could get a bird's-eye view of Grizzelstein, and make his plans accordingly.

"Towards sunset, amidst the chanting of the priests and nuns, the little Mayor walked forth, followed by his faithful, frightened aldermen. The Lady Abbess, who was of royal blood, being the only sister of the cowardly Prince, stood at the city gate and blessed them as they went.

"The Outlaw was watching from the tower. He and his staff were enjoying the joke immensely. The Mayor and aldermen arrived. (How ridiculous they did look in their sackcloth robes, with their chains of office in their hands.) The Mayor himself was holding the key of the city gate.

"They were ushered into the crypt of the church and locked in. There they waited, fearing the worst. Their reception was not encouraging. All that evening there was the greatest consternation in Grizzelstein, for the suppliants did not return. The priests accordingly chanted in the monastery; the nuns prayed in the convent, and the people blasphemed in the streets. What had happened to the Mayor and aldermen? Nobody knew. The men gathered in knots on the town wall and looked across at the mysterious tower of Hanech. Night set in, and camp-fires were lighted by the invaders, and a great brazier was lighted upon the tower of Hanech church. The night was so still that the crackle of these fires could be heard from the town wall.

"At about ten o'clock the faint boom of the tenor bell was heard from the tower. This was followed by another and another, until all eight bells had sent across the valley one single feeble toll. What was the meaning of this? Why did they toll each bell? Was it for some purpose? Perhaps it was some drunken soldier's idea of fun. This was the conversation of the men upon the Grizzelstein wall. And then they saw soldiers moving on the tower, and the sound of sawing came to them; the soldiers were sawing the flag-post down. It was down. And now they were thrusting it through the battlements and making it fast with ropes. And then, in the light of the burning brazier, the terrified townsmen read the answer to their supplications for peace. For the Mayor was hanged from the flag-post—hanged in sight of the town. A dozen soldiers held torches in case the flickering brazier did not give sufficient light. There was no mistaking it—the Mayor was swinging from the flag-post—swinging from the tower of Hanech, and it meant no quarter in the morning to the town. And where were the aldermen—the eight aldermen? Had not the eight bells tolled? One bell for each man—and has not every bell a rope to pull it by? Very well, then—it is all quite simple—eight bells for eight aldermen, and the flag-pole for the Mayor. The aldermen were accounted for—they were all in the belfry ringing-room, hanging in a very neat circle in the centre of the old chamber. The conqueror enjoyed the joke as much as his boisterous soldiers, but no more than the townspeople shuddered at it.

"When the novelty of the Mayor's situation had somewhat worn off, the soldiers left the top of the tower to sleep in the church below, or in the shelter of the tombstones. Pickets were

placed, but they would not be troubled, for Grizzelstein men were
not soldiers; they were just frightened sheep, and they were waiting for the slaughter-men upon the morrow. The Outlaw himself
sat at a table in the ringing-room. On the table he had spread out
his battle plans for the morrow, and around him hung that grisly
circle of aldermen from the bell-ropes. But he was not the sort of
man to be frightened by dead men; he had seen corpses enough
in his day, and had made them too—made them with his sword,
his dagger, his bare hands, and even with his brains—for he could
devise most original tortures, could this conquering robber.

"So there he sat, and there they hung, and little did they trouble
him. And outside the window hung the Mayor, motionless, perfectly motionless, for the night was so very still that nothing dead
could possibly be stirred by the wind; and the pale moonlight,
shining straight through the arched belfry window, silhouetted the
dangling body on the belfry floor. So there he sat with the eight
bona fide corpses and the shadow of another in the very room in
which he worried out his battle plans, having given orders that no
man was to be admitted to the tower.

"About midnight he was sorely irritated, for, not content with
his very precise reply to the town's supplication for peace, out had
come the Lady Abbess to plead for the city's safety. True, he had
granted her an audience, for he had heard that some of these nuns
were devilish fine-looking dames, women who had taken the veil
through disappointment of the very thing they had now sworn to
avoid. But in this case the Outlaw was doomed to disappointment.
Her beauty was not of this world—it made him feel uneasy, and he
just sat silent while she pleaded for her people's lives. She offered
him all the wealth of the convent—the jewels even from the sacred
hangings of the chapel—the plate—the books—aye, everything
of value he could have—but let him keep his men in check, and
not defile the women, for the townsmen were very few and weak,
and they would offer no resistance—they would only curse the
memory of the Prince, her brother, who had turned coward and
left them.

"Now the very daring of the woman, and the fact that he was
afraid of her, irritated the Outlaw still more, and so he summoned

an officer and delivered the Abbess into his hands. 'Take this woman down into the church—give her to my soldiers—a generous present from their chief, for I can find no use for her. Perhaps they can.'

"A few minutes later a derisive shout came from the church below, followed by the agonized scream of a woman.

"'So,' thought the Outlaw, 'she's a woman after all. There's something that will make her scream,' and he laughed and went on with his plans.

"Then the shadow of the Mayor upon the floor began to move. His irritation returned. It was ridiculous. He was giving way to fancies—absurd fancies. There was not one breath of air stirring without—the body could not have moved! But it had—for it moved again—it moved with a convulsive twitch! Could it have been an owl or a bat that had flapped against it and caused it to swing? He got up from his work, dividing the curtain of dead aldermen, and strode to the window. He was not frightened—good lord—no. But he didn't like things that he couldn't understand; that was why he had delivered the woman to his soldiers: he couldn't understand her, otherwise he might have kept her for himself. He now rather wished he had.

"He looked out of the window. The body was hanging perfectly still. A bat was clinging to its hair. It moved downwards and finally tucked itself away behind the dead man's ear. Then a great wet moth crept from the corpse's open mouth and flew into the belfry—striking against the Outlaw's face—and then, attracted by the light upon the table, flew in large circles in and out among the hanging aldermen. Indeed, the night seemed now alive with moths. The Outlaw hadn't noticed them before. Two large ones lay singed and twitching on his battle plan—and then, a bat dropped from the rafter and crawled upon the table, frightened at the light. The Outlaw brushed them from his map and set to work again—but once more the silhouetted body on the floor began to move. The Outlaw took his heavy cloak and hung it over the window, blocking out a great portion of the moonlight from the floor. He then got to work in earnest. He forgot the woman's muffled shrieks and moans in the church below—he paid no heed to the careering circus of insects chased by the bats and banging past the bodies. He was absorbed in his work—his mighty battle plan.

"He had sacked a score of cities in his time, but Grizzelstein appealed to him tremendously. It would be highly entertaining to unlock the gates of the city and just walk in to butcher all the people. Still, it was never his way to be too sanguine. Desperation, he well knew, will often make weak cowards put up a brave and soldierly fight, so it was as well to draw up plans in case of accident. And so with his mind he worked, and with his subconscious mind he listened to the distant laughter of his men and the moaning of the Abbess he had given them. Then his subconscious mind began to hear another thing—a noise of a swinging rope, and grating of the flag-post in the bell-chamber overhead. Yet there was no sound of a wind. The rushlight on the table burned quite steadily, although there were two great arched windows open to the night. The grating noise increased. It continued to increase. Mechanically he stopped his work. It sounded as if the body outside was swinging! Yes! It certainly sounded like it, and looked like it too, for although the cloak of the Outlaw hid the body of the Mayor from the moonlight path upon the floor, the rope was still visible—and the rope was moving backwards and forwards with a tremendous rhythmic swing. With an oath the Outlaw leapt to his feet, and at the same instant a black shadow struck the cloak on the window. Simultaneously, with the noise of a snapping rope, the cloak was torn from the nails and folded itself round the shape that had shot in through the window. The Outlaw looked out—the rope was still hanging, but it was empty—the *body of the Mayor was in the room!!* He tried to call out, but he couldn't. He seemed to have lost his voice. He was petrified with terror. Think of it! The great soldier was terrified. The figure in the cloak rose from the floor. The Outlaw's sword was leaning against the wall. The figure took this in its thin, claw-like hand and dropped it through the window. It fell into the churchyard on the grass. It made no noise. Then the figure shot the bolts of the tower door. It removed the cloak from its head and came through the circle of dead aldermen.

"The Outlaw stepped back till the table was between them,

and looked with horror at the awful face that confronted him. He would not have believed that hanging could have made a face so entirely abominable. The head was puffed and swollen and the neck so thin and feeble that it seemed unable to bear its weight, for the flabby face lolled about from side to side, as if twitched back and forward by some strong vibrating nerve. He could see no resemblance to the Mayor whom he had hanged after sunset, but perhaps that was because the nose was eaten away.

"The creature indicated the hanging bodies, and said in a voice that began low, but cracked into a treble continuously: 'So you have hanged my poor aldermen!'

"The Outlaw's voice returned. He despised fools, and this little Mayor, though excessively horrible to look upon, was a fool.

"'You know that I did. You saw it done!'

"'You are labouring under a slight delusion,' replied the creature. 'You are taking me for somebody else.'

"'I am doing nothing of the kind. You are the Mayor of Grizzelstein—you were unskilfully hanged—you have got off your rope, and you are going to be put back on it.'

"'The Mayor of Grizzelstein lies at the present moment broken and bespattered upon a tombstone in the churchyard below. The rope snapped as it swung, and down he went—my poor old Mayor!' And the creature gave a curious sigh. 'You had ordered that no man should disturb you, so I secreted myself on the roof and climbed down the rope.'

"'But you are the Mayor,' retorted the Outlaw. 'You must be the Mayor of Grizzelstein.'

"'I am not,' replied the creature.

"'Then who in hell's name are you?' cursed the Outlaw.

"'I am a diplomat,' squeaked the creature.

"'You're a madman—filthy—half-alive,' ejaculated the Outlaw.

"'I am the Prince of Grizzelstein,' replied the figure.

"'The Prince of Grizzelstein?' cried the Outlaw.

"'Yes,' said the figure.

"'And what do you want with me?' asked the bewildered soldier.

"'I want to play a game of catch with you—a game of cat and mouse. Go on—run round!'

"And slowly round the table the little swollen-headed, pock-marked creature began to walk, and the Outlaw walked too, keeping the table between them.

"'Yes—I am the Prince of Grizzelstein,' he continued as he walked, 'not such a coward as I am made out. I am a far-seeing diplomat. I knew that my city was helpless to fight against you, and so I went away to Baden-Baden!!! Do you know why I went to Baden-Baden? Come—answer me!' All this as they walked round the table. 'Why do you think I went to Baden-Baden?'

"'I don't know,' faltered the Outlaw as he walked. 'Why did you go to Baden-Baden?'

"'I'll tell you why I went to Baden-Baden,' he said, walking faster and faster. 'But you are quite sure you want to know why I went to Baden-Baden?'

"'Yes,' said the Outlaw, getting out of breath with walking. 'Why did you?' For they were now going at a good pace, though not running—no—they were not running. 'Why did you go? I want to know why you went to Baden-Baden.'

"'Then walk a little faster, or I shall be treading on your heels, and you wouldn't like that, would you?' And the pace increased so much that they almost ran, but the creature continued to talk in that horrible piping, breaking voice. 'I knew and I know that your army would and will be quite useless without you. You are the great commander, is it not so? Eh? Yes—you command—your men are just machines—beasts without brain, egged on by you with hope of spoil and rapine. So knowing that I could not think to stop your army, I began to think of stopping you. And that is why I went to Baden-Baden. You know now, don't you?' The little diplomat was almost shrieking, for by this time they were running.

"'I don't know,' shouted the Outlaw. 'I don't see why you went to Baden-Baden.'

"Suddenly the little man stopped. The Outlaw, who was prepared for a feint of that kind, stopped too. The table was still between them. The little man stretched across it and picked up the rushlight. A moth flew from the light and settled on his face. Its wings began to beat. It clung to the horrible face creeping and fluttering up towards the piece of flesh that was the remnants of a nose. It beat with its wings in the air once more, then slithered from the man's face, and fell with a fluttered thud on to the table. It was dead.

"The Outlaw gasped. The creature laughed.

"'The moth is dead. You know now why I went to Baden-Baden. Look at my face.' And he held the naked flame against his puffed cheek and piece of nose, and there came to the nostrils of the Outlaw a loathsome smell of singeing, putrid flesh. 'My God——' cried the Outlaw. 'What hell's traffic is there in Baden-Baden?'

"'The Devil's Plague!!—the Eating Plague. It's eaten the flesh of a million men—it strikes down the weak—it strikes down the strong—it is Death—and I am Death—and I am going to catch you and kiss you!' And hurling the light in the other's face, and upsetting the table, he leaped straight at the Outlaw.

"The Outlaw dodged behind one of the bodies of the aldermen, swinging it with such force that it pushed the Prince off his feet, but he was up again and running in and out among the bodies of the men—and as he dodged the Outlaw kept swinging the bodies back, to check the advance of the little death man that was after him. Round they went—round and round—playing a game of Death's Catch, and the faster they went, the faster they swung the bodies. Sometimes the little diplomatic Prince would swing himself right round the room on the shoulders of a corpse, then let himself go in the direction of the terrified Outlaw. He shrieked for help, and begged for mercy as he dodged, but that little Thing had no mercy.

"Soldiers were already pounding on the door, but the bolts were strong, and their cries were drowned in the shrieks of the two men as they played their grim game of Catch and Dodge, round and round and in and out—cat and mouse—cat and mouse. And the aldermen swung and jolted on their ropes—and the bells rang and jangled overhead, and the bats flew round—and a screech-owl shrieked—and still the Outlaw dodged and ducked and swung the bodies at the awful thing that never gave up the game. It was mad hell in the belfry of Hanech.

"And then an awful thing happened. The moon went out. It was entirely dark. The game stopped—or rather the tactics stopped.

The Outlaw was afraid to move, for fear of betraying his where-abouts to Death. But Death knew instinctively—but he didn't move for a long time—he enjoyed torturing the Outlaw. And then the game changed. The Outlaw began creeping towards the door—but it wasn't the longing to get free that made him go—it was the longing to find that Thing in the dark and beat it to a pulp, even though it meant death to do it. So the deathly Thing waited by the door, and drawn by the unseen hands of some hideous and fascinating influence, the Outlaw came towards it.

★   ★   ★   ★   ★

"When the soldiers finally broke down the door they found the Outlaw lying dead, and over him was crooning a shape of flesh which bore small resemblance to a man. And from the hole where once a mouth had been, there came a stream of glutinous saliva.

"Then a soldier ran his sword through the thing. The horrible and unspeakable result of that thrust sent him reeling sick against the wall; and as the sword slipped from his hand with a clatter to the floor, the dawn broke over the adjacent city of Grizzelstein."

★   ★   ★   ★   ★

I think our host enjoyed the telling of that story more than all the others. Perhaps because it was of his own choosing, or because the added presence of the Rector and Doctor gave him a larger audience.

One odd effect the story had and that was concerning the Doctor. Although the Rector was more than willing to go up the tower with Carnaby, the man of science stated unblushingly that nothing on earth would make him leave the house. He intended to stay the night. Hogarth willingly agreed to this, for he was again suffering the tortures of the damned with every bone throbbing. He therefore proposed keeping his chair, with the Doctor using my deck-chair on wheels.

I was frankly exhausted, and before Carnaby returned had been put to bed in the Tapestry Room by Nurse Hoadley, who assured me I should sleep well now that the ghost was laid. But I was to find that I had by no means finished with the hateful Porfirio yet.

The moment I turned out my light he was there. I suppose I was asleep: in any case, I dreamt that he woke me, and I could see that this night he meant business. He tried to compel me to follow him, and when I wrestled against his will for hours, or so it seemed, he dragged me from my bed and down the stairs to the Chapel. I could see no heap of rubble on the floor now, and wondered whether Hoadley had cleared it away. But I saw the door that wasn't there. The same door that I had seen when I slept there. Through this he dragged me, past the courtyard and into the orchard. I counted the fruit trees as we passed them: six, seven, eight. Then I looked at him and he had gone. But from beneath my feet I heard a voice—and I knew it was his voice muffled, crying, "Let me out! Let me out!" The very words that she had used. My ankle suddenly seemed to grow strong. I had no need of crutches. I ran to the tool-shed and found the pickaxe which Carnaby had used that morning. His crowbar, too. With these I hurried back, counting the trees to guide me, though I could have found the spot by his voice which went on incessantly, "Let me out! Let me out!" Feverishly I dug with the sharp, flat edge of the pick. I had soon got down into the hard earth some three feet when the steel struck a stone. It was a large flag-stone. I cleared it of earth and then went to the cow-shed to get the lantern, so that I could examine it. When I returned I saw looking up at me Porfirio's evil face. It was carved on what I thought had been the flagstone, but was, I now could see, the heavy stone lid of a great coffin with his face carved upon it. I was about to flee when it moved and a skeleton arm appeared. My head was seized in its bony fingers, and I felt myself being dragged into that grave. I seized the ghastly wrist and wrestled with it, and then from the darkness of the grave a brilliant light leapt up and blinded me. But I clung on to the bone, and then I found it was the bedpost, and Carnaby was standing by me in his dressing-gown.

"Aren't the ghosts laid yet?" he laughed—and oh—how blessed it was to hear it. "I heard you cry out, old chap, and dashed in from Hogarth's room where I was sleeping quite peacefully. He's downstairs, you remember, in the Library. The old frightened doctor's there, too. Do you want to sleep again?"

"No," I cried. "You said, when we'd found the cup, 'We've worked it to a finish.' But we haven't. Put some clothes on quick. Here—help me with my trousers. This damned ankle—do you feel like digging—I know the spot—out in the orchard—do you know what we're going to find?"

"Not an earthly idea," he laughed. "Take it easy."

"We're going to find the top of your bath in the Chapel."

"In the Chapel?" he repeated.

"No. In the orchard. The top of the Chapel bath—the tomb. It's got his face carved on it. The dream can't go back on me this last time. It never has. Hurry."

In less than five minutes I was outside the front door on my crutches, instructing Carnaby what to do. "Pick, crowbar and a spade. I didn't have a spade, but that was a dream. A spade will be quicker. And the lantern from the cow-shed."

"I've got a strong torch. New battery I put in for the trick in the tower. Come on—you shall hold the light and I'll dig where you say. How deep?"

"Three feet, I should think."

"That's easy enough. Here, go steady. It's slippery for scratches. Don't crash on the last lap."

"What the blazes are you two doing?" cried the Doctor from the front door, which we had already left behind us. "Hogarth says, 'What's up?'"

"Going digging," I shouted back.

"Yes——" echoed Carnaby. "Tell him we're digging for the top of the bath."

We heard afterwards that the Doctor went back to the Library very scared, saying, "It's been too much for both of them. Carnaby and the tower was bad enough—but they've got bats in their belfries."

"Now, then, are we right?" asked Carnaby, ahead.

"Two trees farther on—then stop," I answered.

Then I held the torch and he began to dig.

"The only difference so far is that I can't hear his voice," I said. But he was not listening—only digging feverishly. At last I heard what I was listening for—the ring of the steel on stone. "Just the same," I cried, "you're on the stone now. Use the spade. You'll break his face with that pick."

Carnaby went carefully and in a few minutes had uncovered the top of the lid, and from a heap of earth that evil face that had haunted me so long, looked up at us with a smile.

"It's Porfirio," I said. "He's brought us to his grave."

"According to the records," said a voice behind us.

We turned and saw Hogarth leaning on the Doctor's shoulder. They had put on overcoats and followed us. "It's the top of the bath all right—the lid of his coffin which he had prepared against his death. But so the record runs: *'His death was not in the odour of sanctity, for he did much trafficking with the Devil, so that they were constrained to bury the body naked in the earth, face downward, facing fire, the worm and his master the Devil, according to the usage of Holy Church against all sorcerers and heretics. The lid of his coffin shall be placed upon him to restrain him from arising while his consecrated sarcophagos shall be used as a trough for swine-food.'"*

"By now there will be no body beneath it," said the Doctor.

But Carnaby and I held the view it would be as well to remove the lid and see if there was anything of interest underneath. How to remove such a weighty stone was the problem. Carnaby was the only one with us who had strength at the moment, and he was getting weary with continually clearing the stone.

Help, however, came from an unexpected quarter.

The four Indians had heard the noise of the digging and had crossed the field to see. Immediately Carnaby assumed the manners of Ramsbottom, and began to talk to them.

Under his direction they used the crowbar, till they had levered the stone from its earthy bed. Then Carnaby began to dig again carefully. The only thing there, was a crook, but it was firmly fixed in the ground. It needed a deep hole round it before it would give. By the time it was loosened, the bell of the Church began to toll for early service, and the Rector on his way, entered the orchard to see what they were doing.

After some minutes they drew the crook from the ground and found it was surmounting a six-foot staff of steel. The foot end of it had been sharpened like the head of a spear.

"It is his pastoral staff," said the Rector. "It was said of him that no Bishop nor Abbot could lift it other than he. As he faced the Devil with his back turned towards Heaven, they must have plunged it through his heart." He turned to Old Hoadley who had been a bewildered spectator. "Will you go to the Church and tell my curate to proceed with the service, for I think there is more need of me here." Then raising his voice he intoned the Office of Exorcism, while we stood round that grave with bowed heads listening to the Latin prayers. Afterwards, on the way into the old house, Hogarth turned to the Rector and with a surprised expression on his face, he smiled. Then he took the priest's hand in both his and patted it affectionately as he said, "The pain that has been so unbearable has gone. I feel splendidly well. And look, my limbs are all supple again."

"My dear Hogarth," said the Rector softly, "I don't think your house will be troubled further by those two poor ghosts."

*   *   *   *   *

It is now *my* turn to say, "And that's the end of the story." Indeed, I have shelved all my other work and begun to set it down. I have the house very much to myself as Carnaby has gone with Hogarth to London for consultation with the Rightful Authorities. I think the legal ownership of the stirrup-cup will be held in abeyance for many moons. In their absence, Hoadley looks after me as though nothing untoward had happened. He receives constant letters of instructions out of which we learnt that Carnaby had arranged for the Indians' passage home. As to the cup, they still think it has been returned to its rightful owner—the Prophet Himself. I look forward greatly for Hogarth's return, for he has promised to tell me more stories from his collection. But in this volume I am including only those he told between our periods of nightmares. Hoadley has just come in with pleasant drinks before my dinner. I have asked him to drink with me, and he is now raising his glass in that stately way he has. I know he is about to name a toast. I am quite right. He is.

He is saying, "Shall we drink to the Master, sir?"

And I reply, "The very toast I was about to name. To our good friend, Hoadley—the Master—the Master of the Macabre."

THE END

LAUS DEO

ALSO AVAILABLE FROM VALANCOURT BOOKS

MICHAEL ARLEN	Hell! said the Duchess
R. C. ASHBY (RUBY FERGUSON)	He Arrived at Dusk
FRANK BAKER	The Birds
CHARLES BEAUMONT	The Hunger and Other Stories
CHARLES BIRKIN	The Smell of Evil
JOHN BLACKBURN	A Scent of New-Mown Hay
	Broken Boy
	Blue Octavo
	The Flame and the Wind
	Nothing but the Night
	Bury Him Darkly
	Our Lady of Pain
	The Household Traitors
	The Face of the Lion
	A Beastly Business
	The Bad Penny
THOMAS BLACKBURN	A Clip of Steel
	The Feast of the Wolf
JACK CADY	The Well
R. CHETWYND-HAYES	The Monster Club
BASIL COPPER	The Great White Space
	Necropolis
FRANK DE FELITTA	The Entity
BARRY ENGLAND	Figures in a Landscape
RONALD FRASER	Flower Phantoms
GILLIAN FREEMAN	The Liberty Man
	The Leather Boys
	The Leader
STEPHEN GILBERT	The Landslide
	The Burnaby Experiments
	Ratman's Notebooks
STEPHEN GREGORY	The Cormorant
THOMAS HINDE	The Day the Call Came
CLAUDE HOUGHTON	I Am Jonathan Scrivener
	This Was Ivor Trent
JAMES KENNAWAY	The Mind Benders
GERALD KERSH	Fowlers End
	Nightshade and Damnations

CPSIA information can be obtained
at www.ICGtesting.com
Printed in the USA
LVHW081131090122
708138LV00023B/783